Also by J. T. Edson

THE NIGHT HAWK
THE BAD BUNCH
SLIP GUN
TROUBLED RANGE
THE FASTEST GUN IN TEXAS
THE HIDE AND TALLOW MEN
THE JUSTICE OF COMPANY Z
McGRAW'S INHERITANCE
RAPIDO CLINT
COMANCHE

Wormsley sent his right hand across to the butt of his revolver. Swiftly though he moved, he discovered his intended victim was capable of even greater speed. Sufficient, in fact, to counteract the advantage he expected to gain from his weapon having a shorter barrel than that of the more conventional models of the Colt Peacemaker.

Dipping his hand in a smoothly flowing motion, the Texan swept his revolver from its holster, completing the sequence by releasing the thumbed-back hammer. There was a crash of detonating black powder, and a bullet sped through the air. Even as the Storekeeper Colt was coming out of the cross-draw holster, lead entered between Wormsley's eyes and, having ripped through his brain, burst out at the rear of his skull. Killed instantly, he was pitched backward, with the weapon flying from his no-longer-operative grasp. His body sprawled, with arms and legs apart, on the sidewalk. He had at last met a well-deserved fate at the hands of a man he believed to be no more than an outlaw.

No Finger on the Trigger

J. T. EDSON

A DELL BOOK

Published by
Dell Publishing
a division of
Bantam Doubleday Dell Publishing Group, Inc.
666 Fifth Avenue
New York, New York 10103

ISBN: 0-440-20749-5

Reprinted by arrangement with the author

Printed in the United States of America

Published simultaneously in Canada

September 1990

10 9 8 7 6 5 4

RAD

For everybody at Kilaguni Lodge, TSAVO WEST, Kenya with thanks for excellent visits and, mingi Tembo (Tusker Beer) baridi sana. Heri na baraka, yaku-yote!

Author's Note:

To save our "old hands" repetition, but for the benefit of new readers, we have included certain information regarding the Old West about which we have frequently received requests for clarification in the form of an appendix.

We realize that, in our present "permissive" society, we could use the actual profanities employed by various people in the narrative. However, we do not concede a spurious desire to create realism is any excuse to do so.

Lastly, as we refuse to pander to the current "trendy" usage of the metric system, except when referring to the caliber of certain firearms traditionally measured in millimeters—i.e., Walther P-38, 9mm—we will continue to employ miles, yards, feet, inches, stones, pounds, and ounces when quoting distances or weights.

> J. T. EDSON,
> Active Member, Western Writers of America,
> MELTON MOWBRAY,
> Leics.,
> England.

No Finger
on the Trigger

1

A HELLUVA WAY
TO GO ABOUT A CHORE

An earsplitting crash of thunder suddenly rent the air directly overhead, spooking the big claybank gelding already made restless by sensing its rider's lack of concentration!

Coming almost immediately after the sound, a blinding flash of lightning struck one of the scrubby cottonwoods by the side of the trail!

Showering sparks and charred timber in all directions, the trunk of the tree split from top to bottom!

Six foot two inches in height, the rider was as lean as a steer raised in the greasewood country and gave an impression of being just as whang-leather tough. Tanned by long exposure to the elements, the clean-shaven features framed by the neatly trimmed sideburns of his not-long-since-barbered reddish brown hair were too rugged to be termed handsome. However, while generally showing only such emotions as he wished to be seen, it was a face indicative of a strength of will and intelligence that some women found attractive and men either admired or resented.

Even without hearing him speak, to anybody possessed of range savvy, there could be little doubt as to the rider's origins. The indications started with a low-crowned, wide-brimmed black hat of a shape as Texan in style as "Remember the Alamo!" and the Lone Star flag. Less indicative, unless one had known Marvin Eldridge "Doc" Leroy in the days when the Wedge Trail crew was one of many driving large herds of half-wild longhorn cattle to the railroad in Kansas, was his loosely fitting and unfastened brown coat.[1] Its right side was stitched back to leave clear access to the staghorn-gripped butt of the Colt Civilian Model Peacemaker revolver in the carefully designed and positioned holster at the right side of a wide black gun belt. It was the rig of a man who either wanted to foster the belief that he was *very* fast with a gun, or *was*. The rightly rolled multicolored bandanna knotted about his throat, the open-necked blue flannel shirt, and much-faded Levi's pants, their legs turned back in deep cuffs—which could serve as a repository for nails or other small items when performing chores needing them—might have been worn by a cowhand in any cattle-raising state. However, his Wellington leg boots,[2]

1. *We do not claim Marvin Eldridge "Doc" Leroy was the originator of wearing a jacket tailored in such a fashion as an aid to making a fast draw, but his were always converted that way. Information about his earlier career can be found in* Part Three, "The Invisible Winchester," OLE DEVIL'S HANDS AND FEET; Part Five, "The Hired Butcher," THE HARD RIDERS; WACO'S DEBT; Part Five, "A Case of Infectious *Plumbeus Veneficium,*" THE FLOATING OUTFIT; Part Three, "Monday Is A Quiet Day," THE SMALL TEXAN; Part Two, "Jordan's Try," THE TOWN TAMERS; RETURN TO BACKSIGHT; Part Six, "Keep Good Temper Alive," J.T.'S HUNDREDTH *and the* Waco *series.*

1a. *The Wedge Trail crew make "guest" appearances in:* QUIET TOWN, TRIGGER FAST, *and* GUN WIZARD. *They also "star" in their own right in:* BUFFALO ARE COMING!

2. *Such boots were not the modern waterproof rubber variety, but had their legs in a style made popular by the Duke of Wellington in the Napoleonic War.*

with Kelly spurs on their heels, were decorated by the practically obligatory five-pointed-star motif for a man born and making his living on the open-range country between Oklahoma in the north, the Rio Grande to the south, and New Mexico in the west.[3]

Further "signs of origin" were offered by the claybank gelding, which the rider was sitting with the deft ease of one who spent much of his life in the saddle. Close to sixteen hands, the yellowish color resulted from a cross between a sorrel and a dun. Nevertheless, it had the lines of the great Mogollon strain and bore the brand of the ranch in central Texas, which the owner, a Scottish Highlander, Colin Farquharson, had made famous for breeding and selling horses of high quality.[4] In excellent condition, while less suitable for the sudden bursts of rapidity and agility frequently required when working cattle, it was easily up to carrying his weight and the added burden of his belongings for a long distance at a good speed.

Low of horn and double girthed, the rider's saddle was another indication of the Lone Star State. It was designed to meet the particular needs of cowhands who would be spending long hours afork it and intended to hang on to whatever they roped, be it steer, bull, horse, or man. His war bag, carrying spare clothing and other portable items of property, was wrapped in his bedroll beneath a tarpaulin sheet and strapped to the cantle. A coiled lariat swung from the horn and, beneath his left leg, a Winchester Model of 1876 rifle rode with the butt pointing forward to facilitate easy withdrawal on dismounting. The rig was costly, perhaps more decorative than utilitarian with the carving gracing the leatherwork, made by a man famous for such things. A similar grade of workmanship showed in the wide two-eared bridle. It sported fancy stitched leatherwork,

3. *Another example of how completely clothing could identify a man as a Texan is given in:* Case One, "Roan Marrett's Son," ARIZONA RANGER.
4. *Information about some of Colin Farquharson's activities prior to becoming a rancher is recorded in:* .44 CALIBRE MAN *and* A HORSE CALLED MOGOLLON.

and the shanks of the bit took the form of two plump, shapely feminine buttocks and legs.

Although somebody from the East might have believed the rider was a cowhand, such as frequently appeared in photographs or illustrations on the pages of newspapers and magazines east of the Mississippi River, the same would not apply of the person who was better versed with the ways of the West in general and Texas in particular. The most obvious evidence to the contrary for one cognizant of the facts was his footwear. While sharp toed, the heels were low and better suited to walking than working for long hours in the saddle. His hands were obviously hard and strong. However, the palms were smooth and lacking the calluses acquired by frequently having to hang on to a rope against the pull being applied by a powerful and recalcitrant animal.

Jerked by the sound and sight from his reverie, which had been so deep it had prevented him from noticing the threatening signs in the sky, the next thing the rider was aware of was the bony crest of the plunging, terrified horse. Rising too swiftly to be avoided completely, although he instinctively began to turn his head, he was caught with a stunning blow on the side of his face. Bright lights seemed to be erupting inside his skull and, his equilibrium destroyed, he was dumped unceremoniously on the hard-packed ground. Landing awkwardly, with a bone-jarring thump that drove the breath from his body, pure instinct sent him rolling clear of the rearing claybank's steel-shod hooves and, inadvertently, toward the crumbling edge of the arroyo. Freed of human restraint, regardless of its training to halt and stand "ground hitched" and the liberated split-end reins having failed to do so by dangling from the bridle, the panic-stricken gelding took off at a high speed.

This's a helluva way to go about a chore! the Texan thought bitterly as he felt the ground giving way beneath him, but was powerless to prevent himself from toppling over the edge of the arroyo.

The gradient was sufficiently steep and littered with rocks to prevent any such further sentiments!

Already taking a painful battering as he was tumbling over and over uncontrollably, a large rocky outcrop suddenly filled the dislodged rider's vision and a mind-numbing agony robbed him of all coherent thought as he crashed into it. His anguish was short-lived. Something struck his head a glancing blow and he was once more briefly aware of a dazzling coruscation of multicolored lights before he lost consciousness. His momentum took him all the way to the bottom. Sprawled on his back, with arms outflung, he was insensible to the shower of dirt and stones that had accompanied his inadvertent descent.

The thunder continued to rumble menacingly overhead!

Then torrential rain that the gathering black clouds, ignored by the Texan in his reverie, had heralded, began to fall!

*　*　*

When consciousness of a kind returned, feeling as if an army of little men with hammers were hard at work inside his skull with the sole intention of splitting it open, the Texan slowly raised his left hand to make an investigation. Touching his head, it encountered something wet and tackily sticky. Lowering it, he grimaced at the almost congealed blood smearing its palm and fingers. The movement caused him to move his other limbs and discover, as far as he could ascertain from doing so, that all were in working order. However, the throbbing ache from his left side was a cause of greater concern for him. It made even shallow breathing painfully difficult. Hugging at the ribs with his right hand, he tried to sit up.

The storm had moved on, taking the rain with it, but the Texan was in no condition to appropriate the change in the weather. Still soaked to the skin, he shivered uncontrollably in the chilly wind that was blowing. For all that, finding he neither knew what had happened nor who he was, he tried to marshal his battered wits. Disoriented and hurting, despite sensing that to move might add to whatever injuries he had suffered, he could not resist an involuntary attempt to sit up so as to seek out the answer to the first point.

Yielding to the impulse, the Texan quickly discovered, was a mistake. Waves of fresh pain washed over him. Nevertheless,

although unable to hold back the involuntary groan that passed
between his tightly clenched teeth, he persevered with the attempt to obtain a sitting position. This merely aggravated the
situation. His vision blurred and as he shook his head to try to
clear it, he immediately regretted the action. Nausea engulfed
him and he was violently sick. The retching spasms left him
weaker and trembling, this time for perspiration. For all that,
after a few seconds, the roaring inside his skull subsided and he
was able to take stock of his surroundings.

What the Texan saw did not exactly fill him with enthusiasm.
The further wall of the arroyo rose like a sheer cliff, and trying
to climb it even if he was in the best of health would have been
a *very* difficult proposition. Nor, while less close to the perpen-
dicular, was he going to find the other side easy to surmount.
However, by walking or crawling, he must do something to get
out of the strength-sapping glare of the sun. Already the bottom of the dried-up water course was shimmering in the heat,
mocking him and adding to his growing realization that he was
terribly thirsty.

With the thought throbbing through his mind, the Texan
found his eyes were focusing on a small pool of water some
yards to his left!

Just beyond it, a black patch was beginning to form at the
bottom of the sheer wall!

Shade and water!

Lifesavers to a man in the Texan's condition!

Hugging his aching ribs with his right arm, the injured man
raised himself into a kneeling position. From there, he attempted to stand. The effort brought him out in a cold sweat,
soaking his still clammily damp shirt until it clung to him like a
second skin. Nevertheless, gritting his teeth, he forced himself
to stand. On attaining an upright posture, he found his vision
was once again blurring. His world began to spin crazily
around him. Hastily closing his eyes, he almost fell. The sensation passed, but it was some seconds before he compelled himself to force apart the gummy lids so as to take a cautious
squint about him.

Hurt and suffering though he was, the first actions of the Texan on opening his eyes again would have had considerable significance for anybody who knew the West. Despite swaying on his spread-apart feet and showing every movement required an effort of willpower to accomplish, he reached with his right hand toward his right hip and rubbed away the accumulated mud from the holster and the Colt Peacemaker that was still in it. Why this should have happened was easily explained. Sewn inside the top of the holster, a narrow strip of softer leather extended into the rear end of the revolver's frame so that the hammer rested against it and the firing pin passed through a small hole punched in it. The tension of the mainspring against the uncocked hammer kept the pin in the hole and prevented the weapon from being dislodged even by the violent motions to which it had been subjected.

Closing his fingers about the staghorn handle, still acting on instinctive rather than conscious guidance, the Texan eased back the hammer until the withdrawal of the firing pin from the strap liberated the weapon and took it out. Clearly acting by instinct rather than conscious guidance, he brought over his left hand to help clean the hammer, trigger area, and cylinder sufficiently for the mechanism to be operative. With the precaution taken, he returned and secured the revolver.

With the task completed, the man started to move forward. Placing each foot cautiously to counter the effects of the swaying, to which his whole being seemed affected, he watched the patch of shade growing larger and more inviting. At the same instant, he became aware of a dull rumbling sound that seemed to be emanating from within his skull. Suddenly, he found himself suffering a sense of grim foreboding that caused him to hesitate instead of going any closer. He was unable to decide what the cause might be, but he could not fight it off.

Vital seconds passed before the Texan realized that the faint roaring noise, steadily increasing in volume, was not originating from inside his pounding head!

Flash flood!

The two words screamed through the Texan's mind!

Despite a complete lack of recollection with regards to who he was and how he had come to be in such a desperate predicament, the Texan appreciated the full extent of the danger. Only the foolish or ignorant would camp in the bottom of an arroyo. It was not unusual for heavy rains, sometimes falling miles away, to send a thundering wall of water and debris along the bed of the river, which had long since dried up.

Born and raised in the range country, the Texan was neither foolish nor ignorant. Nor, he felt certain, had he been merely camping overnight down there. Instinctively, an appreciation of the potentially dangerous condition caused him to turn his back upon the welcome patch of shade at the foot of the sheer face and make on wobbling legs toward the somewhat more easily climbable slope. His tormented lungs felt as though they were on fire as he retraced his reeling steps and started to scrabble on hands and knees—almost by the tips of his fingers and the sharp toes of his boots—up the rock-strewn incline, but he did not dare to pause and catch his breath.

The distant roaring was growing louder by the second and the Texan concluded he was going to need every ounce of Texas luck to survive!

As his fingers were grasping the corner of a protruding rock, the Texan heard another sound much closer. Again it was one he recognized, freezing the blood in his veins and stopping him dead in his tracks. It also suggested in no uncertain fashion that, bad as the situation had been so far—unless, which he doubted was likely, his ears were playing tricks upon him— there could be *far* worse to come. Looking toward the source of the latest cause of concern, he found that his hearing was functioning correctly.

Under less trying conditions, the Texan might have considered the eastern diamondback rattlesnake lying coiled on the rock and basking in the sun a pretty fine specimen of its kind. Illogically under the circumstances, although he could not bring to mind who he was, he recollected what he had been told by a schoolteacher about such creatures.

Members of the *Crotalidae,* "pit-viper" family, the more

common name, "rattlesnake," referred to the sound produced by movements of modified horny scales at the tip of the tail. The buzzing served as a warning to possible predators or even harmless creatures sufficiently large to damage the snake by stepping upon it inadvertently. However, the rattle was completely innocuous—even beneficial—when compared with its other qualities. Not the least dangerous of these were the fangs, which could be anything up to three-quarters of an inch long and were capable of pumping a lethal dose of poison into much larger quarry than one hurting and slow-moving human being. What was more, as the mouth could be opened a good 180 degrees, they were just as effective if used to stab instead of needing to deliver the bite required by most other kinds of venomous reptiles and, because of their length, the poison could be injected deep into the victim's bloodstream. If that was not sufficient, unlike snakes such as cobras—which could only launch an attack downward and were comparatively slow and clumsy—the S-shaped coiling posture of the rattlesnake allowed it to strike with great speed and accuracy in any direction, including straight up.

Startled by the Texan's sudden and unannounced appearance, that particular rattlesnake was likely to use its fangs any moment now!

Looking at the reptile and listening to the rumbling roar, the Texan rapidly reached the conclusion that he was in one hell of a tight spot. It was going to be a mighty close thing as to which would get him first, the flash flood or the poison-squirting reptile on the rock. Either way, he was sure of one thing. He did not want to die in such a godforsaken place. The trouble being, he could not rightly figure out how he could avoid it. It would either be a slow and agonizing death from the snake's venom, or quicker by drowning. Nor could he decide which way to go would be worse. There was only one small consolation he could draw from the situation. Glancing upward, he saw two turkey vultures were spiraling overhead. Should the snake get him, he was sure to slip back into the floodwater and make the circling pair work a whole heap harder before they could start stripping the flesh from his bones.

"Goddamn the luck!" the man growled, his accent that of one born and raised in the Lone Star State. "If ever a good ole boy from Texas was caught 'tween a rock and a hard place, I'm him. It's just *not* my day!"

2

GO THROUGH HIS POCKETS

After fleeing for about half a mile in panic along the trail, recovering from the fright that had caused it to bolt, and feeling the split-ended reins slapping against its forelegs, the Texan's big claybank gelding had responded to the training it was given at the ranch where it was born and raised. However, it had waited until finding a steep slope that offered some shelter from the rain before coming to a halt. Nor, even after the storm passed, had it moved far. Conditioned to remain comparatively still when ground-hitched, it continued to stand and graze, as much as was possible with the bit still in position, from the grass at the verge of the trail.

Already making their way to investigate the spiraling turkey vultures, as were more of the species *Cathartes aura* converging from all sides, the taller of the two riders coming along the trail was first to notice the claybank. Anywhere west of the Mississippi River in general and on the vast open ranges of Texas in particular, the sight of a saddled and riderless horse was cause for speculation or even concern. Therefore, on seeing it, he brought the animal to the attention of his companion by raising the Winchester Model of 1873 rifle from across his lap and pointing with the barrel. Without waiting to look, the other also lifted a Winchester—albeit a Model of 1876 carbine—to a position of greater readiness and each eased the hammer, set at the half-cock position, which served in lieu of a safety catch, until ready to open fire should the need arise.

The motions and the fact that both riders were carrying shoulder arms in their hands and considered it advisable to set the hammers to the rear in the fully cocked position, while on what amounted to a major road leading to Bonham County's seat, Flamingo, would have been significant to anybody with knowledge of the West. In the vicinity of such a frequently traveled trail, it was unlikely there would be any wild animals of a suitable size—either as predators with designs upon domestic stock, or to be used to supplement beef for food—to warrant the use of the Winchesters. With the possibility of hunting being the purpose of the riders precluded, the implication was that they had reason to believe there might be a need for the firearms as *weapons* and more quickly than would have been possible if these had been reposing in the boot attached to the left side of each saddle.

"I see it, Halcón Gris," the second rider stated. "It's not from our remuda and it isn't what the turkey buzzards are after."

"Nope," grunted the taller, his deep and guttural voice far different from the tones of his companion. "Can't see nobody anywheres close to it, so the buzzards could be after whoever it belongs to."

At first glance, being clad in a round-topped and wide-brimmed black Stetson, loosely fitting brown leather jacket, white shirt with an open neck, Levi's pants, and cowhand-style boots, the smaller rider could easily have been mistaken for a boy. However, despite the short-cropped dark hair showing from beneath the hat and masculine attire, the voice and face were definitely feminine; with breeding and education at odds with such an unconventional mode of dress. Her slender figure, graceful in the saddle, was just beginning to show signs of maturing. Furthermore, there was nothing childlike about the dark-lashed green eyes. They gave an indication that, despite the suggestion of innocence implied by the rest of her beautiful olive brown Hispanic features, Ransome Cordoba had grown up in a mainly masculine society and had come to know the basic facts of life at an early age.

Several years older than the girl, there was nothing even remotely indicative of innocence about the appearance presented by Tom Grey. Plainly visible in the form of a savage slash that started from the hairline above his right eye and cut across the bridge of his nose, a scar ended just below his left ear. It showed up starkly white against skin that was Indian dark and added to the leathery grimness of his aquiline face. His hair, which he kept cut to the length considered de rigueur in cattle country—where presenting an excessively hirsute appearance was considered an abomination—his hair was far more gray than might have been expected at his age. Amber in color with a darker outer rim, his eyes were much like those of the hawk that supplied the first part of his sobriquet, Halcón Gris.

Although clearly a product of two races, experience had taught Grey to avoid making this more obvious. Well worn, his clothing was that of a typical working cowhand and, despite being employed on a *Chicano*[1] spread—albeit one whose owner showed no preference for either race in the selection of men to work the range—more Texan than Mexican in style. In addition to the rifle, he had a gun belt strapped about his waist, with a walnut-handled Colt Cavalry Model Peacemaker in its holster on the right side; but it was not the rig of a fast man with a gun. Nor, despite his competence as a fighter in other ways, would he ever claim to be one. His skills were with the Winchester or the long-bladed J. Russell & Co. Green River

1. Chicano, *a person of Spanish origins residing in the United States.*

hunting knife hanging sheathed on the opposite side to the re-volver.

Riding closer to the claybank, Ransome and Grey studied it with almost equally knowing eyes. Born and raised in Bonham County, the girl knew enough about such matters to decide it was not suitable for working cattle. Neither had its somewhat fancy rig suffered the rigors of hard use unavoidable on the range. Furthermore, while sufficiently impressive to catch the eye—as was generally the prime consideration when making a choice for such a purpose—she felt the animal was more than just some cowhand's "go-to-town" mount selected for looks rather than utility.

"I make the brand C On F," Grey remarked, having drawn similar conclusions to those of his companion and taken them further. Motioning with his rifle to where there was a clearly discernible scar caused by the sign of ownership—the first capital letter superimposed on the second—being burned into the animal's left hip, he went on, "Which same's the hoss spread owned by that Scotch jasper's runs 'round in a skirt out Cowtown way."[2]

"It's called a kilt," Ransome corrected, but without any suggestion of wishing to impress her companion by possessing superior knowledge. "And he's *Scottish,* not Scotch. *Scotch* is a drinking whiskey, although I don't suppose I need to tell *you* that."

"I'm a *tequila* man myself and I don't care what his *skirt's* called by fancy, know-all folks like *some's* I could name," the man declared, showing no trace of resentment. Rather his demeanor was that of an old and well-trusted family retainer, granted privileges by virtue of this long association. "That *Scotch* jasper's still a man to step aside from when he's riled and hosses he sells's're this good don't come cheap."

"Neither does a Winchester '76," the girl supported, having

2. *Cowtown; colloquial name for Fort Worth, Tarrant County, Texas, derived from its long-connection ranching and cattle.*

ridden close enough to discern exactly which kind of rifle was in the rifle sheath. "Whoever's lost him isn't a saddle bum."

"There's worse'n saddle bums hereabouts these days," Grey asserted, subjecting the surrounding terrain to a careful and keen scrutiny. Satisfied there was nothing to cause alarm in the immediate vicinity and reaching to scoop up the dangling reins, he went on, "Anyways, talking's not getting us closer to finding out who-all's lost him. Could be the buzzards know the answer."

Setting their mounts into motion once more, the pair continued along the road. Arriving where it bent along the top of the arroyo, they heard the muted yet growing roar of rushing water and could guess the cause.

"Madre de dios!" Ransome gasped, having the habit of reverting to Spanish when startled despite speaking English with no trace of a Hispanic accent just as much during her everyday life. *"Look!"*

"I *see!*" Grey replied, returning the hammer of the rifle to half cock and thrusting it swiftly into the rifle sheath. Waiting until the girl had just as speedily duplicated his actions with her carbine, he held out the claybank's reins. Waiting only until they were taken from him, he set his big *grulla* gelding moving with a jab from his heels and snapping, "Yeeah!"

Reacting with an equal speed, the girl gave a commanding tug at the claybank's reins and induced the smaller—yet equally well bred—*bayos cebrunos* pony[3] between her legs to follow her companion!

* * *

The Texan wondered whether wishful thinking was causing his eyes to play tricks as he saw the figure of a man bounding down the slope toward him. On realizing the vision was a fact, uncaring of his own desperate predicament, he tried to yell a warning about the second and less obvious peril. All he could manage was an incoherent croaking rasp.

The warning was not required!

3. Bayos cebrunos, *a dun shading to a smoky gray color.*

Regardless of the urgency and the rapidity of the descent he was making, a man like Tom Grey always remained on the alert to his surroundings in case some peril might await the unwary. With his attention drawn by the slight movements it was making, he detected the diamondback rattlesnake. Giving a grunt, he lashed out with his left foot. Striking like lightning, with the mouth opened to its full gape, the poison-dripping fangs passed through the cloth of his Levi's to be halted harmlessly by the leather leg of his boot.

Caught by the kick, the snake hung on to the material for a moment. Then it was flung clear and the rescuer was able to reach down and grasp the Texan's outstretched left wrist in both his hands. Having done so, he realized that the task upon which he was engaged could not be considered anything even close to completed. For one thing, although remaining sentient for long enough to extend the arm and now trying to help in the struggle, the man he was grasping was clearly already too weakened to be of great assistance. Secondly, and far more dangerous, already the forward end of the flash flood was upon them.

At that moment, as he had on more than one occasion since he had obtained them during a visit to El Paso, Halcón Gris had reason to be grateful for parting with the not inconsiderable sum he had paid to purchase his boots. They had served him well in the past and, despite the nature of the terrain underfoot, continued to do so. Bracing his wirily powerful body against what amounted to a dead weight and digging the high heels into the scanty soil of the slope, he found they were giving him just sufficient of a purchase to hold on to the motionless body below him.

However, Grey was uncertain of how long he would be able to continue against the pressure of the water!

What Halcón Gris did not doubt was that assistance was in the vicinity!

Nor was the scar-faced man wrong in his assumption!

Up on the road, Ransome had not even waited to find out what developed. Instead, the moment she had brought her *bayo cebrunos* and the claybank to a halt, she had started to make preparations to render the help she felt certain was going to be needed. Dropping the reins of the big horse, but retaining those of her own mount in her left hand, she swiftly freed the coiled lariat strapped to the apple-sized horn of her single-girthed Mexican-style saddle.

Long experience in handling the sixty-foot length of best Manila rope, its three-strand construction laid extra hard for strength and smoothness, allowed the girl to move swiftly and yet without becoming flurried despite the extreme urgency. Deftly shaking out a loop of the size she knew would be needed for the hooley-ann throw, which her instincts suggested was best suited to her needs, she gave it one quick whirl around in front of her to the right until it was over her head. On being released in the direction of the target, it turned to flatten out as it was descending.

Being developed as a "head catch," which allowed several men to be able to collect horses from a confined remuda at the same time, without disturbing the rest unduly, the loop for the hooley-ann was smaller than would have been needed for some other kinds of throw and, due to the honda sliding along the stem of the rope and taking up the slack, its size decreased as it was in flight.[4] Nevertheless, such was the skill with which Ransome performed the throw, there was still a sufficiently large spread to achieve its purpose.

Watching the loop descend to pass over Grey's head, the girl gave a twitch on the stem, which caused it to tighten about his

4. *A lariat was—and still is—made with one end of the rope being doubled back and spliced to form a small circle, or "eyelet," known as the "honda," through which the other end was passed to form the loop sometimes referred to as a "noose." The section between the honda and the other end of the rope is called the "stem," or "spoke."*

4a. *Although a metal ring can be used for helping form the honda, many men claim such an object might blind an animal and, anyway, would not "set" sufficiently to prevent the struggling captive from freeing itself. A vastly superior precaution and aid is to have a piece of slick leather sewn about the upper end of the eyelet so that the stem of the rope will not burn through it.*

shoulders. Trained by "tie men" who followed the dictates of
Texas in such matters, before the tension came at the other end,
she quickly fastened a knot around the saddle horn instead of
seeking the safety for herself which could have been attained by
applying the half hitch of the "dally"—allowing it to be released hurriedly in an emergency—employed by cowhands in
other states. While she was doing so, she saw that she had not
acted a moment too soon. What was more, even having completed her part by bringing off the hooley-ann throw, the rescue
was still far from being concluded with an equal success. Everything now depended upon her companion and the comparatively small pony between her legs.

With the swirling turbulence of the flood seeming to be making a deliberately thought-out bid at snatching away his burden, in spite of feeling the rope biting into the flesh of his chest,
back, and straining biceps, Grey was thankful for its support.
As the thrust of the current threatened to sweep them both
away, while it was little enough, the help he was receiving from
the other's feeble efforts was playing its part in fending off the
attempt by the churning water to carry them off along with the
other debris it had collected in its rush along the arroyo. Nevertheless, ever a realist, he knew they would not be able to avoid
that fate by their own unaided endeavors.

Above the endangered men, being trained for roping, the
little cowpony had anticipated what was coming when feeling
its rider begin to manipulate the lariat. In fact, it did not even
need the signal given by a nudge from her spurs to start bracing
its forelegs against the weight and pulling, which it experienced
as the loop tightened and the stem snapped taut. Fortunately,
the rains responsible for the flood had lasted long enough in the
vicinity to have softened the surface of the trail, and the sun
had not yet caused it to harden to its more usual rocklike consistency. Therefore, as the rescuer on the slope had already
done, the *bayo cebrunos* was able to dig in its steel-shod hooves
sufficiently to hold firm against the strain that was thrown upon
it.

Regardless of the assistance from above, for close to three

minutes the result of the rescue bid hung in a *very* delicate balance!

Nor, toward the end, was the situation improved by the latest strain to which his already abused and suffering body was subjected, causing the Texan to lapse again into unconsciousness. Feeling the weak movements which had played a small— yet not inconsiderable—part in averting disaster come to an end, Halcón Gris had gritted his teeth and hung on with all the concentrated determination not to be defeated, which was a major factor in his nature. Gazing down in anxiety, Ransome applied all her skill and knowledge to helping the *bayos cebrunos* play its vitally necessary part.

Then, as suddenly as it had come, the first mass of the flash flood was gone. The level of the water subsided and the force of the current slackened. Seeing this, the girl signaled for her mount to start slowly edging backward. Having the pull exerted, sucking in air as best he could against the constriction of the rope, Grey was able to haul the unresisting man a step at a time higher up the slope. Once they were clear of the flow, the girl halted the pony and allowed him to remove the loop. Flexing his sore and aching limbs, then waiting for a few seconds until he had regained his breath, he transferred his grip to beneath the Texan's armpits and resumed the climb without aid. Once at the top, stretching his burden out on the trail, he sank down to recover further from what had been a tremendous physical ordeal.

"I've never seen him before," Ransome commented, after having ascertained there was nothing she could do for her companion, studying the bruised and battered features of the man they had saved. Gesturing toward the blood oozing from the ugly scalp wound, the water having soaked away that which had coagulated, she went on, "Whoever he is, he's going to have a bad headache, if nothing worse, when he wakes up."

"I don't know *who* he is, neither," Grey replied, first tapping the gun belt worn by the Texan with his right forefinger and then drawing the Colt Civilian Model Peacemaker from the holster to look it over. Noticing that an attempt had been made to wipe away the mud which had been gathered during the descent into the arroyo, he emptied the bullets from the cylinder and tested the mechanism by operating the hammer and depressing the trigger. Having done so, he returned the weapon to the rig and continued, "But I sure as sin's for sale in Cowtown know *what* he is."

"It certainly looks as if he might be," the girl admitted, having watched what was being done and being aware of what was portended by the cryptic comment.

The significance of the rig worn by the unconscious Texan had not escaped either of his rescuers. Even the girl was aware that it was the product of a master craftsman well versed in such matters and not merely a highly skilled worker in leather for general purposes.

Battered and bedraggled though he undoubtedly was at that moment, the rescuers felt sure that the man they had snatched from the flash flood was not a cowhand wearing such a rig merely as an affectation. Like his horse's saddle and bridle, his clothing was of good quality and his boots, too, had never been subjected to the rigors of working cattle on the open range. What was more, the examination of the revolver had satisfied Grey that its mechanism had been worked on to ensure an even smoother and faster action than when it left "Colonel Sam's" factory in Hartford, Connecticut. That was a sign of one who knew he must be able to depend upon the complete reliability of his weapon on those occasions when his existence might hang upon a matter of a split second.

"Maybe we should've left him where he was," Grey growled, remembering the threats made by one of the neighboring ranchers to start duplicating the actions of another by bringing in hired guns as a means of dealing with the problem arousing bad feelings throughout Bonham County.

"Maybe we should," Ransome replied, finding herself drawn in a way she could hardly understand by the rugged masculinity of the man lying at her feet. "Only time will tell, Halcón Gris."

"We could maybe speed said time a mite."

"How?"

"Go through his pockets and gear to see happen he's carrying anything to say who he be and what's brought him down this ways."

"We've no right to do that," Ransome protested, despite having a desire to learn more.

"Should I buy a hoss, I'd look it over to make sure it didn't have nothing wrong with it," Grey pointed out.

"This is a man who's hurt," the girl reminded her companion. "Let's get him back to home so we can have him tended."

"You're figuring on taking him back to the spread?" Grey asked.

"It's closer than town, and even if it wasn't, I wouldn't want to trust even a mangy old cur dog to Dr. Grantz," Ransome answered, her tone and expression giving further evidence of the dislike she felt for the man whose name she had mentioned. "Anyways, *you* always say that Juanita's better for tending hurts than any doctor. And having him at the house will give us a chance to find out what's brought him to Bonham County."

"And what happen it's something you won't *like?*"

"I'm sure I'll be able to bear up under it."

"Have it *your* way," Grey assented and, although neither his voice nor badly scarred features suggested any quality of softness, there was something in his eyes that indicated a belief that the girl could do no wrong. "You most always do."

"I do, don't I?" Ransome admitted with a smile. "Find something to make a travois, please, Halcón Gris, and I'll do what I can to make him ready for moving on it."

3
I DON'T KNOW WHO I AM!

"So *that's* what I look like!" the Texan muttered sotto voce, looking into the mirror of the dressing table at his rugged features from which the bruising acquired while falling into the arroyo was beginning to fade and deciding a razor would come in handy to remove the stubble from his chin. "Well, one thing's for sure. I'm not any Mark Counter."

Even as the man saved from the flash flood completed the comment, he found himself puzzled by it. He had no idea of what kind of "marks" were counted, nor why he felt sure this was not his occupation. Giving a frown and shrug, he decided he felt well enough to make a start at finding out who and where he was and how he came to be there.

On first regaining consciousness and feeling as if he was struggling desperately against choking water, which filled his mouth and nostrils, the Texan had discovered it was nothing worse than imagination. His eyes had revealed after a moment of blurred vision that his circumstances had vastly changed and apparently much for the better. The room in which he had found himself was large and cool, with whitewashed walls and a polished timber floor. A cool breeze was filtering through the net curtains, which were draped across open glass-paneled doors and prevented him from being able to see what was outside. There was another door, of solid wood, set in the wall opposite the bed. A washstand surmounted by a mirror and with a jug, bowl, and bottle filled with a yellow liquid and topped by a glass on it was at the left side next to an intricately carved wardrobe. On the opposite wall hung a painting of the Madonna and Child, which might have served as a clue about the people who owned the property if he had not still been in a somewhat befuddled condition. Next to the bed, a chest of drawers and a high-backed chair completed the furnishings.

While gazing about him, the Texan had become aware that every part of his body was aching to some degree. Nor was it hard for him to find out why. His head had throbbed abominably and he had winced as his fingers came into contact with the stitches that had sealed the gash in his scalp. Although he had not been able to see them, he was a mass of bruises and abrasions. The continued exploration by his fingers had encountered a bandage wrapped firmly around his ribs and established this was the only thing he had on. Pushing aside the covers, he tried to sit up. Instantly, a stabbing pain in his left side temporarily robbed him of breath. Sinking back on to the thick and soft mattress, he had wondered what had happened to him.

Only a moment was needed for the Texan to realize just how little he *knew!*

All the injured man's examination of the room had established was that he had no idea where he was!

The Texan could not remember how he came to be in the bed, nor even how he had received his injuries!

As far as the injured man could recall. . . !

With a sense of shock, the Texan realized he could not recollect anything beyond the moment when sentience had returned and he found he was lying bandaged, but otherwise naked, in the bed!

The injured man could not so much as remember his name!

Perturbed though he had been, the Texan had found his attempt to rise and go in search of information proved too much. Slumping back on the bed, he had lapsed into a state of somnolence. Nor had he any idea of how long it had lasted. Even now, although he felt physically much better and was able to leave the bed instead of being compelled to collapse back upon it within seconds of even sitting up, only the memory of a huge woman—with dark brown skin and features that he felt sure could not belong to one of his own race—who had fed him and attended to his needs for the indefinite period since his first recovery seemed real.

For the rest of the time, the Texan had had only uneasy stirrings in his mind and seen vague images. At times a thought had come that he had been sent somewhere to do something; but he was unable to recollect by whom, nor where, or for what purpose. He had an indistinct remembrance of a tall man with a deeply bronzed and badly scarred face holding out a hand toward him, but not why or when. He had a vague memory of a second tall man, but more slender and distinguished looking, speaking to him once. However, he could recollect nothing of what had been said. On occasion there also had been two beautiful young women who were either present or just imagined. He was uncertain which it had been. One was black haired, with olive brown features that seemed to vary between childlike innocence and a wistful greater knowledge. Slightly older, the other was a blond, whose face expressed disapproval. Try as he might, he could not think of who either was. For all that, he was as unable to shake off the belief that the latter was somehow more closely involved in his life than the former.

On waking a short while ago and finding daylight streaming through the lace curtains, despite having no idea of how much time had elapsed since his first partial return to a conscious state, the Texan had discovered his physical condition seemed vastly improved. There was none of the nausea that had plagued him earlier. Even the drowsiness that had kept him somnolent and little aware of his surroundings was gone. At

some time, he had been clad in a long flannel nightshirt and the
bandages had gone from his head and chest. Leaving the bed,
after a brief unsteadiness, he had found soaking his face in cold
water from the jug on the washstand had left him able to think
clearly enough to make use of the mirror of the dressing table.

Turning away after learning nothing of use from seeing his
face and hoping to gain some clue to his identity elsewhere in
the room, the Texan ran his gaze over the clothing in a neatly
folded pile on the seat of the chair by the bed and the black hat
dangling by a fancy *barbiquejo* chin strap from its back. Then
he glanced at the pair of freshly polished boots beneath it and
he decided they all belonged to him. A gun belt with a holstered revolver lay on the chest of drawers. Finding he was
instinctively reaching for the uppermost item of clothing, he
told himself wryly that he obviously had not forgotten *everything* learned in his unremembered past.

What was it they told the bohunk first time he got a pair of
these? the man mused, looking somewhat quizzically at the
garment. You put 'em on with the yellow in front and brown
behind.

Regardless of there being no such color scheme to assist him,
the Texan donned the underpants without needing to think
about how to do so and slipped into the undershirt and shirt.
Then, having donned the Levi's pants and threaded the narrow
brown belt through the loops at the waistband, he turned his
gaze to the chest of drawers. Impelled by a thought he could
not explain, he went over to pick up the gun belt. Noticing
there were some scratches on the holster, which he sensed had
not been there previously, he buckled it around his lean waist.
It was only when he was bending to tie the pigging thongs to
his right thigh that he realized what he was doing. Straighten-
ing up, he concluded the weight of the rig felt both comfortable
and natural.

Whatever his past life might have been, the Texan thought,
the gun belt and revolver had evidently played more than an
insignificant part in it!

Whether for good or bad, the man told himself, he had yet to
find out!

However, the Texan sensed the possession of the rig was in
part responsible for the speculative and even worried attitude of
the beautiful black-haired girl on those occasions when she had
appeared before him!

Even as the man was wondering why he should have aroused
such interest from somebody who he could not shake off the
belief was a total stranger, a movement across the room caught
the corner of his eye!

Turning his gaze in the appropriate direction, the Texan saw
the wooden door was starting to ease open so slowly it seemed
whoever was beyond it had some reason for wishing to avoid
being heard or noticed!

Acting rapidly upon the supposition and without the need
for conscious guidance, the Texan swung around. While he was
doing so, his right hand dipped even more quickly to coil the
second, third, and little finger around the staghorn grips of the
holstered Colt and lift it. Despite his thumb curling around the
spur and drawing back the hammer until the firing pin was
clear of the retaining strap, he refrained from fully cocking the
mechanism, and his forefinger stayed outside the trigger guard
until the four-and-three-quarter-inch-long barrel was clear of
leather and its muzzle turned toward the cause of the action.

Making the draw in a fashion that indicated he was fully
conversant with all its movements, including one very important safety measure intended to guard him against firing prema-
turely and sustaining an injury,[1] the man came to a halt in an
almost-crouching posture on slightly bent legs and with feet
spread to about the width of his shoulders. Held centrally before him at just over waist level, counterbalanced with his left
hand being extended sideways, the Colt was pointing by instinctive alignment toward the cause of the reaction. However,
at that moment, a realization that he had failed to take the

1. *How dangerous failing to take the precaution when making a draw could
be is told in:* THE FAST GUN.

simple yet vitally important precaution of first ensuring the revolver was loaded struck home with sickening force. What was more, the weight of the weapon indicated to his senses that it was not.

A moment later, the Texan realized that having no bullets in the revolver's cylinder was more of a blessing than a potentially dangerous omission!

Framed in the doorway, face showing shock and alarm, was the beautiful black-haired girl who had figured in the man's imagination or—more likely, it now seemed—had actually existed from the vaguely remembered period since the first time he had recovered consciousness!

Aware that the herbal stew with which Juanita had plied her patient for the past three days induced sleep to alleviate pain, Ransome Cordoba had not expected him to be awake. Wishing to avoid disturbing him, she had inched open the door to peep inside. Finding he was on his feet and almost fully dressed would have been sufficient of a surprise, albeit also a tribute to the excellence of the massive part-Mexican–part-Indian woman's ministrations.

However, despite the suspicions that had been aroused by the attire and armament of the Texan, the way the girl was greeted came as a shock. He had moved with the lightning speed of a striking rattlesnake, and the muzzle of his weapon, looking *much* larger than its actual caliber of .45 of an inch, seemed to appear before her in no more time than it took to blink an eye. Although she had never been farther than Brownsville to the east and San Antonio in the west, having grown up amongst fighting men, she was sufficiently wise in such matters to appreciate how grave a peril she had created. Nevertheless, despite having forgotten the Colt had not been reloaded when it was cleaned by Tom Grey and being very startled by the response her unannounced entrance had provoked, she had sufficient presence of mind to avoid any action that might have made the potentially dangerous situation worse.

"Didn't anybody ever tell you it's not polite to *point?*" the girl inquired, forcing herself to stand like a statue in the open doorway and to speak calmly despite the sensation of alarm that assailed her.

Freezing the forefinger with the depressing of the trigger still uncompleted, the Texan lowered the revolver. The knowledge that it was not loaded offered him only a cold comfort. The realization of what might have happened if it had been shook him to the core. Completing the pressure on the trigger and allowing the hammer to sink against the frame under control, he permitted the barrel to sag downward. His left hand was shaking slightly from the reaction as he passed his fingers through his hair.

"I'm *real* sorry, ma'am!" the Texan replied with genuine contrition, admiring the cool nerve displayed by his visitor. Twirling the Colt back into leather with a dexterity that matched the speed of its withdrawal, he went on in what he realized was not the best of explanation, "Coming in so quiet-like, you took me by surprise."

"So it *seems,*" Ransome answered, still employing all her self-control to keep her voice steady and doing all she could to prevent her shaken nerves from making their condition too obvious. Stepping into the room and closing the door behind her, she continued, "But there is no need for you to be alarmed. This is Rancho Mariposa, and you're quite safe here. I looked in to find out how you are."

"I'm some better than I've been for a spell," the Texan declared, wondering whether ignorance of just how narrow an escape she had had or considerable courage was responsible for the girl's behavior. Concluding it could be the latter rather than the former, he went on, "And, like I said, I'm right sorry for throwing down on you that way."

"It was as much *my* fault as yours," Ransome asserted. "I should have knocked before I opened the door, but I didn't want to disturb you if you were still sleeping."

"I haven't been up and around for long," the Texan admitted. "But I felt so much better when I woke, I reckoned I'd get dressed and take a look around."

"Are you hungry?" Ransome asked, wanting to change the

subject, as she could see the visitor was disturbed by what he had done.

"I'm nowheres close to starving," the Texan replied, removing and returning the gun belt to the top of the chest of drawers. "But I could eat a mite, I reckon, ma'am."

"In that case, I'll have Juanita bring up some food," Ransome offered, and watched for any indication of recognition as she continued. "Then my father, Don Jose Fernando de Armijo y Cordoba, would like to come and talk with you if you feel up to it."

"I'd count it an honor to see him whenever he's a mind, ma'am," the Texan asserted, deciding the name he had been given was only vaguely familiar rather than one with which he had had a long acquaintance. "Am I right in figuring I don't belong here?"

"Yes. You had an accident five days ago and we brought you."

"*Five* days back?"

"Five," the girl confirmed. "Your horse was startled by lightning and threw you into an arroyo. Halc—Tom Grey, our *segundo,* fetched you out and we brought you home to have your injuries treated. My nurse, Juanita, has been tending to your hurts and she's as good as any doctor you're likely to meet, but you've been unconscious, or close to it, ever since you got here."

"So that's why things've been seeming mighty fuzzy," the Texan said quietly. "Anyways, it's real good of you folks to've done all you have for me, ma'am."

"We'd have done it for *anybody* in your position," Ransome declared. "That you were a stranger made no difference, Mister . . . Mister . . . !"

Realizing the girl was using a tactful way to find out his name, the Texan opened his mouth. Then he closed it again, and a look of puzzlement close to alarm came to his face.

"What is it?" Ransome asked, startled by the response to her hint.

"That's the trouble, ma'am," the Texan growled, and turned

to stare at his reflection in the mirror on the washstand. "I don't know who I am!"

"I've heard of that happening when somebody's taken a bad fall like you did," the girl claimed soothingly. "But it doesn't last. You still look a mite shaky. Sit down and rest. I bet you'll soon remember everything about yourself."

"It can't come soon enough for me!" the Texan declared vehemently, but sat on the side of the bed. "Aren't I toting anything to say who I am?"

"How would I know that?" Ransome asked, her manner changing from solicitous to cold.

"I can't remember anything except waking up in here," the man replied. "I felt better and got up. When I saw these clothes on the chair, I figured they must be mine and started to get dressed."

"They're what you were wearing when Halcón Gris and I found you," the girl explained, watching for and failing to detect any suggestion that the sobriquet of the *segundo* might mean something to the visitor as she suspected had been the case when he had heard her father's name. "We had *everything* you were wearing cleaned and put your war bag and rifle in the wardrobe."

"Wasn't there *anything* in the war . . . ?" the Texan commenced.

"*Nobody* who is brought injured to Rancho Mariposa is searched, nor are his belongings!" Ransome interrupted, her manner indignant. "Not even if he might be a—"

"A *what,* ma'am?" the Texan queried. He concluded the possibility left unfinished was one that the beautiful girl did not care to contemplate and went on, "Just what do you reckon I might be, ma'am?"

"You seemed to know us when I told you where you were and my father's name," the girl said quickly, being disinclined to supply the requested information.

"Well, not so much *know* as I reckon I've heard your daddy's name. I wouldn't say's I'm from hereabouts, else you'd know me."

"I don't know *everybody* in Bonham County."

"Likely not, ma'am."

"Does the name Teodoro Fuentes mean anything to you?" Ransome asked, watching for the slightest suggestion that she had selected a name better known to the visitor.

"It's kind of familiar," the Texan admitted.

"How about Monocle Johnny Besgrove? Maybe you've heard of him as Sir John, or even 'that limey'?"

"Like that Fuentes jasper. It seems like I *should* know something about him, but I can't call to mind what it might be."

"Brad Drexell, perhaps?" Ransome suggested, naming the third of the ranchers whose property—along with that of her father—formed Bonham County and, although she sensed her only chance of learning anything the man might not want known would be before he was fully recovered from the effects of Juanita's ministrations, feeling bad about what she was doing.

"It's the same's with your daddy and the other two," the Texan answered. "I reckon I've heard of 'em all, but I'll be switched if I can tie a brand to where, when, or why I should have. Anyways, ma'am, you still haven't told me what sort of *hombre* you reckon I am."

"Your guess is as good as mine," Ransome claimed evasively, her face flushed with something close to embarrassment. She realized that, should her suspicions be correct, it would not be tactful to mention them to one who showed every indication of making his living by his ability with a gun. On the other hand, in spite of the speed with which he could draw the Colt and the impression she had gained of his willingness to use it if necessary, her feminine instincts suggested there was something likable about him. Allowing a smile to come, she went on, "I'll go and have food brought up. Then, if you still feel up to it after you've eaten, I'll fetch my father. Only, when we come to see you, I'll shout and kick the door before I open it."

"Just a knock'll do, ma'am," the Texan claimed, also smiling and coming to his feet. Crossing the room, he opened the door and continued, "Maybe between us we can figure out who I am."

"I hope so," the girl replied, and left. Walking along the passage toward the staircase to the ground floor, she thought, And I hope you *aren't* what you seem to be!

Left alone, the Texan found he was once more acting without the need for conscious thought. Instead of returning to the bed, he set about rectifying what could have been a fatal error if he had been up against a real life-or-death situation requiring the use of the revolver. Continuing to allow his instincts to guide him, he slipped the Colt from its holster and, extracting six cartridges from the loops on his belt, fed them into the chambers of the cylinder. While he was doing so, he reflected that the little he had discovered about himself so far was not entirely to his liking.

4

I'M MAKING IT MY
NEVER-MIND

Don Jose Fernando de Armijo y Cordoba was bored. Active by
nature, he resented the riding accident sustained a week earlier
that had left him confined to the house constructed in the Spanish colonial style by his grandfather. Instead of being able to go
out on the range, his view was limited to across the plaza and
what could be seen through the open gates in the high and
sturdy adobe wall that surrounded the buildings. Therefore, he
hoped to be able to relieve his boredom by going upstairs to
introduce himself and, employing tact, satisfy his curiosity with
regards to the injured man his daughter had brought home.
From what he had just been told by Juanita, he considered this
should be possible in the very near future.

In his late fifties, close to six feet tall and slender, the owner
of Rancho Mariposa was still a handsome man. Time had
added an inch or two to his waistline and his once-jet black
hair was liberally streaked with gray. However, his physique
still suggested the strength and energy of a younger man. He

had lived all his life in Texas and was still regarded as a traitor by some people in Mexico because of the stand his family had taken during the struggle to gain independence from Presidente Antonio López de Santa Anna's tyrannical domination.[1] Nevertheless, he invariably wore the attire of a well-to-do *haciendero* from below the Rio Grande. Nor had his selection of such clothing and the retention of his property's original name, albeit using a "Bench C" for his brand instead of the more complicated variety favored south of the border, been held against him by his Anglo neighbors. They were aware that, in addition to having been a most effective scout for General Samuel Houston throughout the earlier conflict, his father had also served with distinction in the same capacity for the United States Army during the Mexican War of 1846. It was equally common knowledge that Cordoba himself was just as active in supporting the cause of the Confederate States, having been with Colonel John Salmon "Rip" Ford and wounded shortly before victory was achieved at the Battle of Palmitto Hill.[2]

At that hour of the morning, were it not for being injured, Cordoba would have been out on the range working with his cowhands. Instead, bandaged and splinted, the broken leg was resting upon the cushions of the wheelchair in which he was seated. This offered him the means to move around the ground floor of the house, and he could hobble up the wide stone staircase with the help of a crutch and the stout black walking cane trimmed with silver bands that rested against either side of it. For all that, inactivity always made him restless, and he had been pleased by the estimation of the visitor's condition he had received from Juanita. Despite its disturbing aspects, having

1. *Although there is no mention of the part played by the ancestors of Don Jose Fernando de Armijo y Cordoba, details of some of the struggle to gain independence for Texas are given in the* Ole Devil Hardin *series.*
2. *Because of the slowness of communications at that period having prevented the news reaching the area, the Battle of Palmitto Hill—ironically won by the force serving the Confederate States—was fought on May 13, 1865, approximately a month after the War Between the States had ended elsewhere.*

been told the man should be fit enough to talk, he was offered an excuse to do something that he could handle in his present restrictive condition.

Seeing seven riders appear approaching the main entrance, having been hidden by the wall until coming into view around the bend in the trail to Flamingo, the rancher changed his immediate plans. He was on the point of calling and asking Juanita to go upstairs to see how the injured man was feeling, but refrained. As they drew nearer, recognizing the man on the high-stepping black Thoroughbred at the center of the group, he became aware of a strange sense of foreboding. There had been a time when visitors from Rancho Miraflores would not have aroused such a sensation. However, having been born and raised in Mexico, the men who had inherited it on the death of his old friend at the hands of cow thieves were not the kind with whom he wished to associate. In fact, because of unacceptable behavior the first time they had paid a call, he had made it known that the one who was coming was no longer welcome in his home.

That Javier Fuentes should choose to ignore the prohibition came as no surprise to Cordoba. Nor was it unusual that he should be accompanied by three Hispanics and three Anglos, all well armed and of less than savory appearance. While the rancher did not know who any of them were, it did not require any great powers of deduction to guess what each would be. As was his own policy, Rancho Miraflores had never differentiated between the two ethnic groups when hiring hands. However, regardless of their range-country attire, he doubted very much if this particular group's experience with cattle went any further than employing a knife and fork on cooked meat. Even before the trouble that was threatening to tear apart the whole of Bonham County, having fired almost all of the old crew, the Fuentes brothers had selected men who were hardcases rather than ordinary cowhands for their replacements.

In his early twenties, although recently there had developed something of an unhealthy pallor in his cheeks and an unnatural glitter in his eyes, the younger of the Fuentes brothers was

tall, slim, and handsome. From head to foot, he was clad after
the latest style worn by rich dandies in the cattle country of
Mexico. His *charro* clothes and high-crowned black sombrero
were costly, with much silver- and gold-wire filigree to flaunt
the family's wealth ostentatiously. The two Colt Artillery
Model Peacemaker revolvers in the fast-draw holsters of an
equally ornate gun belt had fancy silver Tiffany grips. Silver
conchos also decorated his horse's bridle and saddle, its horn
even larger than the norm. While less flamboyant, the plaited
leather quirt dangling by a loop from his right wrist was thick,
vicious looking, and reportedly used at the slightest provocation upon any creature that invoked his easily aroused wrath.

Crossing the plaza and coming to a halt a short distance in
front of the house, the hired hands ranged themselves in a
rough semicircle with the dandified young man at the center. A
vicious jab from the sharp spikes of his spurs' oversized rowels
caused the black Thoroughbred to bound forward a short distance. It was brought to a stop by a savage jerk, via the reins, to
a bit offering a leverage intended to exert control in a most
painful fashion. Despite its elegant lines and evidence of excellent breeding, the animal was trembling and sweating. The look
in its eyes indicated such harsh treatment was so normal as to
be expected and feared.

Watching the exhibition, Cordoba's expression of distaste at
such unnecessarily cruel behavior spoke far more eloquently
than words. Despite his well-deserved reputation for tolerance
and hospitality, there was good cause for the dislike he felt, and
it went beyond the ill treatment invariably inflicted by his visitor upon whatever mount was unfortunate enough to be in use.
Since his arrival at Rancho Miraflores, Javier Fuentes had
proved to be arrogant, spoiled, cruel, and vindictive by nature
and inclination. It was claimed that only his sibling, Teodoro,
and to a lesser degree Dr. Otto Grantz—newly arrived medical
practitioner of Flamingo, as length of residency was judged in
the West—could exercise any degree of control over him when
he flew into a rage.

"*Saludos,* Don Cordoba," the young man greeted. He used

Spanish, although aware that—in spite of retaining the long-established family name for the property—the rancher preferred to have English spoken around Rancho Mariposa. "It's a fine day."

"So it would seem," Cordoba replied in English, knowing his unwelcome visitor to be fully conversant in it. "But I'm sure you didn't ride all this way just to discuss the weather, so to what do I owe the *honor* of your visit?"

"We heard you'd met with an accident and I thought I'd come over to offer you *and yours* my protection," Fuentes answered, still in Spanish, but his handsome face twisted into surly lines.

"I am grateful to you for the thought," Cordoba declared, despite his rich baritone voice expressing no such emotion. He had noticed the emphasis laid upon the words *and yours,* and, knowing who was meant, did not care for it. "But, as I told you some time ago, yours was not an acquaintance I have any wish to continue and I have had no cause to revise my opinion."

"There are some who would say in these troubled times *we* of our race should forget past differences and stick together," the younger man answered, his voice growing harsher.

"A wise decision," the rancher admitted, remembering how both the brothers frequently referred to their Hispanic birthright, although—like himself—the man from whom they had inherited the property had invariably claimed to be a Texan first and a Chicano second. "And one which Sir John Besgrove was expressing only two days ago."

"A *gringo . . .*" Fuentes began, spitting out the second word as if it was a bad taste in his mouth.

"A *friend* who is welcome into my home at any time," Cordoba corrected. "As he was at Rancho Miraflores in the days of your late uncle."

"Our welcome is only to *friends* we can *trust,*" the young man countered. "And, as things stand around here, those who are not our friends must be regarded as our *enemies.*"

"Is that the word of your brother?"

"It is. These are *very* troubled times, *señor,* when a man must choose his side and be prepared to let this be seen. After all, who can tell when and where the rustlers who plague us will strike next? Or whether they will keep on just driving off cattle when there are richer prizes that would bring loot more easy to dispose of?"

Listening to the all-too-obvious underlying current of menace and threat that had come into the Spanish side of the bilingual conversation, the rancher felt his sense of foreboding growing stronger. He was aware that the majority of his crew— every fighting man, to make matters worse—were too far away to let their appearance serve as a deterrent to whatever mischief might be contemplated by the young man. He also wished that he had something far more potent readily available than the single-shot, .36-caliber Remington-Thomas Model of 1858 cane gun leaning against the right side of his wheelchair.

Having been equally aware of the possibility Fuentes had suggested with regards to the activities of the cow thieves,[3] whose operations had cost the loss of human lives as well as cattle and caused much bad feeling throughout Bonham County, the rancher did not care to hear him mention it. The gang had confined their activities to stealing stock and killing anybody who was present so far, but it was only a short step before men so well organized and ruthless might decide to start seeking the more lucrative prospects offered by the ranch houses themselves.

However, wild and vicious as Cordoba knew the younger of the Fuentes brothers to be, he could not believe an attempt to capitalize upon such a contingency was envisaged!

Yet was it beyond the bounds of possibility?

Having all the haughty pride of his well-born Spanish blood, Javier had deeply resented being barred from visiting Rancho Mariposa and pressing, forcing would be a more accurate term, his attentions further upon the beautiful daughter of the house.

---

3. *Although the term "rustlers" was used in the other cattle-raising states, Texans employed the blunter and more accurate description and said, "cow thieves."*

His vindictive nature would have constantly insisted that the affront to his dignity and desires must be avenged. Therefore, either having been prompted by the hardcases—who wanted to gather the loot such an endeavor would produce—or thinking up the plan on his own behalf, he had come to turn the situation locally to his advantage.

Cordoba tried to take comfort from the thought that, his faults in other ways notwithstanding, Teodoro Fuentes would never countenance such an outrage!

The conclusion was weakened by realizing the elder brother might be unaware of what the younger was contemplating!

If an attack was launched and carried out with a cold-blooded thoroughness and lack of concern for taking human lives, there would not be any survivors to point an accusing finger at those responsible!

Even as the rancher was reaching the final summation, light footsteps sounded from behind him and a small hand rested gently on his shoulder. Out of the corner of his eye, he caught the glint of sunlight off the barrel of what he realized was his daughter's Winchester Model of 1876 carbine.

Turning his insolent gaze past her father, Fuentes swept off the heavy sombrero and favored Ransome Cordoba with an exaggerated bow. While doing so, his eyes roamed over her slender figure and made no attempt to conceal the lascivious demeanor that had caused him to be told never to return to Rancho Mariposa. The scrutiny brought two bright spots of color to her cheeks and a look of cold disapproval from the rancher. However, he was amused by the former and paid no attention to the latter.

"In view of what you said," Cordoba commented, the timbre of his otherwise polite tone having an edge like the finest Toledo steel, "perhaps you and your companions would be better employed giving your protection to Rancho Miraflores."

"Uppity old son of a bitch, ain't he, Javier?" inquired the tallest and bulkiest of the white men, his voice harsh and its dialect Kansan. Starting his horse moving forward, he went on,

"I thought you told us he'd act all hoss-pissable, or some such thing, should we come on over and offer to help him out."

"That was what I believed, Señor Coltrane," Fuentes answered, speaking English with a distinct accent for the first time. "Perhaps if I was to introduce you, the hospitality would be granted."

"It's going to be, whether you introduce me or not," the Rancho Miraflores rider stated, his right hand hovering over the walnut grips of a low-hanging Colt Peacemaker. Without looking back, he continued, "Ain't it, boys?"

"That it is, *amigo!*" claimed the shortest, heaviest, and most villainous looking of the Mexicans, in heavily accented English. A wolfish grin twisted at and, although it hardly seemed possible, rendered more evil his unwashed features as he continued, "I was raised to believe *'mi casa, su casa'* applied no matter who it is comes calling."[4]

"Then what says we does something about it?" the biggest white hardcase hinted.

Listening to what was said and watching everything that was happening, Cordoba cared for none of it. Having heard the white man's name and something of the *very* unsavory reputation which went with it, he felt a twinge of fear. Not for himself, but for Ransome. If Asa Coltrane and the others started to force their way into the house, she would try to stop them. Competent as she was with the carbine, she had never needed to use it against another human being, and the rancher was aware of how vastly firing at a target—or even a stock-killing black bear or cougar—differed from facing the prospect of shooting at a man, regardless of how good the reason for doing so. Nor would the fact that she was still little more than a child, and a girl at that, deter the hired hardcases from effectively countering anything they considered to be a threat to their intentions and existence.

4. Mi casa, su casa, *"My house is your house,"* traditional greeting given by wealthy Mexicans when receiving welcome visitors.

"Anybody's comes closer, or tries to pull iron's going to right quick wish he'd never got took with the notion!"

Even as the rancher was trying to think what action he might take to avert the perilous situation, the words in a commanding Texas drawl sounded from somewhere above the porch. They were accompanied by the unmistakable sound of a Winchester's lever-operated mechanism being put through its loading cycle. What was more, he realized, both could only have originated from the injured man about whom he had so much curiosity.

Startled exclamations burst from the hardcases. Jerking his hand away from the Colt, as if it had suddenly become white hot, Coltrane joined the others in looking upward. All any of them needed was a single glance to realize the warning was valid and could be carried out. Held by a bare-headed stranger whose tanned face showed marks of fading bruises, the Winchester Model of 1876 rifle was rock steady and handled with the familiarity which came only from competence in its use.

*   *   *

Having been looking out of the net drapes of the glass-paneled doors leading to a balcony, in the hope of seeing something that might jog his memory into responding, the Texan had watched the riders approaching. Although he was unable to understand why, something in their demeanor had suggested they were not coming for any well-disposed purpose. What was more, instincts he had already learned to act upon—if not entirely trust, after the way he had greeted the girl a short while earlier—supplied the information he needed to decide how to respond. Although he had loaded the Colt, he had not offered to collect it from the top of the chest of drawers.

Having remembered what the girl had told him about the rest of his property, the man had been taking the Winchester from the wardrobe when the recollection of his discovery with regards to the condition of the revolver caused him to check its state of readiness. Finding it was unloaded, he had started to open the war bag before realizing what he was doing. The impulse had proven correct. Taking sufficient cartridges from the appropriate box which was therein, he charged the magazine tube through the slot in the side of the frame. With the precaution taken, he crossed the room and reached the edge of the balcony unnoticed by the newcomers until he addressed them.

"Who the 'something' hell might you be?" Coltrane demanded belligerently, recovering quickly from his initial shock and gaining courage from appreciating numbers still favored his party.

"I'm a man who doesn't take kind to talk like that where a lady can hear it," the Texan replied, having guessed from the bow given by the fancily dressed young Mexican that the black-haired girl was with her father. Such as the deep-rooted repugnance he had acquired in his unremembered past for hearing foul language spoken in the presence of the fair sex, regardless of age and status, he continued, "So, was I you, I'd clean up my language with Miss Cordoba being down there."

"Be that so?" the spokesman for the white hardcases growled, conscious of his reputation of being "wild, woolly, full of fleas, and never curried below the knees." Poking his left thumb against his chest for added emphasis, he went on, "I'm Asa Coltrane and I'll 'something-well' talk how the 'something' I feel like doing, no matter who's listening. Which no god-damned saddle tramp's going to tell me I can't. So you bill out of things that's none of your 'mother-something' never-mind."

"These folks've been good to me and I'm making it my never-mind, all the way from here to there and back the long way," the Texan claimed. Although he did not raise his voice, the threat of retribution was plain in it. "So, being quick-sick of your foulmouthing, I'm saying I reckon it's time you was headed back where you come from, ready to start giving it all that protection your boss reckons'll be needed."

"Who the hell are *you* to be telling us to leave?" Fuentes demanded in English, his voice grating savagely.

"The 'yes' or 'no' to who-all goes or stays's in the hands of Señor Cordoba where the rest of you're concerned," the man on the balcony replied, without allowing the Winchester to sag from its alignment. "But while he's making up his mind on it for you and the rest of your bunch, seeing's how Coltrane's put it down 'twixt me and him *personal,* you'd best tell him to clean out his mouth or turn and get the hell gone beyond hearing distance." Then, proving he had not allowed his attention to be distracted, he growled, "That hand'd better come out *pronto* and *empty,* foulmouth!"

Believing the intervention by Fuentes had diverted the Texan's gaze from him, Coltrane had moved his right hand in what might have passed as a gesture intended to scratch at his ribs beneath the left side of his grubby calfskin vest. However, deducing to whom the final sentence was meant, he glanced up and found the muzzle of the rifle was pointing his way in spite of its holder having started to speak to somebody else. Doing as he was advised, if so mild a term could be applied to what was obviously a command charged with menace, he brought his hand into sight with exaggerated care.

"I'll wait for you back there a piece, Javier," the hardcase claimed.

Tugging on the reins less than gently, Coltrane guided his horse around in its own length. However, the moment his back was turned to the building, he slid the hand beneath the vest once more and closed it around the butt of the Colt Storekeeper Model Peacemaker he carried concealed in an open-fronted spring-retention shoulder holster. Twisting the weapon free, he rotated his torso and started to bring it up. His hope of taking the Texan by surprise proved totally invalid. Flame erupted from the muzzle of the Winchester on the balcony. He screeched as a .45 bullet tore through the brim of his hat and gouged a bloody furrow across the side of his head just above his left ear. Stunned instead of having received a far more serious injury, with the revolver slipping unheeded from his fingers, he toppled limply sideways from the saddle.

Although the rest of the hardcases had expected something of the sort from Coltrane, events moved far too swiftly for them to capitalize upon his actions!

"The next's for you, *boss man!*" warned the Texan, making

the lever of his rifle blur up and down the instant he fired and replenishing the chamber.

"If the gentleman up there doesn't send it into you, I will, *Mister* Fuentes!" Ransome stated, having collected the carbine from the rack by the front door on seeing who was approaching and brought it to her shoulder as soon as the shot sounded from over her head.

"This *isn't* just a walking cane!" Cordoba supported as his daughter was speaking, lifting and pointing his disguised firearm at Fuentes. "It's a *most* effective gun!"

Having seen similar devices and feeling sure the rancher was not bluffing, the young Mexican realized that all three weapons were aimed directly at him. Nor did the thought that none of his men were covered offer him any solace. He was aware that if any of them was successful in making a hostile gesture, he was highly unlikely to see its result. Even if they had been prepared for the intervention from above, they were unlikely to be so concerted in their action that they would be able to prevent at least one shot being fired at him. While the cane gun might miss, he doubted whether the carbine would and felt sure the rifle held by that grim-looking *Tejano* on the balcony would not. For the first time in his life, he was in mortal peril and he discovered the prospect of danger was not to his liking.

"Don't move, *any* of you!" Fuentes ordered, his voice shrill with the anxiety caused by appreciating just how precarious a situation he was facing, but he had no need to speak.

Appreciating the danger, none of the five surviving hardcases attempted to complete the drawing of the guns for which each had reached. Not only did they believe either the girl or the man on the balcony would select them, and not their leader, as a target should they continue, but they saw a massive woman of mixed blood appear in the open doorway from which the girl had emerged. She was holding a double-barreled shotgun in a way which warned she knew how to use it, and at that range it would prove even more deadly than the two Winchesters.

Glancing each side to make sure his words had been obeyed, the young Mexican returned his gaze to the rancher. He was seething with fury at the failure of the plan for revenge he had been assured by Coltrane would work as they had watched every fighting man of Rancho Mariposa depart and have time to be well clear of the area before leaving their hiding place nearby. Nor were his feelings improved by realizing he would be compelled to report his failure to his brother even if the hardcase was only wounded.

"Look to your man!" Cordoba instructed. "Then, as we have nothing further to say and you probably have things of importance to do elsewhere, don't let us detain you any longer. And I would be *obliged* if you would refrain from coming here again. Much as it pains me to say so a *second* time to one who is related to a man I was proud to call friend, you are unwelcome on Rancho Mariposa. Do *not* come back."

5

MY NAME *IS* SMITH!

"You have my gratitude for helping, my friend," Don Jose Fernando de Armijo y Cordoba stated as he and his daughter entered the room allocated to the man she had brought home injured.

"I'm right pleased I could help out, sir," the Texan replied, placing a tray holding used crockery on the floor of the balcony and stepping through the open glass-paneled doors. "Like I said, you folks've treated me real good and I figured something had to be done about those yahoos. Which I reckoned I was pretty well placed to do it."

Almost half an hour had passed since the hardcases with Javier Fuentes had ascertained Asa Coltrane was suffering from nothing worse than a scalp wound that rendered him unconscious. Presented with a strip of white cloth by Juanita, who refused to employ her well-known medical skills by giving further assistance, one of them had used it as a bandage. While the first aid was being carried out, much to their relief, their leader had not responded verbally to the curt dismissal he had received from the owner of Rancho Mariposa. Instead, he had spent the time glowering silently from the Cordobas to the Texan—who had continued to line the Winchester Model of 1876 rifle downward from the balcony—and back. With Coltrane made ready for departure, Fuentes had given the order to ride and led the rest toward the gate still without addressing any comment to the cause of his discomfiture.

Having kept the men from Rancho Miraflores under observation as long as they were in sight, the rancher had taken the precaution of sending one of the youngsters who was in the vicinity of the house to fetch back Tom "Halcón Gris" Grey and some of the hands. Then he and his daughter had gone upstairs to thank their guest for coming so competently to their assistance. They had found him sitting on the balcony, his rifle close at hand. However, although he, too, had clearly been keeping watch, he had finished the meal that Juanita had fetched for him.

"If you are too tired to talk just now . . . ?" Cordoba hinted.

"Shucks, no," the Texan answered. "Happen you've a mind, sit down and we'll visit for a spell."

"That was quite a shot, creasing Coltrane the way you did," Ransome Cordoba praised, having said she would prefer to remain standing, and waiting until her father had transferred the rest of the young man's clothing from the chair to the bed and sat down. "Most fellers would have killed him."

"Could be likely he's lucky I didn't," the Texan declared. "I was figuring on stopping him, no matter how it was done. But I can't say's how I'm sorry things turned out the way they did, it's no easy thing to take a life."

"Have you killed many men?" the girl inquired, but from a—to her—puzzling need to know more about this man she had rescued and not out of idle or morbid curiosity.

"That's *not* a question you should ask, Ransome!" the rancher asserted, his manner stern and showing he disapproved of such a breach of range-country etiquette as the question had been. "You must excuse my daught—"

"No harm's done, nor offense taken, sir," the Texan replied. Then he turned his gaze to the girl and his face was troubled as he went on, "I *reckon* I could have killed a man, or even more than just the one. Hell, you'd think a feller would remember a thing like that, wouldn't you? But it's like everything else, I can't bring to mind whether I have or not."

"Going by what I have heard of him, you would have had no cause for regret if you had killed Coltrane," Cordoba said reassuringly, having noticed the note of tension and concern which came into the younger man's voice and sympathizing with how he must feel about the continued refusal of any recollection of his identity or past life to break through. "He is a killer, hired for that and nothing else."

"It seems I've heard of such," the Texan admitted. Then a look of frustration close to anger came to his face and, clenching his hands into hard fists, he went on heatedly, "Goddamn it, seeing's how I know how to do things like handling a gun, why can't I remember who I am?"

"My daughter told me you had such a problem," the rancher admitted. "While I don't wish you to think I am interfering in your private affairs, haven't you *anything* in your war bag that might tell you who you are?"

"Not a single thing," the Texan replied after having crossed to the wardrobe and carried out a closer examination of the war bag's contents than had been possible when seeking ammunition for his rifle. "You'd reckon a man'd have *something* with his name on it."

"You had on a money belt and a wallet in your pocket," Cordoba remarked, giving his injured thigh a slap expressive of annoyance at having been so remiss in failing to mention the matter earlier. "It was not that we were prying when we found them. Your jacket was in need of repairs and the wallet was soaking. The belt had to be removed so Juanita could attend to your injuries. I took the liberty of locking them in my safe until you recovered, without looking in either."

"That was real good of you, sir," the Texan declared, remembering the girl had claimed neither he nor his property had been searched and, despite the removal of two items which could have solved the mystery of his identity, feeling sure she had spoken the truth.

"Perhaps they have something in them to tell us who you are," Ransome suggested, intrigued by the visitor and hoping to be able to satisfy her curiosity in a way that would not arouse his resentment.

"I surely hope so, ma'am!" the Texan asserted miserably. "Because it riles the hell out of me not to know—Happen you'll excuse my language."

"Your interest is understandable," Cordoba admitted, his manner soothing and waving a hand to indicate he took no offense at the use of the word *hell* in the presence of his daughter. "I have seen such a loss of memory happen before when somebody was thrown from a horse and received injuries like those you suffered. It seems part of the mind still responds to various things that were often done, even though unable to remember personal matters."

"Did those other jaspers ever get back to knowing who they were?" the Texan asked in a worried tone, the comment about the response of the mind reviving the misgivings he had formulated over his obvious skill with weapons.

"Everyone I have known did," the rancher stated, but refrained from mentioning the number was few. "Either it came back to them without help, or something was said or done that caused them to remember."

"Perhaps if you heard your name it would help," Ransome offered. "I know there are so *many,* but we could try some and see if any is familiar."

"I'm game to try *anything*!" the Texan declared.

"You don't look like a Marmaduke, a Wilberforce, or an Algernon," the girl stated, selecting three Anglo first names that had always struck her as slightly ludicrous in an attempt to bring a lighter note to the conversation.

The ploy succeeded!

"Happen I'm any of *them,* ma'am," the young man drawled. "I reckon I'd sooner I *didn't* know."

"It will help if you're called something like Hazeltine, Higginsbottom, or even *Ramsbottom,* although I'm sure you wouldn't want *that* for a name," Ransome continued, looking coy and seeking to relieve the tension further by picking the most unusual English surnames she had heard Sir John Besgrove mention. Having received a nod of approval that told her that her motives were understood by her father, she continued, "But if you should happen to be a Smith . . . what is it?"

The question was provoked by the response to the last, most commonplace, name suggested by the girl!

On hearing it, the relaxed and amused expression left the young man's face and he sat up stiffly!

"Well, I'll be damned if it didn't work!" the Texan said. "My name *is* Smith!"

Prompted by hearing the word, "Smith," the Texan remembered who he was and what had brought him to Bonham County!

While relieved to discover he had a justifiable reason for having developed such competence in handling firearms, the young man also realized he must keep most of the information that flooded back to himself!

Despite the kindness and consideration he had received since recovering consciousness in Rancho Mariposa, the Texan was aware that—the gratitude he felt and the liking he had formed for the Cordobas notwithstanding—they might find themselves with greatly opposing interests in the task he had been sent to carry out!

* * *

The events that were to drastically change the life of Sergeant Waxahachie Smith of the Texas Rangers had commenced when Captain Frank Thornton called him back early from his furlough and gave him the order that had caused him to be on his way to the border town of Flamingo.

Every instinct as a lawman possessed by Smith had suggested the chore ahead would not be easy. For an experienced lawman, particularly one whose well-deserved reputation for tough competence had resulted in his recent appointment as the senior peace officer of a large county, to have taken such a roundabout way when requesting assistance as was his right under the legislature of Texas, gave strength to the supposition. Instead of coming direct, the message from Sheriff Daniel Tobin, which was responsible for his premature return to the headquarters of Company D had arrived via the office of Cyrus Holmes, a member of the state attorney general's legal staff in Austin.

The suggestion from Holmes, which amounted to an order, was for the Rangers to help Tobin look into a spate of cattle stealing affecting not only the ranchers throughout Bonham County but also threatening the well-being of the community, which was its seat. According to the information supplied by Holmes, whoever they might be, the cow thieves were not playing favorites. They were hitting each of the four spreads, all of whom had had men killed during raids, with complete impartiality. However, if the sheriff had any suspicions about who was responsible for the situation—or even the possible identity of the cow thieves—there had been no mention of him having put either into writing.

Despite the dearth of information, the sergeant and his superior had concluded the affair was going beyond a case of cattle stealing in which murder was done. As was only to be expected under the circumstances, because the guilt of the miscreants had not been established, accusation and countercharge were flying back and forth between the ranches. The normally no-more-than-friendly rivalry of the crews, which had never previously become anything worse even though two of them were employed by Chicanos, was rapidly deteriorating into open hostility.

The situation had all the earmarks of a range war brewing!

According to Holmes's letter, although the owners of Rancho Miraflores had suffered like everybody else at the hands of the cow thieves, they had given Tobin another cause for concern. They had announced that, as the law did not appear to be able to offer them the protection for which they paid taxes and were thereby entitled to, they would hire the kind of help necessary to defend themselves.

The Texas Rangers were in accord with Holmes over his assertion that such protection meant hired guns and the possibility of more trouble than the sheriff could hope to handle with his own resources under the conditions that prevailed. Regardless of his considerable experience elsewhere, he was a newcomer and every one of his deputies was born and had grown up around Bonham County. With the best of will in the world, they could not help themselves being swayed by bonds of kin or friendships of long standing with one spread or another.

While Smith had not previously been called to cope with such a state of affairs, his career so far having been spent dealing with other, more conventional forms of lawbreaking, it had always been a prospect that he had disliked even contemplating!

Going by all the sergeant had learned from other Rangers who had been involved elsewhere, dealing with a range war differed greatly from hunting down outlaws. In the first place, for the most part, the majority of the people engaged in it were otherwise law-abiding members of the community. What was more, with *very* few exceptions, the issues behind the conflict were almost certain to be complicated. Generally, there were elements of right and wrong on both sides and each had some cause for grievance against the other. To complicate matters further, even when the source of controversy appeared clear to an outsider relying upon scanty information—like himself—a close examination could prove this was not the case.

Regardless of his misgivings, it was not a fear of responsibility or what might lie ahead that had caused Smith's preoccupation as he was riding along the trail leading to Flamingo!

The fact that he had already attained the rank of sergeant while barely into his mid-twenties was testimony to Smith's capabilities in the special jurisdictional duties of a Texas Ranger. Until being sent out this time, he had handled every assignment with a high level of efficiency that had his superiors giving no small consideration to promoting him higher. There were even some who said he might attain the rank of captain at a far younger age than had previously been achieved.[1]

Because the assignment upon which he was engaged was of a most delicate nature, there was no external evidence to indicate the sergeant was a member of a long-established law-enforcement agency possessing jurisdictional authority all through the Lone Star State.[2] Nor, if it came to a point, would there have been if he had merely been paying a casual visit to Flamingo. Despite the years they had been in existence, the Texas Rangers had never acquired an official uniform. What was more, unless a situation such as the need to provide proof of authority demanded it, the "star in a circle" badge of office—made, as tradition now demanded, from a Mexican silver ten-peso coin—was not displayed openly. It was, in fact, concealed with a document establishing his official capacity in secret pockets of his money belt.

Smith had adopted clothing and an appearance that would, he hoped, create the effect he sought to achieve. Prior to becoming a peace officer, he had worked as a cowhand for long enough to have acquired the skill needed to pass as one. However, he had decided he might learn things faster if he let it be believed he was visiting Flamingo for a more sinister reason than seeking a riding chore handling cattle. When a range war was brewing, it drew hired guns like flies to a rotting carcass and a man could get some idea of the situation by pretending to be one of them. Of course, doing so was not without risks. If either faction thought the other had already taken on the new arrival, its members might consider the most prudent thing

1. *Although Waxahachie Smith did not achieve the distinction, during the Prohibition era, Alvin Dustine "Cap" Fog acquired his sobriquet by becoming the youngest man ever to attain the rank of captain in the Texas Rangers. For further information about his career and how this came about see the* Alvin Dustine "Cap" Fog *series.*
2. *For more detailed information regarding the Texas Rangers, see* Item 17 *of the* APPENDIX.

would be to remove him before he could start earning his pay by taking hostile action against them.

However, such a contingency was not responsible for the perturbation that had rendered Smith less wary than would otherwise have been the case and led to his accident!

The sergeant was aware it had not been his latest assignment that was worrying him. However, while never one to be plagued by self-doubts about his competence, neither was he arrogant nor foolhardy enough to consider himself invincible. He carried scars on his body that would have removed any such delusion before it could take hold. Provided he avoided unnecessary risks and kept his wits about him at all times, he was satisfied that he could take care of himself. Although none had threatened to prove so complex as trying to prevent a range war, or ending it should hostilities already have broken out, he had handled difficult duties before and with enough success to have warranted his early promotion.

Nevertheless, the sergeant had known this occasion was *very* different!

Apart from the assignment, Smith's problem was a *very* old one that had puzzled men down through the ages!

Woman!

In the sergeant's case, the woman was Sally Palmer. Having known each other ever since they were children, until she had been sent East to acquire an education her mother had considered could only be attained there, their friendship had blossomed into something far more intimate when they met again on her return. Unfortunately, although her parents had not objected openly to them becoming engaged, the course of true love had not run smoothly.

While Hector Palmer had conceded that the Texas Rangers were a most estimable body of peace officers and a credit to the state, he had not concealed his belief that he would prefer his future son-in-law to follow a less precarious—and more lucrative—occupation. It was a sentiment that his daughter had quickly come to share. More and more when she and Smith were together, she had complained about him being in a line of work that, as well as frequently taking him away for days, sometimes weeks at a time, was not exceptionally well paid and could prove extremely dangerous.

To a certain extent, the sergeant could understand and even sympathize with Sally's protests, but he believed what he was doing to be important and even essential. Furthermore, he considered it was work for which he was well suited by temperament and training. Certainly he could not see himself settling down, as had been hinted, in a managerial capacity at the hotel owned by her father. He had been a bellhop there as a boy. Although he had fond memories of special events, such as when he had carried up the property of the famous top hand of Ole Devil Hardin's legendary floating outfit, Mark Counter—right bower[3] to its leader, Captain Dusty Fog, an exceptionally handsome Herculean-thewed giant and one hell of a fighting man by all accounts[4]—they were too few and far between to enamor him to the prospect of returning to the hotel business in spite of the status he was promised being higher.

The matter had been brought to a head by Smith having received the early recall from his furlough. Even though doing so meant he would be unable to escort Sally to a ball at which the governor of Texas was guest of honor, knowing only something of the gravest importance would have induced Captain

---

3. *"Right bower,"* second in command. Derived from the name given to the second-highest trump card in the game of euchre.

4. *The event is described in:* THE SOUTH WILL RISE AGAIN.

4a. *Details of the careers of Captain Dustine Edward Marsden "Dusty" Fog and Mark Counter can be found in the various volumes of the* Civil War *and* Floating Outfit *series.*

4b. *We also have the privilege of being official biographer for Mark's grandson, Sergeant Ranse Smith, Company Z, Texas Rangers and two great-grandsons, Deputy Sheriff Bradford "Brad" Counter of Rockabye County, Texas, and James Allenvale "Bunduki" Gunn. See, respectively, the* Alvin Dustine "Cap" Fog, Rockabye County *and* Bunduki *series.*

4c. *The sobriquet of James Allenvale Gunn derives from the Swahili word for a hand-held firearm of any kind being* "bunduki." *It gave rise to the pun that when he was a child he was* "Toto ya Bunduki," *Son of a Gun."*

Thornton to send for him, he had not hesitated before agreeing to go back to headquarters.

Sally had not been slow to react when her fiancé informed her of his intentions!

Smith had been told he *must* decline whatever assignment was in the offing or consider their engagement was at an end!

Nor would Sally listen when Smith had tried to explain his reasons for answering the summons!

On arriving at headquarters, the sergeant had received apologies from his superior for bringing his furlough to an early end. However, Thornton had declared the matter was of great urgency. What was more, while not an adherent to the already often-quoted "one war, one Ranger" train of thought,[5] he was unable to send in more than a single member of his company. Due to circumstances beyond his control, it had to be Smith. With one exception, everybody else was already committed to assignments from which none could be spared. The only other possible alternative, Ranger Talbot Ottoway, was also on furlough. However, he had taken the precaution of ensuring he could not be located and anyway, the captain had asserted in confidence, it was likely some of his other activities would cause his dismissal in the not-too-distant future.[6] On the other hand, Thornton had said, Smith was only in the nature of an advance party sent to reconnoitre the situation. Then, having evaluated his findings, whatever extra help was needed would be provided the moment it became available.

A lesser man might have explained how things stood between himself and his fiancée, but the sergeant had refused to take such a way out. He had sworn an oath on becoming a Ranger, by which he had in effect agreed to take any assign-

5. *According to an often-repeated story, although possibly apocryphal, a sheriff requested assistance from the Texas Rangers to help bring to an end a range war in his county. When only a single Ranger arrived, he was asked why more had not been sent and was told, "Well there's only the one war, isn't there?"*
6. *What eventually happened to Ranger Talbot Ottoway is told in:* SLIP GUN.

ment he was given in the interests of preserving law and order throughout the sovereign state of Texas. Therefore, having been raised to believe a man's word was his bond, he neither could nor *would* refuse when given such a task, regardless of how his private life would be affected.

Although Smith had tried to explain to Sally how strongly he felt on the matter of honor and duty, his words had fallen upon deaf ears. Bursting into a flood of tears, which alarmed him more than would a flow of vituperation, she had declared he could not love her and, therefore, she could see no point in continuing their relationship. Returning his ring, which had cost him a sizable piece of his savings, she had stormed from the room and, even before he left her father's home, had set off for the ball accompanied by a distant cousin highly regarded by her parents.

Regardless of his well-developed sense of duty and responsibility, the sergeant had not found accepting the end of his engagement an easy matter. Sally was the first woman he had loved and, having set her on a pedestal because of this, it came hard to realize she could be so lacking in understanding of his position.

Such a frame of mind was hardly the best when a man was setting out to deal with a difficult and potentially dangerous situation!

In fact, regardless of five days having elapsed, Smith was still brooding upon the matter to such an extent he had failed to notice the change in the weather and was caught unawares by the bolt of lightning that struck the cottonwood and resulted in his present involvement with the people at Rancho Mariposa.

6
THESE ARE TROUBLED TIMES

"Smith!" Ransome Cordoba said, eyeing in a speculative fashion the man she had helped to rescue.

"Smith," the Texan repeated, showing no resentment over the slight suggestion of skepticism that had tinged the girl's voice as she spoke the single word. "Given first pick at the remuda, it's not the name I'd have snaked out of the bunch. You should see the looks I get when I sign it on a hotel register."

"That's because you belong to a *very* large family, Mr. Smith," Don Jose Fernando de Armijo y Cordoba put in quickly, darting a prohibitive glance at his daughter as she had once again come close to crossing the boundaries of range-country etiquette. While she had not gone as far as inquiring, "Is that your *summer* name?" she had made it plain she suspected it might be.[1] He felt certain the response he had elicited

---

1. *In the Old West, if a person experienced doubts when another gave a name by way of introduction, the only way to express them and reduce the chance of provoking a hostile response was to ask, "Is that your* summer *name?"*

when first mentioning the name had been genuine. However, like her, he was hoping to learn more; but in a way that lessened the chance of their visitor taking offense. "The desk clerk probably realizes he has had many of your kinsmen visit the hotel."

"Being a *Mr.* Smith does have its advantages," the girl admitted, guessing why her father had intervened. "For one thing, it's better than having to write Hazeltine or Higginsbottom."

"Or Ramsbottom comes to that," Sergeant Waxahachie Smith drawled.

"*Anything* would be better than *Ramsbottom,* I'd imagine," Ransome remarked, realizing she still had a liking for the Texan in spite of her misgivings about how he might earn his living. "An, if you don't mind me saying so, you don't look like a Marmaduke, Wilberforce, or even an Algernon."

"Why, thank you 'most to death for that, ma'am," the sergeant replied, concluding the girl had made her latest comment as a form of apology for the breach of western etiquette she had come close to committing. "Only, seeing as my folks saddled me with Waldo, I wouldn't say what I've got is a whole heap better."

"*Waldo?*" the girl queried.

"*Waldo,*" Smith confirmed, truthfully. "My momma had me called it to keep us in good with my rich Aunt Sarah-Rose, then I'll be switched if she didn't die and leave all her money to my high-toned Cousin Jervis."

The reply given by the sergeant was proof that, despite his condition for the past few days, he had not lost the quick wits that brought him through many a dangerous predicament. In addition to having been reminded of his identity, he had remembered that he had been sent to Bonham County to carry out an assignment and still needed to ascertain more of the facts about the current situation. Therefore, he must not allow himself to be swayed by personal feelings. He had been rescued by Ransome and the *segundo* of the Rancho Mariposa, brought to the house, and given care and attention. What was more, he had liked everything he had so far seen of her father. However, he was too experienced to fall into the error of allowing himself to be swayed by first impressions or considerations of personal gratitude.

Nor did the events of the day change anything!

The incident with the men from Rancho Miraflores suggested to the sergeant that there was trouble between the two spreads. Regardless of the dislike he had taken toward Javier Fuentes, his sense of duty and training as a peace officer would not permit him to ignore the possibility that Cordoba could have supplied provocation for the hostility. Nor did the kindness he had received rule out the chance that the rancher was involved in the cattle stealing. As far as outward appearances and action went, one of the most pleasant and generous men whom he had ever met had proved to be the head of a ruthless gang of counterfeiters operating from the Texas Panhandle country. Therefore, his personal feelings notwithstanding, he had quickly appreciated the need to avoid revealing anything which might expose his identity and suggest the reason he was in the vicinity.

Smith's career as a Texas Ranger so far had been spent further north in the state and, wanting to retain anonymity as an aid to carrying out his assignments, he had done all he could to ensure his name had not been given prominence on reports of the incidents in which he had participated. Even on the few occasions when he was mentioned, it had never been by the name he was given at birth. His dislike for it had caused him to select and introduce himself as Waxahachie, having been born and spent his childhood in that town, until he and everybody else of his acquaintance rarely thought of him in any other fashion. Nevertheless, wanting to avoid the chance of anybody around Bonham County having heard of him, it had been his intention to use an alias on his arrival at Flamingo.

Unfortunately, because of his memory returning so suddenly, the sergeant had been unable to prevent himself from declaring his surname was Smith. While it had been too late to avoid supplying that much information, he was hoping to avoid being identified correctly by giving his much-disliked first name and that the Cordobas would overlook the connection if they should have heard of him in his official capacity.

For his part, despite being grateful for an intervention that had saved his daughter and himself from a fate he did not care to contemplate, the rancher was filled with a similar wariness. He had duplicated the summations of his daughter and *segundo* with regards to the injured man's clothing and armament. Nor had the conversation so far served to give any definite proof of the way in which Smith made a living. As they were terms in common use throughout the Texas range country, saying, "Given first pick at the remuda" and "snaked out of the bunch" could mean nothing more than that Smith had heard them and hoped their employment would make him appear to be a cowhand. All the other indications suggested he was in some form of employment dependent upon his ability to handle a gun. However, Cordoba realized such skill had never been the sole prerogative of *pistoleros valientes* hired to fight other men's wars. Knowing the kind of opposition against which they were likely to find themselves in contention, many peace officers acquired a similar proficiency with weapons. That was particularly true of those who, instead of being men already domiciled in an area and elected to a local office for expediency, made a profession out of law enforcement.

"My apologies for being so remiss, sir," the rancher said, knowing the former kind of professional gunfighters in particular could be *very* touchy and resentful of prying into their private affairs and activities. Although he hoped to learn more, particularly whether the Texan might have been on his way to take employment with one of the other ranchers, he was willing to adopt a more roundabout route than that of his daughter to produce the information. Reaching under the left side of his black bolero jacket, he brought out a leather case and opened it to display half a dozen brown cigars. "If you would care to smoke, I can assure you these are excellent."

"Well no, sir, but thank you right kind' for asking, sir," Smith refused politely. "I stopped smoking, drinking, and chewing tobacco when I was twelve 'cause I found they was stunting my growth and costing me *money*. Only I never did grow any taller, nor managed to save a lick of the money I didn't spend buying them. Don't let that stop you lighting up, though."

"Thank you, sir," the rancher said, selecting a cigar and, having replaced the case, taking a box of matches from his pants pocket. Applying the flame he created and sucking in the smoke appreciatively, he blew it out and inquired in a matter-of-fact tone, "You know how you come to be here?"

"Miz Ransome told me this morning," the sergeant confirmed, looking at and rising to give a bow to the girl. "You've got my gratitude, ma'am, and I'd admire to thank the gent who helped you to his face now I'm well enough."

"You may do so as soon as he returns from the range," Cordoba promised. "And please sit down again, sir."

"*Gracias,*" Smith drawled, and lowered his rump onto the bed. "I reckon I will."

"We of Rancho Mariposa are always willing to help anybody, stranger or friend, whom we find in difficulties," Ransome declared, meeting the sergeant's gaze without giving any indication of the pleasure she had experienced at his words. Instead, before her father could think of a more tactful way in which to seek the same information, she went on, "By the way, *Mr.* Smith, now your memory has come back, do you remember why you were going to Flamingo?"

"I've never been there, *Miss* Ransome," Smith replied, and in spite of the slight emphasis on the honorific, again showing no sign of objecting to a question bordering on what would be considered an invasion of privacy anywhere west of the Mississippi River. Exuding an air of regarding the explanation sufficient, he continued, "And my friends call me Wa—*Wal* on account of they say I've neveɪ had any dough."

"Are there many places you've never been?" the girl queried, hard pressed not to show her amusement at the explanation of the sobriquet.

"A whole heap here, there, and about a ways," the sergeant

admitted. "But I hope to get around to them all afore I'm through. What kind of a place is Flamingo, anyways?"

"Much like any other border town," Cordoba supplied, darting another glance of prohibition at his daughter and watching for any suggestion that his visitor knew more about the local situation than was suggested by the question. "It was once a haven for smugglers. In fact, during the War Between the States, it was the western boundary of the region through which the Ysabel Kid and his father, of whom I don't doubt you've heard, used to run supplies purchased in Mexico to the Confederate authorities.[2] However, when peace came, the efforts of the U.S. Cavalry and Guardia Rurale put an end to the smuggling. Now, like everywhere else in the range country, it derives much of its present income from cattle—or, at least, it *did.* These are troubled times, my young friend, troubled times."

"Like this morning," Smith hinted. "With that Fuentes jasper?"

"That is more of an unexpected offshoot from the trouble," the rancher estimated. "Cattle have been disappearing all through Bonham County and anybody who happens to be with them is *killed.*"

"Cow thieves aren't known for wanting to have folks see them at their wide-looping," the sergeant pointed out, guessing there was something more significant behind the mention of the killing. "Fact being, I've heard tell they've been known to throw lead at whoever saw them."

"That is true," Cordoba confirmed. "But usually they are just shooting with the intention of driving off the men riding herd. Those around here do *more* than that. With one exception during their first raid, they've made *certain* they never left a living witness."

"Who was this 'one exception'?" Smith queried, satisfied he could raise the point without showing more than the interest

2. *Some details of the career of the Ysabel Kid and his father, Big Sam Ysabel, are given in the* Civil War *and* Floating Outfit *series.*

that would be expected of anybody in his position who was merely making a casual visit to Bonham County. "And why didn't they finish him off?"

"It was Teodoro Fuentes," the rancher replied. His voice became tinged with bitterness and regret as he continued, "They killed his uncle, who owned the Rancho Miraflores, and he was knocked off his horse by a bullet striking a watch in his left breast pocket. They must have thought he was dead instead of merely being knocked unconscious. In every other case, perhaps because they learned of this error, they have ensured *everybody* near the herd they were stealing was killed by checking the bodies and—taking the appropriate action should anybody only be wounded."

"Sound like real mean son of bi—*hombres,*" the sergeant said, making the alteration to the description as he remembered the girl was present and despite realizing the full implication of the way in which the last part of his host's comment had been phrased.

"They *are*!" Cordoba confirmed with feeling. "And, as you saw earlier, there are always those who will try to take advantage of any kind of situation. Whether Javier Fuentes thought up the scheme or was led into it by Coltrane and the others, he was using the thefts as an excuse to settle a grudge against me and mine."

"So there's no trouble between the spreads?"

"Nothing of *that* kind."

"I'd've thought that with all the cattle stealing and killing going on feelings'd be running more than mite high?"

"They are. But, with the exception of the Fuentes brothers, we are all acquaintances of long standing."

"All *friends,* huh?"

"I'll admit I've had differences of opinion with Brad Drexell in the past," Cordoba replied, watching for and failing to discern any suggestion that the visitor knew and might even be going to work for the man he mentioned. "But they've always been settled amicably. And now, with *everybody* losing cattle and having had men shot down by the cow thieves, there isn't any reason for one ranch to be suspect more than any other."

The conversation was interrupted by the sound of hooves approaching!

"It's Halcón Gris and some of the boys," Ransome reported, having darted across to the open glass-paneled door and looked over the balcony. Glancing pointedly at Smith, she went on, "Sheriff Tobin's with them. I wonder what's brought him out here?"

"We could call him up and find out," Cordoba suggested. "Of course, only if our young friend here feels up to receiving another visitor?"

"That'll be fine with me, sir," Smith assented, being interested in meeting the peace officer responsible for his assignment in Bonham County. "Unless he's come for something personal, that is."

"If he has, we can go to another room," the rancher declared. "Ask the sheriff to come up, Ransome."

"And Halcón Gris?" the girl inquired.

"Again, only with our guest's permission," Cordoba replied.

Receiving a nod of concurrence from the sergeant, who remembered having heard her use the sobriquet when referring to the ranch's *segundo,* Ransome stepped onto the balcony and called for the two men to come upstairs. Having done so, she returned and went to open the door. In passing, she threw a look at Smith to try to discover whether he was worried by the prospect of meeting the sheriff. She decided that if he was, he hid it very well. He continued to lounge on the bed and did not so much as glance at his gun belt.

Even without seeing the badge of office worn by the older of the men who came into the room, the sergeant would have known which was which. Juanita had told him enough to allow him to identify Tom "Halcón Gris" Grey. Studying Sheriff Daniel Tobin, he concluded he could be looking at himself in another twenty or so years. He also decided that he liked what he saw.

Carrying a tan-colored Stetson in his right hand, tall, lanky,

yet moving with a suggestion of whipcord strength, the sheriff
of Bonham County had dark hair turning gray at the temples.
A neatly trimmed moustache accentuated a firm mouth with
grin quirks at the corners and the oak brown face had a similar
hint of a dry sense of humor in its otherwise composed and
unemotional lines. He wore clean range clothes, sufficiently in-
expensive to suggest he was honest enough to be living on his
salary alone, with a walnut-handled Colt Artillery Model
Peacemaker in the tied-down holster of a gun belt, which had
probably cost nearly as much as the rest of his attire put together. His gray eyes went from Smith to the gun belt on the
chest of drawers and back, but their scrutiny was redolent of
wary interest rather than hostility.

"Miss Ransome tells me's how I owe my worthless neck to
you, Halcón Gris," the sergeant stated after Cordoba had carried out the introductions. "And I'm hoping I'll be able to buy
you a drink, or six, in town for doing it."

"I take that kind," Grey replied, but his demeanor was more
neutral than friendly. Clearly, like the girl, he was reserving his
judgment and awaiting developments before responding with
friendship to a man who was still, he suspected from her attitude, an unknown quantity. "Not that I'm a drinking man,
mind."

"None of us ever are," Smith drawled, admiring rather than
resenting the attitude of the dark-faced cowhand in showing
such strong loyalty to the Cordoba family. "But the offer goes
and I'm hoping you'll take it up as soon's we can get it done."

"Don't think I'm not pleased to see you, Dan," the rancher
remarked, having watched the byplay between his guest and
Halcón Gris. "I always am, except perhaps at tax-collecting
time, but has something special brought you out here today?"

"It could be," the sheriff admitted. "Has young Javier Fuentes and some of the Rancho Miraflores hands been around here
this morning?"

"They came," Cordoba admitted.

"Peaceably?" Tobin asked.

"They *left* that way," the rancher claimed evasively. He had no desire to have the incident become a matter for intervention by the law, or to cause Grey and his crew to go in search of revenge. Despite what had taken place, he could not forget that the Fuentes brothers were kin to an old and trusted friend. What was more, particularly in the prevailing conditions, he felt certain that Teodoro would ensure nothing else of that kind was even contemplated by Javier, much less being given the support of their hired hands. "Do you have any reason for thinking it would be otherwise?"

"There was some talk around town," the sheriff replied. However, he had no intention of admitting he had been told by a saloon girl that the younger Fuentes brother and some of the hardcases from their ranch had been discussing coming to Rancho Mariposa with some undisclosed mischief in mind. "So, seeing's how I've not had my butt on a saddle for a spell, I figured I'd drop on over and see if there was anything in it. Met Halcón Gris and some of your boys on the way in and he reckoned he'd been told there was some fuss at the house 'n' concluded they'd best drop by to ask the why-all of it. We didn't see Javier and his bunch on the way here, though."

"They've probably gone straight back to Rancho Miraflores," Cordoba guessed.

"Could be," Tobin admitted, knowing such a route would have removed the need for the men to ride along the trail to Flamingo. "Was there any trouble?"

"Yes," the rancher confirmed, even though he had no desire to have the affair taken further, but being unwilling to try to deceive a man for whom he had developed a liking and respect. "Asa Coltrane got arrogant and our visitor here was compelled to crease his skull with a rifle bullet."

"Just *arrogant*?" the sheriff queried.

"There's some's might even've called it *threatening,*" Smith declared, as the peace officer darted a look in his direction.

"*Threatening?*" Tobin queried.

"I'd even go so far's to say it was *most* threatening," the sergeant estimated. "Leastways, that's what we'd call it back to home happen a jasper started pulling a gun without a whole heap more call than he'd been given."

"Coltrane pulled a gun on you?" the sheriff asked, although he was aware that the hardcase was quite capable of such behavior; particularly if believing it was safe to do so.

"It looked to me like he was doing nothing else but," Smith affirmed. "Although I *could* be wrong and he was only scratching for a seam squirrel 'n' brought out that hid-away Colt Storekeeper by mistake. Which being, I'll apologize most humble should our trails cross again."

"That *could* be what caused the `mishap,` Dan," Cordoba claimed as the sheriff's gaze swung his way. "Anyway, in the interests of peace and quiet, I'd rather the whole thing was forgotten."

"How'll Coltrane feel about it?" Tobin challenged.

"I'm sure Teodoro Fuentes will *persuade* him to see it *my* way," the rancher answered. "In fact, when he hears, I'm willing to bet he'll be taking his brother and the others severely to task for coming here."

"Huh huh!" the sheriff grunted, although he shared Cordoba's unspoken suggestion that the elder of the brothers had not been aware of the younger's intentions. "*Happen* I see him, I'll ask how he feels on it."

"I'm sure he'll be as willing as I am to say all is forgiven and forgotten," the rancher declared. Then, directing the words more to his Indian dark *segundo* than the local peace officer, he went on, "and I certainly *don't* want it taken any further by *anybody.*"

"Then I'll see's Teodoro and Javier know how you feel on it," Tobin promised, and turned his attention from Cordoba in a way that showed he considered that aspect of the affair was closed. "I seem to mind Halcón Gris telling me on the way here's how the banging-around you got falling into that arroyo had made you forget who you was, young feller."

"It *had,* " the sergeant admitted. "Only Miss Ransome got to picking out what could be my name. Well, sir, she's cut Hazeltine, Higginsbottom, and Ramsbottom from the herd, which last I was 'special pleased to see gone.[3] Then, comes her getting to mentioning Smith, dog my cats if I didn't remember who I was. *Waldo* Smith. You'll find it in our family Bible, but not in Bible Two."

"Halcón Gris allows you're riding a big C-on-F Mogollon-strain claybank gelding," the sheriff commented, showing no sign of being aware what was meant by "Bible Two."[4] "Did you buy it from Colin Farquharson hisself?"

"No, sir," the sergeant lied, having decided to offer a clue that would satisfy the local peace officer or at least suggest a means by which verification of his bona fides could be ascertained without his true identity being made public. "I got him from a dealer in Austin, only I lost the bill of sale. Tell you what, though. Happen you telegraph the *dealer,* Mr. *Cyrus Holmes,* and ask him happen he remembers me, I seem to recollect the number on it was, eleven, twenty-three, sixty-one."

"Eleven, twenty-three, sixty-one, huh?" Tobin repeated, giving no indication of having noticed the slight emphasis on certain words and being aware that the Cyrus Holmes of Austin who he felt sure was meant had never been a dealer in horses. He also concluded the numbers would allow him to confirm his supposition that the young man had come in response to the request, which circumstances had required was sent by a less direct route than would normally have been the case, for assistance from the Texas Rangers. "I'll do just that, Mr. Smith, happen you're staying around here for long."

"It will be for a few more days at least," Cordoba stated, suspecting there was more to the references to the claybank

3. *We apologize to any of our readers who are called "Ramsbottom" and can only say in exculpation this is the name used in the documents upon which we have based this narrative.*
4. *"Bible Two," also sometimes known as the "Black Book"; the list of fugitives published annually for the Texas Rangers and said to be read by them far more frequently than the real Bible.*

than appeared on the surface and also knowing the meaning of "Bible Two." "Our young friend isn't in any shape for traveling just yet, even as far as Flamingo, and you can find him here until he is."

7
YOU'RE A *MYSTERY,*
MR. SMITH

"Howdy, ma'am," Sergeant Waxahachie Smith greeted, entering the stables at the rear of the Spanish colonial–style house. Fully dressed, he was carrying his war bag, bedroll, and Winchester Model of 1876 rifle. "Come to make sure I'm leaving?"

"Yes," Ransome Cordoba replied before she could stop herself, and blushed as she realized the instinctive response might be considered both impolite and ungrateful.

"Serves me right for asking," the Texan drawled cheerfully.

"Yes, it does," the girl confirmed, irked rather than relieved by the visitor appearing to be more amused than offended at her answer.

Four days had elapsed since the unpleasant visit by Javier Fuentes and the Rancho Miraflores hands. There had been no more raids by the cow thieves, but this was explained by their habit of only striking on occasions when there was sufficient rain to wash away their tracks. The weather had stayed fine.

However, the time had not been entirely uneventful for the sergeant.

Smith had been grateful that Don Jose Fernando de Armijo y Cordoba had insisted he stayed at Rancho Mariposa until he was fully recovered from his ordeal at the arroyo. He was aware that, particularly after having antagonized the younger of the Fuentes brothers and Asa Coltrane, he would need to be in the best of health before arriving at Flamingo. Being allowed to remain in the room where he had regained consciousness, he had had the privacy to resume the routine he performed every day when circumstances permitted to ensure he retained his physical fitness. This included squeezing a pair of U-shaped metal springs he had had made to keep up the strength of his hands and doing some exercises he had seen as a bellhop being performed in her room at the hotel by a woman who was famed throughout the West as "Madam Bulldog."[1] In addition to practicing his draw, he had exercised by twirling and juggling the revolver. Far from being an affectation to be shown off and impress people, the latter were intended to increase his dexterity in handling the Colt Civilian Model Peacemaker. He was also allowed to shoot at targets outside the wall surrounding the house and was satisfied that he had not lost the accuracy he had acquired with the revolver and Winchester.

Although Smith had become on excellent terms with his host and learned enough to feel sure he must look elsewhere for the leader of the cow thieves, he was less well received by the majority of the people around the ranch. Still suffering from the pangs of his broken engagement, he was not so receptive to Ransome's charms as might otherwise have been the case. Nor was he in the mood to pander to feminine whims, such as her obvious desire to learn more about him and thereby be given cause to increase her partially developed liking. To have done

1. *Further information about the career of Charlotte "Madam Bulldog" Canary is given in:* Part One, "Better Than Calamity," THE WILDCATS *and its two "expansions":* THE HIDE AND HORN SALOON *and* CUT ONE, THEY ALL BLEED.

so, particularly if he had confided that he was a member of the Texas Rangers on official duty in Bonham County, would have improved relations between them. However, despite being satisfied her father was victim rather than instigator, he did not wish to let her have information that she might inadvertently divulge and allow the truth about him to reach the men he would be hunting.

Ransome had continued to have mixed feelings about the man she had rescued. While she had found herself liking him for his dry sense of humor, good manners, and rugged manly appearance, she was far less enamored of him refraining from supplying any information about his past, and over the indications that he made his living by skill with a gun rather than ability in working cattle. Nor was she any better pleased by the way in which he treated her. He was always respectful, but his attitude invariably implied he regarded her as a child and she considered herself to be a full-grown woman.

From what the sergeant had seen of the ranch's crew and heard about the precautions to be taken against leaving the house, he had decided the Cordobas had little need to fear further visits by Javier Fuentes. None of them were hired gunslingers, but—no matter whether Anglo or Chicano—they were tough, intensely loyal to their employer, and possessed of sufficient fight savvy to be able to hold up their end in time of trouble. However, even Tom "Halcón Gris" Grey had shown to anybody who knew cowhands that they did not consider Smith was suitable for complete acceptance into their circle. Although he was able to discuss the cattle business with them, his footwear in particular indicated he did not earn his living from it as they did. They had treated him politely, out of respect for Don José's wishes and the part he had played in driving off the men from Rancho Miraflores, but made it clear they did not regard him as being one of them.

For his part, the sergeant had made no attempt to ask questions that might have aroused suspicions and, perhaps, lead to open hostility. He was just as incommunicative on the few occasions when a member of the crew had tried to acquire information about his past activities and future intentions as he had been with Ransome. Justified as he considered the reticence to be, even more so than in the case of the girl, it had been another barrier to him having gained acceptance by the cowhands.

Shortly after noon on the day following the unwelcome visit by the younger Fuentes, a man from Rancho Miraflores had arrived with a letter for Cordoba from his employer. Teodoro Fuentes had written to offer an explanation for the misapprehension that he claimed had arisen over the reason for Javier's visit. He stated that it was made with a genuine intention of rendering whatever assistance might be needed as a result of the rancher's incapacitated condition, but had been expressed badly and the situation was exacerbated when the rest of the party had grown annoyed by the less-than-courteous way in which they were received. There was an apology for the behavior of Coltrane and gratitude that the "visitor" had shown such commendable restraint in inflicting only a minor wound. The letter had finished by saying that, as far as its author was concerned, the matter was closed and he hoped the recipient would feel the same. Replying, Cordoba had given his assurance that he, too, was willing to forget the incident, but regretfully must continue to ban Javier from visiting his home.

During the same afternoon, a deputy had brought a message from Sheriff Daniel Tobin. It, too, was addressed to Cordoba, saying that Teodoro Fuentes had visited the office and given the same explanation for the behavior of Javier and the hardcases, declaring he had instructed all his crew to consider everybody at Rancho Mariposa in the same friendly fashion as had always been the case. The sheriff had claimed everything pointed to the older brother having been unaware of whatever the younger had planned, so was trying to avoid trouble between the two spreads; a point of view with which Cordoba had stated he was in agreement. The letter had asked that "Waldo Smith" be informed a telegraph message from Cyrus Holmes in Austin had confirmed the existence of the "bill of sale" and ended with a suggestion that he call in to see Tobin on his arrival at Flamingo for "a friendly chat."

Referring to the request for Smith to visit the sheriff, the rancher had been relieved to discover it was neither unexpected nor a cause for annoyance. Instead, the sergeant had commented that peace officers always liked to know who was arriving in their bailiwick and, in fact, he was generally the recipient of a similar summons most places he visited. Although Ransome had clearly disapproved of the allusion to his supposed occupation of hired gunfighter, he had received a smile that suggested his shrewd and worldly host suspected something of the true situation. However, he had not offered to confirm whatever supposition Cordoba might have formed, and the subject had been dropped without further discussion.

Each day, Juanita had come to attend to the sergeant's head wound. On her visit the day before, stating she was satisfied it would be safe to do so, she had removed the stitches she had inserted to seal the gap in his scalp. Deciding he had delayed for long enough, he had stated his intention of leaving in the morning. Although Cordoba had suggested a longer stay, he said he felt he should be on his way. He explained that he intended to stop over in Flamingo for a few days, then go and find somewhere else he had never been before to see what it looked like. The explanation was accepted without question and, learning that one of the hands was going into town, he had asked for a message to be taken to the sheriff telling of his intention to arrive the following afternoon. This was arranged and he was guest of honor at dinner that evening. His attempts to thank the Cordobas for their kindness had been brushed aside, as was his offer of payment, although both had clearly been appreciated.

Packing ready for moving out, Smith had decided he was as well equipped as when he had set out for Bonham County. All the clothing he had been wearing when thrown into the arroyo had been washed and, where necessary, repaired. Although his J.B. Stetson hat had not come through the accident unscathed, being of good quality, it had been restored to its previous condition with the help of one of Cordoba's house servants skilled in the art of steaming and reshaping headgear. In fact, except for a couple of scratches on the front of his holster that a liberal application of saddle soap and boot wax could not entirely conceal, his attire gave hardly any sign of his ordeal.

"Do you have everything you need for your journey?" Ransome inquired.

"Yes, thanks, ma'am," Smith replied, putting down his bedroll and resting his Winchester on it by the side of the stall in which his claybank gelding was standing. "Juanita gave me a big enough breakfast to last me until I hit town this afternoon."

"Will you be staying long in Flamingo?" the girl asked, watching the sergeant stroll to where his double-girthed saddle and its bridle were sharing a small wooden burro with her own and her father's rigs.[2]

"That depends."

"Upon what?"

"What I find there," Smith drawled, truthfully as far as it went.

"There isn't much to attract *anybody,*" Ransome claimed. "I only visit it on a Saturday to collect our mail and whatever supplies might be needed."

"*Every* Saturday?" Smith queried, picking up the saddle and bridle.

"It's only rarely I miss," the girl replied. Seeking to give the impression she was only passing on a piece of information that might be of interest, she went on, "There's a dance at the schoolhouse in the evening. *Anybody* who's so minded can come."

"I'll keep that in mind, ma'am," the sergeant promised, re-

2. *Burro: in this context, a small wooden structure like the roof of a house upon which a saddle would be rested when not in use. Being so dependent upon his rig, a cowhand preferred to use a burro when one was available instead of laying it down or hanging it by a stirrup.*

2a. *Despite the misconception created by Western movies—even the late and great John Wayne being an offender—a cowhand would never toss down his saddle on its skirts. If no burro was available, he would either lay it on its side, or stand it on its head, somewhere it would be safely clear of anybody inadvertently stepping upon it.*

turning and opening the gate to the stall. "Happen I'm still around town, that is."

"Then you may *not* still be there?" Ransome hinted, noticing the claybank showed none of the fear of its owner that had been obvious between Javier Fuentes and the black Thoroughbred.

"Could be, then again, maybe not," Smith drawled. Starting to prepare the gelding for travel, he went on, "I've long since learned there's only *two* things certain in this world of ours. You're born and you die. Everything 'twixt and 'tween, from whether you're born rich 'n' handsome—which I've only got *one*—or dirt poor 'n' ugly and die happy or painful, it's *all* just chance."

"I hadn't realized you were born *rich,* Mr. Smith," the girl remarked, watching the Texan working and reluctantly deciding he was as skilled at throwing a heavy saddle onto the back of a big horse as any cowhand she had come across.

"My momma thought I was right pretty, Miss Ransome," the sergeant stated gravely. " 'Course, I can't but admit she liked horned toads and hellgrammites."

"I think you're *almost* as good looking as either of them," Ransome assessed. "Anyway, there will be a dance and I *may* see you at it."

"Yes'm," Smith conceded. "You just may at that. But I'd best warn you, I'm not the world's *best* dancer. Nor even the one hundred and twelve thousand, three hundred and sixty-first, comes down to it."

"I'll keep that in mind," the girl promised, sounding just as sober as if she had been given information of the greatest importance and wondering why the number quoted seemed familiar.

With the saddle and bridle in place, the sergeant led his horse from the stall. He picked up and slid the Winchester into its boot and, having fastened the bedroll to the cantle, walked toward the open doors of the building with the big animal following on his heels like an enormous hound dog. Once outside, glancing around him, he decided there were any number of places he would less like to live. Then, recollecting how being engrossed in memories of another woman had almost caused his death prior to his arrival at Rancho Mariposa, he shrugged off the thought. Swinging astride the gelding's broad back, he controlled the high spirits created by several days' rest and good feeding with the deft ease of one long accustomed to handling such a powerful mount.

"Well, it's time I was going," Smith drawled. "Thanks again for everything, Miss Ransome. "Bye now, you-all!"

"Good-bye," the girl replied, watching the sergeant as he crossed the plaza and, having removed his hat to give it a flourish directed between herself and her father seated in the wheelchair on the porch, passed through the main gate. As he disappeared from view, she shook her head and said quietly, "I wish I could like you as much as I know Poppa does, but you're a *mystery*, Mr. Smith, and with the way things are around Bonham County, I don't like mysteries no matter how well spoken they might be."

*   *   *

Riding slowly along the main street of Flamingo, toward where it opened out and formed a large central square, Waxahachie Smith studied his surroundings with a careful gaze. He did not know how long he might be staying, but was aware that upon such an assignment a knowledge of the town's geography would prove useful and might even help him stay alive.

Shortly before the sergeant had come into view of the town, a glint of light had caught his gaze. It proved to be a signal from Sheriff Tobin, intended to attract his attention. Meeting for a discussion in the concealment of a small clump of shrub oaks, he had been told of the situation that resulted in his being sent to Bonham County. He had not added greatly to his sum of knowledge.

To help Smith form a better understanding, Tobin had sketched a map of the county on a piece of bare ground. Roughly shaped like the upper half of an octagon, with Flamingo being at the center of the baseline formed by the Rio Grande, the area was divided into four close-to-equal segments. The Fuentes brothers' Rancho Miraflores held the eastern quarter bordering the river. Cordoba's Rancho Mariposa came next, then the property owned by Sir John "Monocle Johnny" Besgrove and that of Bradford "Brad" Drexell extended to the border in the west. Except for the sparing of Teodoro Fuentes in the first raid, no spread had suffered more, or less, than the rest. Furthermore, when questioned by the sheriff about the extent of his injury, Dr. Otto Grantz had claimed he—the only victim to survive in any attack—had been extremely fortunate to escape with his life.

However, what had happened to the stolen cattle was a complete mystery!

Despite assistance from the sheriffs of the adjacent counties and the Guardia Rurale in Mexico, there was nothing to suggest they had been taken out of Tobin's bailiwick. This implied to the peace officers that, after putting his own brand over those on the stolen animals, the man responsible was holding them in a remote part of his range until they could be sent away as part of otherwise legitimate herds. Nevertheless, trying to select a possible suspect had been fruitless. There was no way that any of the brands used by the four ranchers involved—Bench C, C̲, Cordoba's Rancho Mariposa; Rafter F, F̂, —its earlier owners also having selected an easier mark of identification than the so-called skillet of snakes, or greaser madhouse variety generally used in Mexico—Fuentes's Rancho Miraflores; the Union Jack, ⊠, "Monocle Johnny" Besgrove; B Bar D, B-D, Brad Drexell—could be converted into another without the alteration being instantly discernible.

Tobin had said frankly that his decision for requesting outside assistance to deal with the stealing of the cattle was motivated by the conditions that prevailed in his bailiwick. Being new to the area, he had kept on the deputies employed by his predecessor. While he had no reason to doubt their honesty, all were local men and each was in some way connected with one spread or another. Experience elsewhere had taught him that he might not be able to count upon them to act with impartiality. Nor, on account of the distrust that had arisen, would the ranchers and, more particularly, their crews be likely to take kindly to an investigation by a man whose sympathies might be with another spread. Therefore, he had considered it advisable to seek the aid of a man—or men—who would be beyond such suspicions.

Admitting there had been no open hostility between the spreads as yet, with the possible exception of the visit to Rancho Mariposa—which he was inclined to believe was an ill-conceived act by Javier Fuentes rather than organized aggression—the sheriff had said there was an undercurrent of veiled animosity amongst them. Despite being of long standing, being directed mainly against Besgrove and, because of their friendship, Cordoba, that of Drexell was more latent than active. Regardless of the amiable relationship that their predecessors had always shown toward their immediate neighbor and the Englishman, although it was less amicable with the owner of the B Bar D, the new occupants of Rancho Miraflores had established they had no desire to continue such a state of affairs. However, even they had taken no action beyond warning they would not tolerate trespass upon their range.

Due to the situation being so unsettled, Tobin had declared, he was concerned by the number of hired gunfighters who had started to drift into Flamingo. Although none of them had given signs of having been hired by any specific employer, he suggested that Smith—pretending to be one of their kind—might learn why they had arrived and whether this had any direct bearing upon the stealing of the cattle. Such was the course of action decided upon. To prevent any suggestion of their acquaintance becoming known, the peace officers had taken separate routes on parting and the sergeant rode slowly to allow the sheriff to reach the town before him.

While clearly a thriving and prosperous community, to Smith the seat of Bonham County looked only marginally different from hundreds of other such towns scattered across the range country. Only those on the banks of comparable rivers offered similar facilities for paddle-wheel steamboats or other freight-carrying vessels to be loaded and unloaded, but they all supplied much the same amenities elsewhere.

As was the general case, the central square was the hub of all business activities. The bank stood adjacent to the large building housing offices for the sheriff, other county officials, and the jail. At its other side, with an equally solid construction giving an air of permanence and profit, was the undertaker's. Glancing at it in passing, Smith concluded wryly it was one establishment sure to prosper regardless of how much trouble was occurring locally. Opposite them, just as sturdily built and well maintained, was the International Hotel. To the right of it, the premises where the *Flamingo Herald-Tribune* was published stood between the Mercantile Emporium and the Highlander Saloon. A large Spanish mission-style church, obviously long established, and a much newer white-walled frame schoolhouse took up one side, being faced by assorted premises also catering for the various needs of the population and surrounding district.

Living accommodations for the citizens, predominantly a mixture of whites and Chicanos, were divided roughly into two halves. The poorer section of the community straggled in the direction of the Rio Grande's muddy banks. Uptown stood the newer residential area occupied by the more affluent members of the community, several of whom were Hispanics. Each offered means of relaxation, in the form of saloons and other places of entertainment, graded in the style best suited to the pockets of their most usual class of customers.

Taking in the sights as he went by, while everything appeared peaceable enough on the surface, Smith could understand why the sheriff had expressed concern. At least a couple of well-armed men where loafing outside each of the saloons he passed. The majority were dressed after the fashion of cowhands. However, if employed at all, he knew they were extremely unlikely to be hired in such a beneficial capacity. In fact, they and those who favored other sartorial styles reminded him of wolves resting until deciding the time had come to go hunting. Their scrutiny of him was just as wary and he felt sure that none of them believed he was in the neighborhood hoping to obtain work herding cattle. Having no doubt that he could end up by finding himself in opposition against at least some of them, it was a relief to decide he had never seen any before and conclude they were ignorant of his official status.

Bringing the big claybank gelding to a halt in front of the International Hotel, having accepted Tobin's suggestion that it would serve as a good base from which to bring himself to the attention of those interested in hiring gunfighters rather than ordinary help, Smith dismounted. He was about to toss the reins over the hitching rail when a youngster came across the sidewalk and, by offering to take his mount to the livery stable, proved to be engaged upon a means of earning spending money he had sometimes followed at the same age. While agreeing to the arrangement and reaching into his pants pocket for a coin, he glanced to where two men wearing the style of clothing favored by professional gamblers were coming from the main entrance. What he saw warned him that he was unlikely to be ignored. The shorter was a stranger to him, but he recognized the taller and did not doubt this would be mutual. Hoping to avoid the trouble he felt sure would be forthcoming, he lowered his head and turned as if meaning to remove the bedroll from his saddle.

The hope did not achieve fruition!

"Well, what do you know, Tommy, it's *Whit Stokes*!"

8

YOU KNOW ME AS "SMITH"
"*John* Smith"

Hearing the words, Sergeant Waxahachie Smith felt a mixture of relief and annoyance!

While it seemed the taller of the men was still unaware of Smith's true identity, which was to his advantage, the circumstances of their last meeting were not calculated to arouse friendly feelings. He had been working undercover to infiltrate a gang flooding Texas with counterfeit money, and Herbert Wormsley was one of those involved in passing it via games of chance. However, it was a personal matter that had aroused animosity between them. Smith had intervened while the gambler was living up to one aspect of his unsavory reputation by assaulting with fists and feet the saloon girl who had the misfortune to be his current mistress.

The sergeant felt sure that the thrashing he had administered to Wormsley, who had tried to resist his intervention, would not be forgotten!

"You've got me mixed up with somebody else, mister,"

Smith claimed, swinging his gaze to the speaker and stepping away from the boy and horse. "My name's *not* Whit Stokes, nor ever has been."

"I'm not surprised you're saying *that*, what you *did*!" Wormsley asserted, shoving back the flap of his black cutaway coat to leave unimpeded access to the ivory handle of the Colt Storekeeper Model Peacemaker in the cross-draw holster of his gun belt.

"Why'd that be, Bert?" inquired the second man, his manner that of a sycophant rather than a social equal.

"You mind how the law jumped that 'green goods game' I sent and asked you to come and sit in on up Lipscomb County way last year?" Wormsley asked, and, having received a nod of confirmation, continued. "Well, this here's the son of a bitch who sold us out to the Rangers afore you got there."

"That's a *hard* name, *hombre,*" Smith said quietly, noticing the boy was showing a ready grasp of the situation and starting to lead the claybank away without waiting to be paid.

"You want me to call you it again?" Wormsley inquired, the thought of how narrowly he had avoided arrest and lost a lucrative source of revenue being less motivation than remembering the beating he had taken at the hands of the newcomer to Flamingo.

"I *wouldn't*, was I you," the sergeant advised, knowing there was no chance of avoiding the confrontation and wanting to give the youngster time to get clear of the line of fire if possible. He was aware that several people were watching what was going on and, showing a typical western appreciation for the potential danger, either taking shelter or standing still beyond hearing distance. "It casts a bad light on my momma."

"Ain't *nothing* bad enough can be said about a tail peddler's sired a whelp to sell his *amigos* to the law!" Wormsley claimed. "Don't you reckon so, Tommy?"

"I thought this was just 'tween you and me," Smith drawled, his appearance seemingly relaxed despite him being tense and completely ready to take action. "But, seeing as it don't look to be, you won't mind *my* good buddy back there taking cards, I reckon."

Although the sergeant was not a trouble seeker by nature, the role he had elected to employ on his latest assignment required that he proved himself tough and unwilling to "take no sass, but 'sassparilla'." What was more, he had felt sure he would be called upon to prove himself before he was accepted in the character he was playing. That he was to be allowed to do so against a man who only evaded inclusion on the pages of the Texas Rangers "Bible Two" because of lack of proof rather than innocence of crime, removed any slight inhibition he might have felt. Nor, he was certain, could he avoid locking horns with Wormsley. Certainly, even if to do so would not have been detrimental to his assignment. Letting it be seen he backed down would be unlikely to avert a confrontation.

Having drawn his conclusions as soon as he was addressed by Wormsley, Smith had assessed the danger he was facing. He knew the taller of the pair to be a competent gunfighter, but felt sure the same did not apply to Tommy. Nevertheless, aware that the pair of them working in conjunction could prove too much for him to cope with, he attempted a hoary old trick in the hope of lessening the odds against him.

Unlike when trying to avoid recognition by Wormsley, the sergeant saw his latest ploy was working with the second gambler!

Convinced there could be an undiscovered threat close by, Tommy swung his gaze in the direction indicated by Smith's brief nod. However, guessing what was intended, Wormsley did not duplicate his companion's involuntary reaction. Instead, suspecting the reason for the trick, he sent his right hand across to the butt of his revolver. Swiftly though he moved, he discovered his intended victim was capable of even greater speed. Sufficient, in fact, to counteract the advantage he expected to gain from his weapon having a shorter barrel than that of the more conventional Models of the Colt Peacemaker.

Dipping his hand in the smoothly flowing blur of motion he had shown when surprised by Ransome Cordoba, Smith swept the revolver from its excellently designed holster. This time, however, he completed the whole of the sequence by releasing the thumbed-back hammer. There was a crash of detonating black powder and a bullet sped through the air. Even as the Storekeeper Colt was coming out of the cross-draw holster, lead entered between Wormsley's eyes and, having ripped through his brain, burst out at the rear of his skull. Killed instantly, he was pitched backward with the weapon flying from his no-longer-operative grasp. His body sprawled, with arms and legs thrown apart, on the sidewalk. While he had successfully evaded the consequences of numerous infringements of the law until that moment, including having beaten to death one of his mistresses, he had at last met a well-deserved fate at the hands of a man he believed to be no more than another outlaw.

Satisfied there was nothing more to be feared from Wormsley, Smith swiftly recocked his Colt while swinging its barrel toward the second man. He found he had been correct in his assessment of Tommy's character. Although the shorter gambler's attention had been brought back, his reactions were too slow for him to pose any threat at that moment. Staring into the muzzle of the revolver as it was directed his way with great speed and menacing precision, he was equally alarmed by the coldly grim face of the Texan behind it. Much to his consternation, he found his fingers were unable to complete drawing his own weapon and, knowing the kind of company he had been keeping, expected to join his companion on the sidewalk at any moment.

"Leave it in leather!" Smith commanded, ready to shoot again if the need arose and hoping it would not.

"S-Sure, Mr. St . . . ," Tommy assented, the coldly drawled words restoring motion to his hand and allowing him to snatch it clear of the revolver. Recollecting how the Texan had disclaimed the name supplied by Wormsley, he made what he hoped would prove a suitable apology. "I wasn't figuring to draw down on you, *mister*."

"I'm right pleased to hear *that*," Smith declared with mock joviality. "And to make sure you won't be getting the notion later, didn't I hear you say something about how you was figuring on leaving Flamingo *real* soon?"

"Y-You sure did!" the gambler promised, without remarking that no such declaration of intentions had passed his lips. "I was only saying in there's how I reckoned I'd be heading out as soon's I'd got my gear together."

"Then I wouldn't want to keep you talking when you're so all fired set on pulling up stakes and going," Smith asserted, glancing along the street to where the sheriff and two deputies were approaching at a fast walk. Noticing nobody else was offering to come closer, even the boy with his claybank was remaining a short distance away, he decided he had better try to prevent his supposed criminal activities from being mentioned. Returning his gaze to the obviously frightened gambler, he continued, "There's but one thing, though."

"What'd that be?"

"I surely hope that, when the great seizer there asks you what happened, you don't let on *why* Wormsley was all set to call me down. 'Cause what was between us was *personal* and nothing to do with that 'green goods game' up to Lipscomb County. Fact being, the law got on to us 'cause *he* talked too much when he was in liquor, not through me selling out to 'em."

"Bert allus talked too much when he was drunk," Tommy claimed truthfully, deciding his deceased companion could have had some other cause of animosity, but wanted to put the blame for the betrayal and breaking up of the counterfeiting gang upon the Texan as a means of obtaining his assistance in settling whatever was the real trouble between them. "You can count on me to say the *right* things, Mr. St—*mister!*"

"I'm real pleased to hear it," Smith declared, returning the staghorn-handled Colt to its holster. However, there was still an undertone of menace in his voice as he went on, "Just mind that you do like you say. And another thing . . ."

"Y-Yeah?" the gambler inquired.

"Don't you mention the name Wormsley called me to *any-*

body at all!" the sergeant commanded. "Should you be asked, you know me as Smith. *John* Smith!"

* * *

"Excuse me, sir!"

Hearing the words while accepting the key to the room he had taken at the International Hotel, Waxahachie Smith looked around. He had just arrived to check in after being treated in a way intended to give support to his pose as a gunfighter seeking employment. Having first questioned the onlookers, including the surviving gambler, Sheriff Daniel Tobin had escorted the sergeant to the jailhouse ostensibly to check whether he appeared upon a wanted poster. On arrival, they had conducted a conversation calculated to convince the deputies who were present that they had never met before.

Tall, slim, tanned by the elements, the speaker looked to be in his early forties. Showing strength of will, the undefinable aura of one long used to leadership and a sense of humor, his features were clean shaven. He moved with the erect carriage of a soldier and the gait of cavalryman. Although the gun belt he had on was not suitable for really fast work, the sergeant felt sure the walnut-handled Colt Artillery Model Peacemaker butt forward in a high cavalry-twist holster was far from being a mere affectation. Despite the Texas cowhand's-style clothing he was wearing and absence of any such aid to vision as had produced the sobriquet, going by the upper-class British accent in which the words were uttered, Smith deduced he was Sir John "Monocle Johnny" Besgrove.[1]

1. *A popular misconception in the United States all through the nineteenth century was that all members of the British upper class wore monocles. This could have been helped to gain strength as a result of a few like the Earl of Hawkesdon, known as "Brit," who did so. See:* RIO GUNS.

1a. *Having learned of the supposition, the very competent British criminal, Amelia Penelope Diana "Benkers" Benkinsop wore a monocle as an aid to creating the character she was playing at one period during her visit to the United States in the mid 1870s. See:* Part Three, "Birds Of A Feather," WANTED! BELLE STARR. *Further information about the visit is given in:* BEGUINAGE IS DEAD! *and* Part Five, "The Butcher's Fiery End," J.T.'S LADIES.

"*Me,* sir?" the sergeant inquired.

"*You,* sir," the Englishman confirmed. "Could you come into the bar and give me a few seconds of your time over a drink?"

"I'm not so all-fired *busy* that I can't," Smith declared. "Nor ever have been's I can call to mind."

Turning from the desk, after having arranged for his belongings to be taken to his room, Smith felt a sensation of being watched, which he had come to know was reliable. Glancing around in a casual-seeming fashion, his gaze went to the entrance to the dining room from where he estimated the scrutiny was being conducted. However, there was nobody in sight and he concluded that, having suspected his purpose, whoever had been watching had withdrawn beyond his range of vision. Deciding against going to investigate, he accompanied the Englishman into the barroom.

"May I ask whether you're planning to stay hereabouts, Mr. *Smith*?" Besgrove inquired, having exchanged introductions and ordered the drinks.

"Sheriff had some notion's how I *shouldn't,*" the sergeant replied. He had noticed that, as so often happened when he used his genuine surname—particularly when, as now, he added a spurious John—a slight emphasis was put on it by the Englishman and he concluded he had given the desired impression of using an alias. "Only I pointed out's how all the witnesses, including the *amigo* of the jasper I shot, allowed I'd had to do it in self-defense. Which being and seeing's how I've enough money on hand to stop me being a vagrant 'n' burden on the civic fathers, I reckoned there wasn't nothing *legal* to give him the right to tell me to leave town."

"And he accepted it?" the Englishman asked, knowing the sheriff was not the kind to be frightened by any man no matter how competent with a gun.

"Wasn't too all fired eager, first off," Smith admitted. "But he come 'round to my way of thinking when I told him's how I was within my rights under Article Eleven, Twenty-three, Sixty-one of this here sovereign state of Texas's legal rulings and me 'n' my lawyer cousin had already taken one sheriff to

law under it and got ruled for favorable, which cost his county
a heap of compensation money and him his badge. Anyways, I
don't reckon you've asked me in here just for the pleasure of
my company, pleasurable though it is."

"I haven't," Besgrove conceded, the explanation having confirmed his supposition that there was more to the newcomer
than was the case with the usual run of hired gunfighters. "I
trust you'll not think I'm taking too much of a liberty, but are
you here in search of gainful employment?"

"I'm always willing to *listen,* at least, when I'm being told
about it."

"Would you be willing to work for me?"

"Doing *what*?"

"I've made arrangements to purchase a large herd of cattle in
Mexico and I'd like to hire you to ensure the money for them
reaches their owner."

"Don't you have any of your own crew you can send with
it?"

"Naturally I'll be sending along enough of my cowhands to
handle the herd. But they aren't trained fighting men, and,
going by what I saw out there, you *are.* So I'd like to have you
with them as a guard."

"Uh huh!" Smith grunted. He knew ranchers occasionally
bought herds below the border to help supply the meat-hungry
East, but realized there could be more involved where the offer
he had received was concerned. *"Sounds easy enough."*

"You're far too intelligent to believe *that,"* Besgrove stated
with a smile. "Which is the reason I'd like to hire you."

"Why *me*?" Smith queried. "I've only just hit town and,
what I've seen 'round and about, there's plenty of others you
could've taken on."

"I want a man who not only knows how to shoot, but when
not to shoot, and you proved on the street that you know *both.*
Anybody who takes even less money than you'll be guarding
into Mexico is likely to have to fight to keep it. So I want a man
along who can fight, but won't go out of his way to make
trouble. I believe you fill my needs. Are you interested?"

"Well, now, I'm kind of being one of the idle rich at the moment. So I wasn't figuring on hiring out for a spell. Tell you what, though. Leave it a couple of days, less'n time's pressing heavy on you, then we'll talk again."

"As you wish." The Englishman sighed and reached inside his loose-fitting jacket. "May I pay you a retainer as an option on your services?"

"Nope," Smith refused. "I don't *never* get myself so obligated I'd be obliged to take on a chore happen something else comes up to make me want to say no to it. Tell you what, though. Should I decide *against* taking on, you'll be the *first* to hear."

"I'm obliged to you for that, sir," Besgrove stated, finishing his drink and holding out his right hand. "And I hope you will come around to accepting my offer, but I must know by Monday evening at the latest."

"You'll know one way or the other by then," Smith promised, deciding he liked the look of the clean-cut Englishman without allowing this to change his objectivity. "Thanks for the drink, sir. Now I reckon I'll be getting up to my room."

Parting company with Besgrove in the entrance lobby, the sergeant found the dining room unoccupied and the desk clerk was absent. Going up to the first floor and turning along the passage, he ran his gaze over the masculine figure leaning a shoulder against the wall at the door of the room for which he had received the key and concluded this was the unseen observer. Clad after the style of a working cowhand, a supposition given credence by the less than "professional" style of his gun belt and its holstered Colt Cavalry Model Peacemaker, the man was of medium height and thickset. Looking to be in his late forties, solidly fleshed, there was an air of command about his deeply bronzed and heavily moustached face that suggested his identity to Smith.

"Howdy, Mr. Drexell," the sergeant greeted.

"Did Monocle Johnny point me out?" the rancher inquired, his accent that of a native-born Texan.

"Nope," Smith replied. "Somebody was watching us going

into the bar and, finding you up here waiting for me, it doesn't take the know-how of a Comanch' medicine man to figure that somebody was you and who you must be."

"You called it right as the injun side of a horse," Bradford Drexell declared, extending a large and hard hand to be shaken. "Would you be open for hiring?"

"Not right now."

"No offense meant, but would that be 'cause you're already hired on someplace?"

"Nope. It's 'cause I've got enough money not to need to work. I wouldn't want you to think of me's being *lazy*, though. My momma always claimed I was *bone idle* and, like it says in the Good Book, Eleven, Twenty-three, Sixty-one, don't *never* make a liar of your momma."

"Which surely wouldn't be the right 'n' honorable thing to do, it being in the Good Book," Drexell admitted, trying to remember whether he had heard that particular biblical quotation mentioned in the past. Although unable to recollect having done so, being a shrewd judge of character, he was duplicating Besgrove's summations with regards to the man he was addressing being *very* different from the usual run of hired gunhands. "But would you be willing to *think* about taking on a chore?"

"I'm always willing to *think* about work, even though I've *never* taken kind to doing any," Smith claimed. "But whether I said yes or no to a chore would depend on what I was being asked to do and how *urgent* it'd be for me to start at it."

"What I want is for you to ride my range."

"As a *cowhand*?"

"I've got all the cowhands I need. Good fellers, but they're not trained gunfighters. Happen it comes to shooting against the cow thieves who're working hereabouts, I want a man like you to lead them."

"Why *me*?"

"I saw the way you handled things on the street. You're damned fast, but you only downed the one of them. The rest of those . . ."

"Hired guns?" the sergeant offered, as the explanation was ended with something close to embarrassment.

"Hired guns," the rancher confirmed. "No offense meant. The rest of 'em who're around town would've dropped the other tinhorn as well, just for being there. And that's *not* the kind of help I aim to hire. The last thing I want is for some innocent cowhand getting made wolf bait just 'cause he's on my land. Will you take the chore?"

"Give me to Monday to decide whether I am to go or stick around," Smith requested. He concluded that on the surface his visitor's primary reason for wanting to hire him was much the same as that of the Englishman. Having accepted he was what he was pretending to be, each apparently believed he would prove less likely to provoke trouble than any of the other hired guns around the town. However, he did not discount the possibility that one or the other had an ulterior motive for seeking his services. "I'll let you know then for certain."

9

I'M NOT TOTING A GUN

"Thank you, Mr. Smith," Ransome Cordoba said, having just completed a round dance and joined in the applause for the small band on the rostrum. As usual when attending the weekly dance, her hair and dress were Anglo rather than Hispanic in style. "By the way, how far off being the world's best dancer did you tell me you were?"

"Far as I can bring to mind offhand, I said I wasn't even the one hundred and twelve thousand, three hundred and sixty-first," Sergeant Waxahachie Smith replied. Taking the girl by the arm and escorting her to where the rest of her party were gathering after having been on the dance floor, he continued, "Why?"

"You're *much* too *modest*," Ransome asserted, having found the man she had helped to save earlier in the week to be light on his feet and well versed in the steps of the varsouvianna, in which he had been her partner. "After dancing with you, I'm sure you *must* be the one hundred and twelve thousand, three hundred and sixty-first."

"Why, thank you 'most to death for those kind words, ma'am," Smith drawled. "And I hope you'll let me have another dance tonight?"

"I *think* my feet can stand it," the girl assessed. "Will you join us?"

"I reckon I'll just sort of drift around and be sociable first," the sergeant answered, having already discovered the attitude of the Rancho Mariposa's hands had not warmed to any great extent and wanting to avoid any suggestion that he might be present as a member of their party. "Excuse me, please, ma'am."

"You're excused," Ransome confirmed, disengaging her arm and joining the five young men, led by Tom "Halcón Gris" Grey, who had arrived with her.

Walking away from the girl, Smith glanced around in the hope of discovering some clue to the strange circumstances in which he had found himself!

In spite of the interest aroused by his eventful arrival at Flamingo, except for having received the two offers of employment, Smith had not made any noticeable progress in his assignment. Hoping to capitalize upon the notoriety he had forced upon him, he had spent Friday visiting saloons and other places that he considered might prove informative. As was the case in other towns, the barber from whom he received a shave and the hostler at the livery stable where his claybank was accommodated had proved to be useful sources of local news and opinions. Unfortunately, what little he had learned from them and elsewhere only deepened the mystery.

In fact, although Smith could hardly believe this was the case where such a competent and experienced peace officer was concerned, as a result of his findings, he had begun to wonder whether the request for assistance from the Texas Rangers was premature.

As no further theft of cattle had been reported, either the cow thieves had ceased operations or their activities could merely have been curtailed due to the continued good weather. What was more, it seemed Sheriff Tobin overestimated the threat of a range war erupting.

Despite Smith having received the offers from Sir John Besgrove and Bradford Drexell, he had not heard anything to suggest there was going to be open friction between them or with either and the other two local ranchers. Going by what he had gathered in conversations with the genuine professional fighting men around the town on Friday, none had been summoned by a specific employer. Instead, they had picked up news that there could be lucrative employment in Bonham County and, things being quiet elsewhere around Texas, had come to look into such possibilities as the area might offer. Some were talking of leaving, as no offers of work appeared to be forthcoming.

According to the barber and the hostler, while the present occupants of Rancho Miraflores were generally disliked, this appeared to be on account of less-than-sociable behavior and an insistence upon keeping others off their range. However, the hardcases hired by the new owners had never mingled with, much less sought to cause trouble for, the cowhands of the other ranches when visiting Flamingo. Furthermore, despite having taken on such men, the fact that the Fuentes family had suffered the first loss of human lives and cattle prevented there being any reason for the present incumbents of the property to be suspected of implication with whoever was responsible for the killings and thefts.

On Friday evening, using the pretense of obeying an instruction to report his decision with regards to remaining in Flamingo for longer than he had stated during the previous interview, Smith had attempted to seek enlightenment from Tobin upon the reason why outside assistance was sought. He was informed by the deputy on duty at the office that the sheriff had left upon some undisclosed urgent private business in the next county and would not be returning until Monday evening at the earliest.

Based upon what the barber had told the sergeant when he

raised the subject, the dance Ransome had mentioned was a popular source of entertainment in Flamingo on Saturday nights. Although the Fuentes's hands ignored it, contingents from the other ranches always attended. Therefore, by Saturday—in addition to not having been averse to seeing the girl again—Smith had already concluded it could offer him an opportunity to study at first hand the attitudes of the various crews toward one another.

Furthermore, while taking his midday meal at a small cantina on the fringes of Flamingo's poorer section which had become a rendezvous for the hired gunhands, something the sergeant had learned suggested his presence at the dance might prove more than just informative. After paying a genuine compliment to the excellence of the chili con carne, a dish to which he was partial, he was informed by the Chicano owner that word had been spread for "men like him" to wait around as employment would be forthcoming shortly. Asked for details, the man had claimed he knew nothing more than he had received a sum of money from an unknown source. It was accompanied by instructions to supply food and drinks as an inducement to stay for those who were short of cash and thinking of leaving to look for work elsewhere.

Disturbed by the information, Smith had paid particular attention to the behavior of half a dozen cowhands from each of the three crews when—arriving along the trails that radiated from the town to serve as long-established and accepted boundaries between the properties—they had accompanied their respective employers into Flamingo on Saturday evening. In every case, while five were young, there was an older man present. There was none of the wild dashing about on their horses and reckless indiscriminate discharging of revolvers which had so frequently been recorded as normal activities of their kind when visiting a town for relaxation.

Aided by experience in other parts of the Texas range country, Smith had realized there were two reasons for the ommission. Firstly, it was not pay night with the attendant possibility of drinking "not wisely but too well." More important, however, was the fact that most of them had been born and raised in the area. While they might whoop it up in an irresponsible fashion elsewhere, especially after having completed the long and arduous work involved in making a trail drive, they tended to refrain from doing so in their hometown except upon very rare occasions.

Not only had the groups from the three spreads come in quietly, the few cowhands who called at various saloons did no more than take a couple of drinks on the premises and buy others to carry away in concealment before going on foot to the schoolhouse. Even the latter purchases had not been excessive. What was more, prior to entering the main classroom, all who were armed had surrendered their visible weapons to the deputy sheriff standing at a table just inside the open front door. As Smith had not been asked to give up his holstered Colt, it was obvious their actions were voluntary or in response to orders given by their respective employers. Nevertheless, despite what appeared to be evidence to the contrary, the good behavior of the cowhands failed to dispel the conclusions he had arrived at earlier.

Inside the large room, which had had its desks removed and a large clear space made available for dancing, the crews remained in their respective groups—each with its coterie of friends and relations who lived in the town—instead of mingling with one another. Nevertheless, the sergeant still could not detect any indication of why Tobin had considered it necessary to ask for assistance. Having failed to find any suggestion of trouble elsewhere, he had started to wonder whether it was sought as an aid to quelling another kind of problem that should have been the sole province of the local peace officers. However, there was not even any sign of the hostility that sometimes developed as a result of rowdy behavior on the part of cowhands antagonizing the citizens.

As he had told Ransome was his intention, being willing to act upon his suppositions, Smith started to try to "be sociable." Prior to his enrollment in the Texas Rangers, he spent two years as deputy marshal to a peace officer whose family had

had a long association with the enforcement of law and order throughout the Lone Star State.[1] An important part of his education from Marshal Sherman Tragg of Waxahachie had covered the signs to watch for when seeking to locate possible troublemakers. However, it was soon obvious that his pose of being a hired gunfighter was successful. Nobody was objectional to him, but there was a lack of cordiality from the people in the room who showed no sign of adherence to any ranch crew, which was all too obvious to anybody with his knowledge of such matters. It was the same with the cowhands. As yet, neither Sir John Besgrove nor Bradford Drexell had put in an appearance, and their respective crews showed a similar disinclination to that of the Rancho Mariposa hands toward accepting his company. Nevertheless, he concluded that—with one exception—they were little different in character from those hired by Don Jose Cordoba.

"Do you know why Mexicans make refried beans?"[2] asked a loud voice with a North Texas accent. "It's 'cause no *greaser* can ever do anything *right* the *first* time!"

Hearing the words, Smith knew without looking the speaker was the exception. Despite wearing a gun belt with its holster empty, indicating that—like the rest of the group from the B Bar D—he had surrendered the weapon it had held on arrival, he had already struck the sergeant as being worthy of extra attention. Addressed by one of the cowhands as "Cousin Cyrus," his attire was much the same as the others and his face bore a tan indicative of much time spent outdoors. However, Smith's keen gaze had detected a bulge under the left side of his

1. *As is recorded in the* Alvin Dustine "Cap" Fog *and* Rockabye County *series, members of the Tragg family continued to be active in the law enforcement of Texas during the Prohibition era and still are to the present day. Some details of two earlier members who served as peace officers are given in:* SET A-FOOT *and* BEGUINAGE IS DEAD!

2. *Refried beans: a Mexican dish generally made from the mottled variety of kidney beans known as "pinto," which have had spices added and are cooked until attaining a consistency similar to what are sold in the United Kingdom as "mushy peas."*

loose-fitting jacket, which could have significance. What was more, a careful look at his hands had established they bore none of the roughness acquired through working cattle. Against that, he gave the impression of being a man possessed of much good humor and a desire to be the "life of the party." He was a regular visitor to the punch bowl on a table between where his party and the men from Rancho Mariposa were standing. Although its contents were non-alcoholic, like others among the cowhands and townsmen—albeit more frequently than anybody else—he surreptitiously added to the contents of his glass from a flask he produced out of his hip pocket. Perhaps provoked by these additions, jokes and puns flowed from him almost continuously in stentorian tones. Some were less than flattering to the mentality of Englishmen. Others, like the latest, had been just as derogatory about Hispanics. They had provoked annoyed glances from the crews of the Rancho Mariposa and the Union Jack. However, Grey and Besgrove's foreman—as Smith deduced the oldest of the group from the former ranch to be—had prevented objections being made.

Ever since they had parted, Ransome had been watching Smith. She had noticed the less-than-sociable reception he was receiving, but had been too occupied elsewhere to do anything about it. However, at last she found herself free from the various friends and acquaintances amongst the townspeople with whom she had been in conversation and, being without a partner, decided to offer him an opportunity to ask her for the next dance. With that in mind, she started to walk across the floor toward where he was standing. Although she realized she would have to pass the cowhands from the B Bar D, despite the way they had stayed clear of the other crews, she thought nothing of it. Except for the one with the loud voice, she knew them all and had never found them in any way objectionable in their behavior.

"How's about you and me having the next dance?" asked the joker, after having glanced at the main entrance and stepped with a slight teetering motion away from his companions to confront the girl.

"No, thank you," Ransome replied. She decided the man's attitude and tone were suggestive of one who had drunk more than was seemly, but sought to avoid causing offense by the refusal. "I—"

"Well, I'll be switched!" Cousin Cyrus said, before the girl could claim she already had a partner. "We let your kind take up white folks' land 'n' live over here in Texas, so how come we ain't good enough for you to dance with?"

Spoken in an even louder voice than was used for the jokes, the words carried sufficiently to be heard all around the room. Every conversation ended and a silence that could almost be felt descended. It was like the still that frequently came before a violent storm erupted.

Such was the shock caused by the insulting words, nobody spoke or moved for almost ten seconds!

Color flooded into Ransome's cheeks, but she could hardly believe her ears. She was aware that animosity existed between some Anglos and Chicanos. Nor, she realized, was it only the former who preached racial antipathy. In addition to some other Hispanics, despite hiring a mixed crew of hardcases, the new owners of the Rancho Miraflores always professed a dislike for white men in general, and Texans in particular. However, regardless of the Fuentes brothers' attitude, Bonham County had generally enjoyed a cordial relationship between its two main ethnic groups. Certainly, until that moment, she had never been subjected to any such adverse comment with regards to her racial origins. What was more, the cowhands of the B Bar D had always treated her with politeness and respect.

After the surprise died down, there was a more noticeable reaction to the comment from the other occupants of the room than was being shown by the girl. A growl of anger rumbled from the throat of Grey, and it was echoed in an equally furious way by every other member, white and Chicano, of the Rancho Mariposa's party. A similar indignation started to be shown by others in the classroom who did not belong to the party from the B Bar D. Even the latter looked startled by the remark Cousin Cyrus had made. Nevertheless, as was generally the trait of cowhands, their instincts caused them to be ready to stand by him as one of their own in the face of the obvious hostility from people who did not ride for their brand.

Watching and listening to the response, Smith realized the situation was grave and potentially dangerous. Wondering why the deputy sheriff who had been at the front entrance to the schoolhouse was not coming to intervene, he glanced around. Discovering the peace officer was nowhere in sight and the firearms surrendered by their owners were left unattended, he concluded that he must take action personally in an attempt to prevent the situation he had envisaged from happening. He was equally aware that he could not announce his official status as a means of averting the trouble that would certainly be forthcoming unless it was nipped in the bud without delay.

"Happen you'd waited for Miss Cordoba to finish, 'stead of sounding off that way, *hombre*," the sergeant announced, in as loud a voice as the other man had used and advancing before anybody else could move or speak, "she'd have told you she'd already gotten the next dance spoken for."

"How's that come to be any of your never-mind?" Cousin Cyrus demanded, swinging his gaze around and teetering slightly on his heels as if just a little the worse for liquor. Then, glancing pointedly at the holstered Colt worn by Smith and giving the impression of realization coming, he went on, "Hey, though, ain't you that hired gun's Cordoba's took on?"

"*Nope!*" the sergeant denied emphatically. Knowing cowhands, he appreciated the necessity to refute the suggestion that he was employed by Cordoba and, therefore, aligned with the Rancho Mariposa's party. He noticed from the corner of his eye that they had halted on receiving a signal to do so from Grey. However, despite this passive response, the rest of the B Bar D men would be willing to give support to one of their number if they thought he was being threatened by a hired gun from another spread. "I've not been 'taken on'—as *you* put it— by *anybody*, but I'm the feller who's spoken for Miss Cordoba's next dance."

"You are, huh?" Cousin Cyrus said, his manner defiant.

Once again, he turned his gaze to the staghorn-handled Peace-maker in the holster of the well-designed gun belt. Then, making a gesture that indicated his own unburdened rig and then Ransome, he continued, "*I'm* not toting a gun, but I ain't too scared neither to say there's some's might reckon any gal's been raised right 'n' proper ought to be more choosing about who she dances with."

"There's some's reckon's how a feller shouldn't expect a *lady* to dance with him when he's got *liquor* on his breath," Smith countered, despite suspecting the drunkenness was a pose. He also guessed, should he or the Rancho Mariposa's party make an objection over the comment about the girl's selection of a partner, the reference to him being armed was intended to ensure the support that the B Bar D party would feel honor bound to give one of their number who was not. "And you act like you've been pouring from your hip flask into your punch real frequent."

"Are you saying I'm *drunk*?" Cousin Cyrus demanded.

"Was I you," the sergeant answered, "I'd hate like hell to have folks think I'd talk that way to a lady when I was *sober*."

"Well, if that don't beat all!" Cousin Cyrus claimed, and glanced at the cowhands to his rear. "This *gunny* allows it ain't right for us to take a li'l drink when we're so minded, Cousin Tule, fellers. Maybe he reckons there should be a law again' it."

"There *is* a law against it," Smith claimed, giving the B Bar D crew no time to respond to what was clearly a request for backing. Then, being aware that cowhands were often impressed by what appeared to be a knowledge of the law far in excess of their own, he adopted a method he frequently employed to imply he possessed it. "Leastwise, Article Eleven, Twenty-three, Sixty-one of this here sovereign state of Texas's legal rulings say it's again' the law to bring drinking liquor into a schoolhouse.[3] But that don't make no never-mind to *me*. As far as I'm concerned, there's *nothing* wrong with *anybody* tak-

---

3. *The combination of numbers were, in fact, Sergeant Waxahachie Smith's date of birth. Americans put the month first, then the day and the year.*

ing a li'l drink, nor even more than one. Not 'less'n it makes the
jasper go to mean-mouthing a *lady* without waiting to hear her
tell why she couldn't have the *next* dance with him."

"What's going on here?" demanded an authoritative voice.

Smith identified the speaker without needing to take his gaze
from the apparently drunken man, who he sensed had made a
similar recognition and did not care for it. What was more, he
could see the members of the B Bar D crew were regarding the
arrival of the newcomer with mixed emotions. All were showing relief, but the one who claimed kinship with the cause of
the disturbance in particular was also clearly disconcerted by
seeing his employer crossing the room.

"Well!" Bradford Drexell growled, having left his plump and
matronly-looking wife in the doorway and advanced swiftly.
He came to a halt between Smith and Cousin Cyrus, but did
not address either of them. "What's coming off here, Merle?"

"I reckon Tule's cousin's been putting a touch too much
strengthening juice in his punch, boss," replied the foreman of
the B Bar D, to whom the question was directed. "He talked a
mite out of turn to Miss Ransome and this gent set him to
rights on it."

"Talked out of turn, huh?" the rancher growled. Having noticed the flush on the girl's olive-skinned cheeks and the menacing attitude displayed by the men from the Rancho Mariposa as
they stood in a rough crescent a short distance behind her, he
concluded that whatever was said had been offensive to her. His
gaze swung briefly to Smith, but the sergeant did not speak
and, in fact, appeared to have lost interest in the affair. "Just
how much of 'a mite' was it, Merle?"

"It was only the liquor talking, boss. Cousin Cyrus didn't
mean *nothing* by what he said," the still-worried-looking cowhand claimed before the foreman could answer. His voice took
on a tone close to pleading as he went on, "Did you, Cousin
Cyrus?"

"I *allu* . . . ," the man began, his former teetering and suggestion of being drunk having disappeared. Glancing over his
shoulder at the cowhands to his rear, he saw nothing to suggest

they would support him further and, giving a shrug, he continued, "I reckon not."

"Then you'd best say you're sorry to Ran—*Miss Cordoba,* should there be any need for it," Drexell stated. "And, seeing as you're so all-fired fond of 'strengthening juice,' you'll likely want to be heading for someplace where it's more fitting than here to drink such."

"Sure, Cousin Cyrus," the cowhand supported, as a dark flush crept over the face of the man who had received what was clearly an order to leave the dance. "Let's go over to Barney's and you can tell me about the folks back to home over some of his good sipping whiskey."

"I'll come with you, Tule," the foreman stated rather than offered, reading correctly what was meant by the slight jerk given by his employer's head. "There's a few things I want to talk over with Barney."

Letting out a noncommittal grunt, Cousin Cyrus swung around without obeying the first part of the instructions he had received or even looking at Ransome. Accompanied by Tule and with the foreman following close behind, he walked away showing none of the earlier signs suggestive of having become objectionable because of drink. As he went, what sounded like a mutually given sigh of relief arose from the onlookers. Then talk and other interrupted activities were resumed, but in a more subdued fashion.

"I don't know what was said, Miss Ran—*Cordoba,*" Drexell said, having watched the trio until they had collected their revolvers and left the building. "But, seeing as how he was here along with my boys, I'll apologize for him."

"No apology is necessary, *Mr.* Drexell," the girl replied, a touch of sorrow in her voice. Despite the way Cousin Cyrus had behaved, she remembered how—although they had never been on as close terms as her family was with Besgrove—her first name would have sufficed, and she would have been less formal when addressing the rancher prior to the animosity aroused by the cattle stealing. "I'm sure it was only the drink talking and he didn't mean anything by his remarks."

"Happen he did," Drexell growled, without asking what the remarks had been, "he can haul his butt off the B Bar D pronto, no matter that he is Tule's kin come a-visiting." Then, giving a short bow to Ransome, he turned his attention to the remainder of his crew and, nodding to where his wife was approaching, said with the quiet determination that they knew meant he would brook no refusal, "Don't you bunch go 'strengthening' your punch anymore. Ma's looking a mite peeked, so we'll be pulling out soon."

"Keep our boys together and drinking the punch just the way it comes from the bowl, Halcón Gris!" Ransome commanded, being aware that the Rancho Mariposa's crew, too, had been indulging in the "strengthening" of the otherwise innocuous brew and swinging around to look from one to another of them. She knew them too well to believe they would be willing to let the incident pass without seeking to take reprisals against the man who had treated her in such a disrespectful manner and she had no desire to let it be the cause of trouble between them and the cowhands from the B Bar D. Then, giving a well-simulated yawn, she went on, "Anyways, I'm getting tired and reckon we'll head for home after the next dance."

Although he made no attempt to join in the conversation, Smith considered the supposition he had formulated upon learning the hired guns were being persuaded to remain in Flamingo could be correct. The incident suggested that, as he had envisaged, the dance had been used in an attempt to provoke open hostility between the crews of the local ranches. However, he was too experienced a peace officer to draw the obvious conclusion that Drexell was responsible. In fact, he felt there were indications that implied this was not the case. From what had been said, the potential troublemaker was not a member of the B Bar D crew but merely visiting a kinsman who happened to work there. Certainly, despite the way he was dressed, Cousin Cyrus did not have hands indicative of his having worked with cattle. What was more, although his gun belt was of no better quality than those of his companions, the bulge under the left side of his jacket indicated he had a short-barreled revolver concealed there and the sergeant had hoped to be given an excuse to discover in what kind of rig it was carried. Smith knew it was a favorite ploy of gunfighters—even some who were on the side of law and order—to wear a weapon in plain view, but to have a second that could be produced unexpectedly from concealment.[4] Unfortunately, the intervention of the rancher had come before the examination could be performed.

On looking from one crew to the other, Smith could see the decisions to take an earlier-than-usual departure were not meeting with approval. He sensed that, in their attempts to avoid trouble, Ransome and Drexell were building up rather than reducing the animosity that the incident had aroused. He believed he could persuade the girl to delay her departure while they were dancing and hoped to have the opportunity to try to dissuade the rancher after the music ended.

The sergeant did not have a chance to carry out his intention. Even as he was about to step forward and ask Ransome for a dance, there was an interruption. On the rostrum, the leader of the band was about to signal for the other musicians to play. However, at the sight of some new arrivals, he suspended the movement.

Although wearing a brown suit of the latest Eastern style, instead of his more usual Western attire, it was not Sir John Besgrove who caused the reaction. Nor, despite clearly being twins, were the pair of red-haired young cowhands bringing up the rear of his party responsible. Realizing who it was by the rancher's side, the leader was sufficiently impressed to refrain from starting the music. What was more, if the low exclamations that swept around the room were any indication, the recognition was widespread.

Five foot eight in height, with immaculately coiffured black

4. *One gunfighter who occasionally relied upon such a ploy was Major Bertram Mosehan, leader of a special force of peace officers whose purpose was to counter the activities of an exceptionally dangerous criminal organization in Arizona Territory; see:* WACO'S BADGE.

hair topping a regally beautiful well-bronzed—yet far from leathery-skinned—face, the woman who had caused the reaction would have stood out in any company. Although in her early forties, such were the magnificent curves of her close-to-hourglass figure, she contrived to make the plain yet clearly expensive black two-piece traveling costume and mauve blouse she had on seem as revealing as the most daring evening gown. Her expression and demeanor suggested she was a person with whom it would be *most* inadvisable to take liberties or trifle.

"Ah, Ransome, Emily, Drexell," Besgrove said, escorting his companion to where the girl was still standing close to the rancher and his wife. "I'm delighted to find you all here. May I present my cousin, Freddie Fog."

10
HIS NAME *IS* SMITH

"Well, *Mister* Claybone!" Teodoro Fuentes said in English with no trace of an accent, looking at the man who entered the dining room of the house that he frequently visited when in Flamingo, shortly after midnight. His voice was cold, even disdainful, as he continued without sitting down on the comfortable chair from which he had risen when the other came in, "I hear you didn't achieve *anything* at the dance."

Even to a casual observer, it would have been obvious who wielded the authoritative power at the Rancho Miraflores!

And why!

Despite being some ten years older, with receding close-cropped black hair, Teodoro had a strong resemblance to the build and obviously pure aristocratic Castilian features of his sibling. However, his face had none of the unhealthy pallor and suggestion of debauchery shown by Javier. Instead, it was set in lines indicative of a harshly unyielding and unforgiving nature that would never be tempered by mercy, and he exuded an aura of an almost fanatical intensity. Expensive and of excellent cut, his *haciendero*'s attire was somber black and completely unadorned by even a single strand of gold or silver filigree. He had on an excellently designed and manufactured black gun belt, which was polished until given a close to mirrorlike gloss. It was a rig that, provided its wearer was competent in such matters, would allow an extremely fast withdrawal of the rosewood-handled Colt Civilian Model Peacemaker in the cross-draw holster on its left side.

"Are you sure you weren't followed here?" inquired one of the other two occupants in the room—both of whom had also stood up and remained on their feet—before the rancher could be answered.

The question was put, in tones redolent of something close to alarm, by the man of obvious Hispanic origins who owned the property. However, despite the luxurious nature of his surroundings and being dressed expensively and in good taste—although some people would have considered the number and size of the rings he wore on all his pudgy fingers was excessively ostentatious—he was just as clearly from a stratum further down the social scale than that of Fuentes. Of medium height, in his late forties, thickset, albeit running to fat, he would have been recognized by practically everybody in Flamingo as Don José Lorenzo Rabena. Despite the honorific that now preceded his name, there were rumors that he had made his fortune from border smuggling and even less savory activities, but nothing had been proven. Nor were assertions that he now owned, or at least controlled, a variety of business any better substantiated. What was *known* was that he operated a bank patronized mainly by members of his own race and was spoken of as a leading member of the Chicano community.

"Were you?" the rancher demanded when the newcomer refrained from supplying the information.

"Of course I wasn't!" stated the man who had been called Cousin Cyrus, but whose real name was Moses Claybone, not troubling to hide his resentment at it being thought that he would overlook such a basic precaution. "Do you reckon I was born yesterday?"

"I'd been told you were *good,*" Fuentes answered, darting an accusatory glance at the other white man who was present before returning it to the newcomer. "But you didn't manage to do *anything* at the dance."

"I'd got everything going along the way I wanted until that goddamned gunny of Cordoba's cut in!" Claybone objected sullenly, having a genuine antipathy toward Mexicans in spite of his current employer being of that race. "That knobhead, Tule, had accepted me's one of his kin from up Texarkana way and I figured I could easily stir up some fuss."

"But you *didn't* 'stir up some fuss,' as you put it!" Fuentes pointed out.

"Like I said, Cordoba's gunny cut in," Cousin Cyrus answered. "And he hadn't handed over his gun when he come in like the cowhands from all the spreads."

"Neither had you," the rancher growled. "At least, not the one you're still wearing under your left arm."

"I'd got it," Claybone conceded, although he had believed his habit of carrying a concealed weapon had escaped the notice of his employer. "Only I reckoned's he knew I had and, way he took out Bert Wormsley, I wasn't figuring to stack up against him when he was ready to copper my bet unless I'd got an edge. I might've done something, seeing's how I'd got those yahoos from the B Bar D ready to back me, but Drexell come in and stopped me cold."

"How?" Rabena asked.

"He as good as told me to get out," Cousin Cyrus admitted, but only after he had waited until Fuentes showed signs of impatience over his refusal to respond to the other Hispanic.

"And you went?" the rancher stated rather than inquired.

"Way things'd turned out," the would-be trouble causer replied, his earlier bonhomie having been replaced by a surly expression, "there wasn't *nothing* else I could've done. Drexell's crowd showed they was going to do what he told 'ems."

Happen I'd gone against him, not even that yahoo I slickered into thinking I was kin would've stood by me."

There was justification for the tone of bitterness in Claybone's voice!

As the would-be trouble causer had claimed, up until the intervention of "Cordoba's gunny," the scheme upon which he was engaged had been progressing smoothly. Arriving at the B Bar D ranch house at noon, having been supplied with the requisite information when hired, he had led Tule to believe he was a distant relation from North Texas and was invited to accompany the contingent attending the dance. It was his intention to provoke an incident leading to violence before Bradford Drexell, who had been diverted to the International Hotel by a fake message from a prominent cattle buyer, rejoined the party. Having employed what a later generation would call "ethnic" jokes of a derogatory kind to stir up animosity amongst the groups from the Rancho Mariposa and Union Jack, he had waited until seeing the deputy in charge of the deposited weapons was decoyed away as he had been assured would happen. Fortune had appeared to be favoring him. Realizing even Cordoba's *segundo*—who had kept the rest from showing their resentment for his jokes—would not remain passive if the girl was treated with disrespect, he had taken advantage of her approaching to do so. Unfortunately, "John Smith" had stepped in and the appearance of their employer had prevented "Cousin Cyrus" from persuading the men he was with to start trouble.

"They're loyal to Drexell, that's for sure," Dr. Otto Grantz supported, it having been on his recommendation that Claybone was hired. Under different conditions he would not have tried to excuse his nominee, but he had an ulterior motive for wanting to avoid having the elder of the Fuentes brothers begin to doubt his judgment. "I'd say you played it the only way you could under the circumstances."

Big, heavily built, there was nothing of the friendly small-town medical practitioner about the latest speaker. In fact, he did not have an appearance calculated to fill patients with the belief that he would be kindly and understanding. Beneath his plastered-down blond hair, which reeked of bay rum, his sallow features were less than pleasant and a thick moustache stained with nicotine did nothing to soften their lines. Furthermore, having a slight Germanic accent, his voice was too harsh to produce a soothing "bedside manner." As a result of his physical shortcomings, while he had proved to be competent in all aspects of his profession and far more up to date in his knowledge, he had failed to build up the liking that his predecessor had established all through Bonham County. Nevertheless, his dark brown suit and white silk shirt were of a quality that indicated he either had independent means or earned a very good income in spite of his unprepossessing demeanor.

"I *did*!" Claybone asserted, cold challenge in his manner. "There wasn't a chance of me trying anything else. I might've done something with that damned fools's took me for one of his kin, but Drexell wig-wagged for his foreman to come with us when we headed for the saloon. It was soon plain I couldn't get either of 'em liquored up enough to do anything."

"How did you get away from them?" Fuentes wanted to know.

"Said I felt like some she-male company and aimed to go to the cathouse for it," Cousin Cyrus explained. "The cow nurse allowed he didn't have enough money to go with me, so I told him's how I'd see him back at the spread. Fact being, he looked like he was more pleased than sorry to see me leave. There was one thing, though . . ."

"What was it?" the rancher was compelled to ask as Claybone showed no sign of continuing until somebody raised the subject.

"Cordoba's gunny was watching when I left the saloon," Cousin Cyrus obliged, in the manner of one conferring a favor. "He followed me to the cathouse, but I ducked out the back way and made damned sure he didn't shag me here. Well, I've come and now I'll take my money and head back there."

"Your *money*?" Fuentes asked, placing his hands behind his

back in a posture he frequently adopted. "And what money would that be?"

"The pay you owe me," Claybone supplied, his manner charged with menace.

"I said you'd be paid when your work was finished," the rancher pointed out, a spot of darker color coming to each of his swarthy cheeks. It was a warning to anybody who knew him well that his never-too-even temper was approaching the point where it erupted dangerously. "And, from what you've told me, you've done *nothing* to earn it."

"I did all I could," Claybone asserted. "It wasn't *my* doing's Drexell didn't stick around the hotel like he should've."

"That still doesn't entitle you to—" Fuentes began, but was not allowed to continue with, "the full amount."

"I *allus* get paid, *greaser*!" Cousin Cyrus snarled, starting to ease open the near side of his jacket with his left hand and move the right in that direction. "So you can haul out the *dinero* and . . ."

While speaking, Claybone was watching the rancher's posture. In his considered opinion, it was not a position to make the best use of the potential for speed offered by the well-made cross-draw rig. What was more, believing all Mexicans to fight with knives rather than revolvers, he doubted whether Fuentes had the ability to bring out the Colt with any speed regardless of the gun belt's excellent design. Satisfied upon those points and just as convinced he had nothing to fear from the other two men present, he was going to draw his concealed gun and insist upon receiving the money he had been promised even though he had failed to complete the task he was given.

Already annoyed by the failure of the scheme he had concocted and the less-than-respectful manner in which he had been treated by Claybone, as well as being just as much of a racial bigot, Fuentes was in no mood to yield to such a demand for payment, particularly when it came from a gringo. However, although he could handle the revolver with considerable proficiency, he was disinclined to take chances against a professional gunfighter. Therefore, he had put his hands in a position that he hoped would produce a sense of false security. Satisfied this was achieved, he made his play and the manner of his response justified one of the conclusions drawn by Cousin Cyrus.

The rancher made no attempt to bring his right hand from behind his back and across to the Colt. Instead, it was already holding a weapon when it came into view. Despite his supposition with regards to the way in which Mexicans fought, the movement took Claybone by surprise. Although he started to reach for the Merwin & Hulbert Army Pocket revolver as soon as he realized some form of hostile action was being commenced, he had not even touched its butt when he learned he was at least partially correct in his assumptions.

Coming into view, Fuentes's right hand was holding the knife that he had slid from its place of concealment on his left wrist beneath the sleeve of his bolero jacket. Giving a twist to his torso, he flung the weapon with the speed and skill that told of long practice. Hissing through the air, its six-inch-long spear-point blade penetrated the center of Claybone's throat. Aided by the impetus of the throw, the razor-sharp edges of the twin cutting surfaces sliced onward to sever his jugular vein and windpipe.

Although Cousin Cyrus managed to clutch and bring out his revolver as he was stumbling backward, the wound he had received was sufficiently potent to render its use impossible. It slid from his fingers and they rose involuntarily to join his other hand in reaching for the hilt of the weapon protruding from his flesh. Instinctive though the movement was, wrenching free the blade merely served to aggravate his predicament. The removal allowed his life blood to gush out in its wake and, a sudden weakness overcoming him, he spun to sprawl facedown on the floor. Watched by the other three men, none of whom—not even Grantz, regardless of the Hippocratic oath, which tradition required was sworn by all members of the medical profession prior to qualifying as a doctor—offered to render any assistance, Claybone's body jerked spasmodically for a few seconds before becoming limp and motionless.

"Huh!" Fuentes grunted, after having crossed to roll his victim over and, extricating the knife, he cleaned the blade on the lining of the unfastened jacket. "It seems, *Doctor,* that you are no better at picking a reliable man than you are at curing Javier's . . . problem."

"Shall I get Dumb Ox in here?" Grantz asked, trying not to show he was impressed by the deadly prowess that he had never suspected, and referring to the rancher's massive mute servant-cum-bodyguard who was on guard in the entrance hall and had admitted Cousin Cyrus. He was seeking to change the subject from his shortcomings in curing Javier Fuentes of an addiction to cocaine. Despite having supplied morphine to alleviate the problem, he had never subscribed to the prevailing medical belief that it served as a harmless and nonaddictive potion to substitute for the noxious narcotic used by the younger of the brothers. Nor, as he augmented his income to no inconsiderable extent by his patient's need for more cocaine, was he eager to effect a cure. "We'll have to get rid of the body."

"So we will," Fuentes agreed, returning the knife to its sheath. Waving his now-empty hand toward the corpse, he continued with no more emotion than if he were discussing something of no importance, "And he might be more use to us now than he proved while he was alive."

"How?" the doctor asked.

"I'll have his body stripped, mutilated, and taken into the barrio," the rancher explained. "Then, when it's found, it'll be assumed he was robbed and murdered there. That ought to get the B Bar D gringos stirred up and, with the right kind of prompting, they could even go in after revenge."

"Would that serve our purpose?" Rabena inquired.

"Any trouble between our people and the gringos serves our purpose," Fuentes claimed, and his gaze swung to Grantz. "What's bothering you?"

"I was thinking about that gunny who stopped Claybone's tricks," the doctor answered, seeking to ensure that the subject of Javier's problem was not raised again. "It's not the first time he's billed into your affairs, Teodoro. So who is he and what's his game?"

"He calls himself 'John Smith,' but that's likely a summer name," Rabena supplied, preventing Fuentes from pointing out that the visit by his brother to the Rancho Mariposa had not been made at his instigation. Possessing the means to obtain information from the local ranches as well as many places around the town, he continued, "Seems his horse got spooked by lightning and threw him into a draw on the way here and he was hauled out by Ransome Cordoba and that 'breed *segundo* of theirs. They fixed his hurts and let him stay at the hacienda, which'd be their way, but I haven't heard anything to suggest he's working for Cordoba."

"It could be that Cordoba hired him to try to find out about the cow thieves," Grantz suggested.

"It *could*," the banker conceded, his tone implying he considered this unlikely. "But he hasn't been asking any questions about it at the Cantina del Chili Con Carne, or anything else much, for that matter."

"He moved in quickly enough when Claybone tried to use the Cordoba girl to start trouble," Grantz pointed out, remembering what had been said about the events at the dance.

"I can't gainsay that," Rabena conceded, almost grudgingly as—sharing Fuentes's antipathy for those who did not belong to their race, albeit generally concealing it better—he resented having a gringo so deeply involved in their affairs. "But he only danced with her once and the men from the Rancho Mariposa who were there didn't treat him like a friend."

"I've heard that cowhands don't take to professional gunslingers," the doctor claimed. "Even when its one who's been hired by their boss."

"That's always the way I've found it to be," Fuentes affirmed, and gestured at the body. "In fact, our friend here only got by because he wasn't wearing a fast-draw rig and that fool of a gringo at the B Bar D was dumb enough to fall for him reckoning to be his kin. But it's this Smith *hombre* who interests me right now."

"Like I said, I haven't been able to find out whether he's been taken on by Cordoba or not," the banker confessed, in response to a pointed glance from the rancher. "But I heard Monocle Johnny and Drexell both tried to hire him."

"Why *him*?" Grantz asked. "They've not taken on any of the other gunslingers we've got waiting around town."

"They must think he's something special," Fuentes estimated. "And, thinking of how he handled Javier and those fools at Rancho Mariposa, I'm inclined to believe the same. Yes, there's more to this man Smith—if that's his name. . . ."

"His name *is* Smith!" announced a voice with a Texas accent, speaking with conviction.

Swinging around, the three men looked at the speaker who was standing in the open doorway. He was tall, handsome, albeit with a somewhat sullen cast of features and in his mid-twenties. Dressed after the style of a successful professional gambler, he wore a gun belt decorated by silver *conchos* with a pearl-handled Colt Civilian Model Peacemaker in a low-hanging Missouri Skintite holster.

"You sound very sure, Mr. Ottoway," Fuentes remarked, without offering to introduce the newcomer to his companions.

"I am *sure*," the man declared, glancing at the body on the floor. Instead of asking any questions, he went on, "He's Sergeant Waxahachie Smith and he's in the same company of the Rangers that I w—*am*."

"*You* are a Texas Ranger?" Rabena almost gasped, too surprised to have noticed the way in which the last word had been changed.

"I'd show you my li'l ole silver 'star-in-a-circle' badge, but . . ." Talbot Ottoway replied, swinging a gaze filled with mockery at the clearly startled Hispanic banker and letting the response end there.

"Why didn't you let me know they were sending somebody in?" the rancher demanded, also having failed to attach any significance to the way the newcomer's previous comment had ended.

"I didn't know myself until I got back to headquarters, like you said I should," Ottoway answered. "The captain looked more than a mite surprised to see me afore my furlough was over, but I let on I was just passing through and dropped in to pick up any mail's might have come."

"Why were the Rangers called in?" Rabena asked, showing consternation. "Has news of what we are doing reached them?"

"Seems your Sheriff Tobin figures all the cattle stealing and murdering in his bailiwick's like' to start a range war," Ottoway replied, wondering exactly what was involved and feeling sure it went far beyond the reason he had given. "So, like every local John Law can, he's asked for help from the Rangers."

"And you've been sent to help this Smith?" the rancher guessed, contriving to avoid showing his relief at hearing that the real reason for the killings and the theft of cattle was not under investigation.

"The hell I have!" Ottoway denied, but he had no intention of admitting he had been warned by Captain Frank Thornton on his arrival at headquarters that his career as a Texas Ranger was likely to be terminated in a less than satisfactory fashion unless he tendered his resignation. Nor, wanting to add to the not-inconsiderable sum of money he had already been paid by the rancher for supplying the information and assistance made possible by his official position, did he wish it known he had done so rather than face too close a scrutiny of the activities that were responsible for the demand. However, realizing he had been too vehement in his response, he went on in a less aggressive fashion, "I nosed around and found out that Smith'd been sent."

"Just him?" Fuentes asked.

"Thornton doesn't have anybody else on hand," Ottoway replied. "Nor, what I heard, is he likely to for another week at the soonest."

"Is he good, this Smith?" the rancher inquired, deciding the information explained why the man in question had dealt with the situation at the dance in the manner reported by Rabena.

"Good enough," the former peace officer stated, relieved that none of the trio had thought to raise the subject of why he had not been sent to assist Smith. "He's one real smart son of a bitch and he's come out the winner on some other mighty tricky chores."

"Then he might . . ." Grantz began.

"Not if he gets killed first," Fuentes purred.

"If he *does,*" Ottoway put in, "you'll right quick wish he *hadn't*!"

"Why?" Fuentes asked, impressed by the earnest way in which the warning was delivered.

"You don't kill *any* Ranger without asking for more goddamned trouble than you can handle," Ottoway answered. "And that'd go even more so with Waxahachie Smith."

"Why *him*?" the rancher queried.

"He's a right popular feller and not only with our company," the former peace officer explained. "And soon's word got out that he's dead, even should it be made to look like an accident, there'll be more Rangers than you can shake a stick at headed down here to find out the why of it. Once here, they'll move heaven and earth to get at the truth and won't stop until it's got. Then God help the feller responsible, because they'll nail his hide to the wall no matter how they do it."[1]

"You believe it's *that* serious?" the rancher queried.

"I'm telling you it *is,*" Ottoway declared.

"Then we won't *kill* him," Fuentes decided, and glanced at Grantz. "But we'll fix things so he won't be in any condition to go on with his investigations and, by the time somebody gets here to replace him, we'll have achieved our purpose and they'll have other things to keep them *fully* occupied."

---

1. *The trait of making a determined effort to avenge the murder of a compatriot was still retained by the Texas Rangers in the Prohibition era; see:* THE RETURN OF RAPIDO CLINT AND MR. J. G. REEDER.

11
THIS WON'T HURT YOU

"Where's everybody, *amigo*?" Sergeant Waxahachie Smith asked, finding the Cantina del Chili Con Carne's dining room unoccupied except for the owner when he entered at noon on Sunday.

Although the International Hotel offered excellent food, considering his time had been spent in a comparatively unproductive fashion the previous evening, Smith had come to the small cantina with the joint purpose of having his favorite kind of a meal and trying to discover whether there had been any further instructions for the unemployed hired guns from their mysterious benefactor.

The night before, taking advantage of the interest aroused by the arrival of Sir John Besgrove's party, the sergeant had made for the saloon that was patronized by the men from the B Bar D. Satisfying himself that the foreman was present to ensure the cowhand was not led into mischief, as he had assumed would prove the case when seeing the signal Bradford Drexell had made, he had continued to keep watch from an alley across the street. When Cousin Cyrus had left alone, he followed in the hope of learning who was behind the attempt to provoke trouble between the ranch crews.

Having delayed entering the brothel for a few minutes, so as to avoid letting the man he was after suspect his intentions, Smith had learned he made an error of judgment. Cousin Cyrus had left by the rear door and there was nobody around who might have been able to supply information about the direction he had taken.

Realizing his hope of discovering something of use about the activities of the would-be trouble causer would not be fulfilled, the sergeant had returned to the schoolhouse. On reaching the main classroom, he had found the groups from the Rancho Mariposa and the B Bar D were still present. What was more, there appeared to be a much more relaxed atmosphere than when he had taken his departure. Watching what was going on, he concluded the improved state of affairs was produced by the people who had come in with Monocle Johnny.

Nor was Smith unduly surprised that such a thing had happened!

Not only was the beautiful woman related to the rancher, she was the wife of the already-legendary Captain Dustine Edward Marsden "Dusty" Fog[1] and had acquired quite a reputation on her own account. A scion of the British aristocracy, she had elected to come to the United States and employ the alias, "Freddie Woods," for some undisclosed reason.[2] Despite being

---

1. *Details of the career and special qualifications of Captain Dustine Edward Marsden "Dusty" Fog can be found in the* Civil War *and* Floating Outfit *series.*
2. *The members of the Hardin, Fog, and Blaze families with whom we have consulted decline to say why Lady Winifred Amelia "Freddie Woods" Besgrove-Woodstole—as she was before her marriage to Dusty Fog—decided to leave England and live in the United States of America under an assumed name.*
2a. *Mrs. Fog appears as "Freddie Woods" in:* THE TROUBLE BUSTERS; THE MAKING OF A LAWMAN; THE GENTLE GIANT; THE CODE OF DUSTY FOG; BUFFALO ARE COMING!; THE FORTUNE

in what was still basically a "man's world," her capability had enabled her to own and operate the best saloon in Mulrooney, Kansas. In addition, having been elected as mayor, the policies she had caused to be adopted had ensured a standard of honesty and fair dealing that was the exception rather than the rule in the other trail-end towns along the intercontinental railroad. Furthermore, since her marriage had brought her into a clan of considerable importance in Texas, she had proved to be a powerful influence upon the affairs of the state; particularly where its major source of income, the cattle business, was concerned.

Studying the way in which Drexell in particular was behaving, Smith had decided all he had heard about Freddie Fog's personality and diplomatic skill was correct. The rancher was talking amicably with Besgrove and Ransome Cordoba. What was more, there was a mingling of the cowhands from the three ranches, which had been conspicuous by its absence prior to the sergeant leaving. From various remarks he heard passed among them, he had guessed the change partially came about by the presence of the two red-haired youngsters who had arrived with the beautiful woman. If their references to her as "Aunt Freddie" were any guide, they also were part of the powerful Hardin, Fog, and Blaze clan. Furthermore, other comments implied they worked on the OD Connected ranch and, as such, were able to indulge the local cowhands' wishes to hear about the exploits of the spread's floating outfit, which had earned its members—now no longer as active as in earlier years—a legendary status among their kind.

Although Ransome had introduced Smith to Freddie and mentioned how his intervention had helped smooth over a potentially dangerous situation, he had not been invited to stay in their company. In fact, it had been made obvious by Besgrove and Drexell that his presence was an embarrassment. Therefore, rather than do anything that might have threatened the improved state of affairs, he had made his excuses and with-

HUNTERS; WHITE STALLION, RED MARE; THE WHIP AND THE WAR LANCE *and* Part Five, "The Butcher's Fiery End," J.T.'s LADIES.

drawn. Satisfied there was no danger of hostilities breaking out amongst the crews, he had left the schoolhouse.

The search that the sergeant carried out in the hope of finding Cousin Cyrus had proved fruitless, and he had decided to end it by visiting the Cantina del Chili Con Carne. Taking a couple of drinks and declining a meal, but promising to have lunch there the following day, he had learned the offer of free food was still in effect and a number of the professional gunfighters were taking advantage of it. However, failing to discover anything else of interest, he had elected to call it a day and returned to the International Hotel. His room was at the front of the building and he had watched from his window the departure of the ranch crews. As had been the case during the later part of the dance, the groups from the spreads had behaved in a far more friendly fashion. He had noticed that, although the foreman and Tule were present, Cousin Cyrus was not with the party from the B Bar D.

Indulging in the luxury of having nothing of special importance demanding his time, the sergeant had slept late that morning. Rising, he had carried out his routine of exercises and taken a bath. By doing so, he had been too late for breakfast in the hotel and had come to the Cantina del Chili Con Carne as promised to the owner with the dual purpose of partaking in his favorite kind of meal and finding out whether there had been any further developments of interest to a "hired gun."

"You are too early, *señor*," the owner replied, his fat face wet with sweat.

"For a meal?" Smith queried.

"The food has just finished cooking, *señor*," the owner answered, hoping the watch he had kept on the street and his having only unfastened the door when he saw the Texan approaching had not been noticed.

"Could be the weather's scared everybody except me off," the sergeant suggested, having observed dark clouds suggestive of an approaching storm while walking from the hotel.

"Many of my customers go to morning mass, *señor*," the Mexican explained, forcing himself to try to appear his usual

jolly self. He was alarmed by the instructions he had received a
short while earlier from a man whom he was in no position to
refuse. Furthermore, there were three obvious hired guns waiting in the kitchen and they had warned what would happen to
himself and his wife, held by them, if he should fail to produce
the desired result. "The rest don't get up this early, and you are
the first to come."

"But not the last, you hope," the sergeant drawled.

"Not the last, I most surely hope," the owner agreed, still
compelling himself to sound jovial. "And what can I get for
you?"

"A bowl of your excellent chili con carne, *amigo,* and refried
beans on the side," Smith ordered, wondering whether the
slightly agitated attitude of the Mexican was caused by having
news he considered might not be received well by a hired gun.
"I'll follow it with pecan pie and some coffee."

"Muy pronto, señor," the owner declared and, frightened in
case his state of perturbation might warn the Texan that something was wrong, he scuttled away rapidly to avoid being asked
any further questions.

Brought as promptly as was promised, the steaming bowl of
reddish brown chili con carne and the pile of refried beans on a
plate proved to taste as good as their predecessors eaten by
Smith at the cantina. Being hungry and enjoying the meal, he
did not notice the way in which the owner repeatedly glanced
toward the door of the kitchen and then to the front windows.
Pushing away the empty crockery, he was about to ask for the
dessert he had ordered when he became aware of an over-
whelming feeling of dizziness. Shaking his head, he placed his
hands on top of the table and tried to rise. He found that his
legs refused to support his weight and a strange lethargy was
creeping over him. Before his brain could register that more
than one pair of swiftly moving footsteps were approaching,
blackness descended and he crumpled forward. He did not feel
himself lifted by two of the hard-faced men who had been waiting for his collapse, or being carried toward the kitchen from
which they had emerged.

* * *

"It's no use blaming *me,* Javier!" Dr. Otto Grantz claimed, showing no sign of concern over the wrathful way in which his visitor was eyeing him. "I have to pay the high price my suppliers ask."

"Then why not take it *without* paying?" hinted the young Mexican, his dilated eyes and the twitching of his unhealthily gray features showing the symptoms of being in need of what a later generation would term "a fix."

"Because, my young friend," the doctor replied, in the manner of one explaining something to a far-from-bright child, "despite having to live and work in this benighted land, I have no desire to have my life brought to an end. Especially such a one as would be my fate if I was stupid enough to try what you suggest."

"I've got the men to protect—" Fuentes began.

"Your brother has the men," Grantz corrected.

"Asa Coltrane and some of the others do what I tell them!"

"So I've heard. And I've also heard how *well* they did when you tried your game at Rancho Mariposa."

For a moment, the doctor thought he had pushed his visitor too far!

Raw, close-to-animal rage, twisted at Fuentes's face and he lurched from his chair with his far-from-steady hands hovering over the butts of his guns!

"Who'll get it for you if anything happens to me?" Grantz inquired, contriving to keep his alarm from showing.

"You aren't the only one selling it!"

"True. But can *you* find somebody else?"

"I-I . . ." Fuentes croaked, realizing he did not have another source of supply and sitting down again. "May all the saints damn you to hell!"

"That might worry me, but I've never believed in their existence," Grantz purred, satisfied the danger had passed. "However, at this moment, our problem is *you.* Clearly the morphine isn't serving its purpose. Therefore, you must have more cocaine. Unfortunately, as I've told you, it costs a great deal of money."

"My brother—" the young man commenced.

"Will only pay the price of morphine," the doctor countered. "Ach! If I only had enough money of my own!"

"How do you mean?"

"The people who supply me have a large quantity they want to dispose of."

"How *large* a quantity?"

"It would not only last you for at least two years, there would be enough left over for you to sell the rest of your friends when you get back to Mexico City and more than cover the cost."

"What would the cost be?" Fuentes asked.

"Two thousand, five hundred dollars," Grantz replied.

"Where would I get that kind of money?" the Mexican demanded.

"The same place you tried before, perhaps," the doctor suggested, then glanced at the clock on the instrument cabinet of his reception room. Picking up a bunch of keys from the top of the desk at which conversation was taking place, he unlocked a drawer. Watched by his visitor, whose tongue ran across clearly dry lips, he removed a small box. "Here, this will last you a few days. However, it is the *last* I have until I can raise the money to buy more."

"And if I bring you the money?" Fuentes asked as he snatched the offering with an almost pathetic eagerness. *"All* of it?"

"Then I will buy the whole supply and your problem will be solved," Grantz promised, hoping the young Mexican would not think to ask what he was expecting to gain from the purchase. "Now you'd better be going. By the way, don't the Cordobas . . . ?"

"Those high-and-mighty bastards, ordering me from their house like I was some stinking peon!" Fuentes spat out, the worst of his temper always being aroused by any reference to the people who owned the Rancho Mariposa. "One day I'll pay them back for the way they've treated me!"

"And who can *blame* you?" Grantz inquired, his manner sycophantic and giving no indication that it had been his intention to revive such memories and sentiments. "Don't they come to evening mass here in town every Sunday, like the good Catholics they are?"

"Yes," Fuentes admitted, but was clearly puzzled by the question.

"And there're quite a few places between here and their hacienda where an ambush could take place," the doctor elaborated. "By the cow thieves who've been raiding around here, I mean."

"Yes!" the young Mexican said, an appreciation of what had been meant by the words now striking him, and he nodded with vigor. Coming to his feet, he went on as he started to make for the door. "Yes, they *do* and, who knows, those cow thieves might make another raid tonight."

"It certainly looks like their kind of weather is coming up," Grantz admitted, darting a glance from the window to where the black clouds were moving across the sky. "And perhaps it would be better for you to get going. It looks like there's rain coming and I don't doubt you've got quite a few things to do before mass ends."

"That I have," Fuentes confirmed, the ravaged lines of his handsome face taking on an expression of evil. "And you can let your suppliers know that you'll take all they have off their hands."

"That was *close.* He's getting more edgy by the day," Grantz breathed after his visitor had left and he was going into the room that served as an operating room when he had surgery to perform. "This business isn't going the way Fuentes planned. So, providing that young hophead gets the money, it'll give me a stake to get as far away from here as I can travel, should things go wrong."

The arrival of Javier Fuentes had been expected by the doctor!

Like many of the crowd of wealthy young radicals to which he belonged, the Mexican had started to try to counteract a sense of inadequacy by smoking marijuana; which he and his kind had insisted was harmless and even beneficial. The effect had been obtained for a time, but—as was all too frequently the case—he had found its potency diminishing. Complaining of this deficiency and acting upon Grantz's suggestion, although Teodoro was unaware of where the responsibility lay, he had turned to the vastly more potent and effective cocaine.

Knowing how much of the soul-destroying white powder Javier had purchased at their last meeting, the doctor had realized the stock was deplete and had anticipated there would be a need to replenish it. Since hearing of the abortive visit to the Rancho Mariposa and guessing its real purpose accurately, he had been contemplating how he might acquire a larger sum than had already accrued from his services. Having planted the idea in the receptive mind of the young Mexican, which he knew to become even less stable when reminded of the well-justified humiliation suffered at the hands of the Cordoba family, he had donated just enough of the potent narcotic to ensure sufficient bravado would be aroused for it to be acted upon.

Already involved in the political activities of the Fuentes brothers in Mexico, Grantz was helping with the most ambitious scheme so far attempted. He had been instructed to precede them to Texas and, without allowing their association to be known, set up a practice in Flamingo. The death of the previous medical practitioner shortly before his arrival had allowed him to do so without that particular complication arising. Despite his failure to "cure" the younger brother's addiction—which, to give credit where it was due, was the last thing he wanted to do with such a lucrative patient—he had already been of one service to the elder sibling by virtue of his profession and was to do something else, this time in the surgical line, that morning.

While waiting for the arrival of the men he was expecting, the doctor thought about the development he had heard was threatening the scheme upon which he was engaged. From

what he had been told by Rabena a short while earlier when
they met to discuss the part he was soon to play, providing the
Texas Ranger fell into their hands, there was a danger of the
hostility amongst the other ranchers—which was so essential to
their plans—being brought to an end. The banker had been
requested by Monocle Johnny Besgrove and Brad Drexell to
send a messenger who would be trusted to ask Teodoro Fuentes
to join them in a meeting intended to organize a roundup covering all their spreads and satisfy everybody that none had
stolen stock upon it. Aware of what the result would be, the
doctor and his fellow conspirator also wondered why they had
not heard the body of Moses Claybone had been found.[3]

Grantz's thoughts on the subject were brought to an end by
hearing a buckboard draw to a halt at the side door. Opening it,
he discovered the plan to capture Waxahachie Smith was successful. While a third was clearing, keeping watch on the ends
of the alley between the surgery and its nearest neighbor, two of
the hired guns—who, although actually hired by Fuentes, had
been in town pretending to be waiting for an employer—carried
the unconscious Texas Ranger inside. Closing the door behind
them, he told them to lay their victim upon the table he used
for operations and, when this was done, to go into the next
room until he called for them. Left to himself, he removed his
jacket and rolled up his shirtsleeves. Then he meticulously
scrubbed his hands and arms up to the elbows. Having done so,
he crossed to the table and ran his gaze over the instruments of

3. *Teodoro Fuentes had outsmarted himself. After being subjected to the
mutilation he had described, the body of Moses "Cousin Cyrus" Claybone
was taken by "the Dumb Ox" to be left in the poor section of Flamingo
known as the barrio near the cantina of an otherwise disreputable Chicano
who, Jose Lorenzo Rabena had declared, would be in opposition to their
scheme. Unfortunately for the plotters, the owner found the corpse shortly
after it was deposited. Deducing how the dead man had earned a living from
the condition of his hands, the Chicano had believed his body had been left
by an equally unscrupulous business rival in the hope that the other hired
guns around Flamingo would come to take revenge under the misapprehension that he was murdered in the cantina. To avoid this, the owner took and
sank the corpse—suitably weighted—in a deep stretch of the Rio Grande.*

his trade, which he had placed in a position convenient for them to be selected and used.

The previous evening, on hearing what was planned, Rabena had remarked a couple of well-aimed blows from an ax or meat cleaver would achieve the desired result. Grantz had replied with pompous dignity that he was a doctor, not a butcher. He did have pride in his skill, which was considerable regardless of his otherwise dubious professional ethics, but this alone had not provoked the response. No matter how the enterprise turned out, he wanted to be able to claim he had acted in all good faith when two men brought him a third who he had assumed to be a hired gun like them. When, or if, questioned by the authorities, he would say they had told him that their companion had been hurt in an accident and, as a result of his examination, he had decided there was only one way to act if he was to save the victim's life.

Checking upon Smith's condition, the doctor sought for any suggestion that the drug he supplied to be used at the Cantina del Chili Con Carne had failed to produce the desired effect. At the conclusion of his examination, he felt sure that he could carry out the operation without there being any chance of a premature return to sentience.

"This won't hurt you," Grantz remarked to the motionless and uncomprehending sergeant as a crash of thunder heralded the commencement of a storm. "At least, not until you finally regain your wits and, provided my orders are carried out, that won't be for some days."

Swabbing Smith's right hand with disinfectant, but—the inadvisability of breathing on the patient not yet having been appreciated by the medical profession—without attempting to cover his own mouth and nostrils with a cloth, Grantz selected one of the razor-sharp scalpels that were his pride and joy.

Making the first incision an inch or so above the point at which he proposed to make the amputation, with the elements giving what seemed a Wagneresque accompaniment to the foul deed he was performing, the doctor sliced through the epidermal layer down each side of the forefinger toward the palm and carefully peeled back a section of skin between the knuckle and the first joint. Continuing to exercise the utmost care, he snipped through subcutaneous tissue, tiny blood vessels and tendons encased in their own lubricating sheaths until he reached the actual bone. Once the phalange had been separated from the metacarpal bone that was part of the intricate structure of the palm of the hand, he folded the peeled-back section of skin over the wound to form a protective pad. This he secured with tiny stitches, which would have elicited a sigh of envy from the most expert seamstress, and, laying the severed finger aside to be destroyed when he was finished, he covered the hand with an equally neat wrapping of spotlessly clean bandages. Working just as carefully and unhurriedly, he repeated the procedure on his "patient's" left forefinger.

Without even waiting to wash his hands, or noticing the storm had blown over while he was completing an excellent—albeit totally unjustified—piece of surgery, Grantz called the two men from the other room. Giving one a bottle of dark brown liquid, he told them to carry out the rest of the instructions they had received from Fuentes. Waiting until they had taken his "patient" outside and he heard the buckboard moving off, he set about removing all the evidence of the operation he had performed.

12

SOMEBODY IS GOING TO LIVE TO REGRET *THIS!*

Despite there being a threat of rain to follow that which had fallen earlier in the day, Ransome Cordoba was in a happy and contented frame of mind as, feeling warm in the waterproof garments common sense had dictated she put on, she sat by her equally protected father in the buggy that they always used when attending evening mass at the Catholic church in Flamingo. She would have preferred to travel on horseback to and from the service, but he insisted that decorum required she wore feminine attire unsuitable for riding.

The unpleasant incident at the previous night's dance had filled the girl with a sense of foreboding. However, the intervention of the man she still only knew as Waldo Smith had prevented what might easily have developed into open hostility and involved everybody present, not just the contingents from the Rancho Mariposa and the B Bar D. What was more, the arrival of Mrs. Freddie Fog had served to cause Bradford Drexell to forget his differences with Sir John Besgrove. Nevertheless, regardless of Ransome stating her father would be in full agreement, the men had claimed they considered it would be more tactful if the most important issue they had discussed was held in abeyance until she could tell him of it. Agreeing, she had gone home at the conclusion of the dance and, waking him up, had satisfied herself that her assumption was correct.

Considering only good could come from the proposal, Don Jose Fernande de Armijo y Cordoba had traveled with his daughter to Flamingo that morning instead of waiting until later in the day as would normally have been the case. They were accompanied by Tom "Halcón Gris" Grey and half a dozen cowhands who were of the Catholic faith and always attended evening mass with them. Although the distinguished visitor had not been present, the Cordobas and the other two ranchers had held a most productive meeting in the main dining room of the International Hotel.

The proposal of checking their spreads in an attempt to ascertain how serious the losses from the cow thieves had been and to prove none of them were holding rebranded stolen stock on their respective ranges had been agreed on without hesitation as far as the Texan, British, and Chicano ranchers were concerned. As further evidence of their good faith, Cordoba and Monocle Johnny had declared their wish that Drexell should serve as roundup captain.[1] However, Teodoro Fuentes had done no more in response to the invitation to join them than send a message promising to give the suggestions he had received his consideration. He said he would inform them of his decision later.

Much as the girl had hoped she would have a chance to renew her acquaintance with Smith, who she was growing convinced was far from the hired gunslinger he had led her to assume him to be, she was not granted the opportunity. Asking about him at the reception desk on her arrival and after the meeting was over, she had been informed on each occasion that

1. *The duties of a roundup captain are described in:* THE MAN FROM TEXAS.

he was not in his room. However, his property was still there and this implied he had not taken his departure from the area.

Because of the threat of rain, dusk had come early. However, as the party was on the familiar trail that separated the Rancho Mariposa from the Union Jack, there was sufficient light for them to travel without needing the lanterns of the buggy to supply extra illumination. Due to the inclement nature of the weather, like their employer and his daughter, all the cowhands had donned and fastened slickers over their Sunday "go to town" clothes. Amiable chatter was passing between them and nobody was giving the slightest thought to the possibility of danger.

The ambush came as a complete surprise!

Passing along a stretch of the trail with gentle and bush-covered slopes on each side, the group were caught by a withering blast of rifle and shotgun fire delivered from fairly close quarters on the left and right!

Caught by a charge of buckshot, fired from sufficiently near to ensure all nine .32-caliber balls impaled his body, Cordoba was slammed sideways. By doing so, he inadvertently saved his daughter from a worse fate than the one which overtook her. Filled with the rage he had developed toward the girl and her father, Javier Fuentes had planned to satiate his lust upon her before she was finished off. However, the impact she received caused her to move into the path of an approaching .44.40-caliber bullet. Ripping through the side of her head, it killed her instantly. The reins slipped from her no-longer-responsive grasp and, driven into panic by the commotion, the spirited horse drawing the buggy lunged forward in a wild gallop that threw her from the seat.

Nor, with the exception of their *segundo,* did any of the cowhands fare better. Lead from six weapons on one side and five at the other was slashing indiscriminately into man and beast. Despite the places of concealment selected amongst the bushes, the red flare of muzzle blasts would have served to locate the positions of their assailants, but the information was of no use. Impeded by their slickers, they could not have brought out their holstered revolvers even if they had had more stable seats than the saddles of their frightened and pitching horses. Not everyone was killed outright, but all were struck by bullets and thrown from their mounts before any could arm himself and fight back.

Sharing the dislike of his companions for suffering bodily discomfort when it could be avoided, Grey had taken a similar precaution to avoid getting wet. What was more, as a result of the much-improved state of affairs that had arisen from the successful outcome of the meeting, even he was not as alert as usual. Nevertheless, there was one difference. Unlike the cow-hands, he did not have his rifle in a saddleboot. The omission had aroused no comment. When riding, unless it reposed across the crook of his left arm, he invariably carried his Winchester Model of 1873 repeater suspended—by a rawhide loop attached to a "carbine ring," which he had had fitted on purchasing it[2]—from his saddle horn. He had explained the habit to anybody who pointed out the disadvantages of such a means of transportation by asserting, "I'd sooner have to dry and clean her after every shower than not have her *real* handy should she be needed sudden-like."

Taken just as unawares as the rest of his companions, Grey nevertheless responded with a speed that would have gladdened the hearts of his Chihuicahui Apache warrior forefathers. Leaving the back of his plunging horse by his own volition, he contrived to snatch the rawhide loop of the rifle from the saddle horn and take it with him. What was more, he alighted on his feet and, although he staggered a couple of paces, retained his equilibrium. Snapping the metal butt plate to his right shoul-

2. *Being shorter than rifles, like handguns—see Item 3 of the Appendix— carbines were intended for use by mounted soldiers. To offer greater accessi- bility when on foot or in the saddle, many types designed with mainly mili- tary sales in mind were equipped with a swiveling metal ring attached to the side of the frame. This could be coupled to the hook—generally brass, which could be given a bright polish for ceremonial purposes, where the army and navy were concerned—fitted on a leather strap, allowing the weapon to be suspended across its user's left shoulder and to hang by his right side.*

der, he sighted along the barrel to where the muzzle blast for a
spread of buckshot that took the life of a cowhand indicated the
position of the man responsible. His Winchester cracked the
instant he was sure of his aim and, regardless of the speed with
which the discharge was made, he achieved success. A cry filled
with anguish rose from the bushes, followed by the sound of
something heavy crashing to the ground and the thrashing of
limbs working with a spasmodic lack of control.

Despite the fury he felt over what was happening to the rest
of his party, especially the Cordobas, Halcón Gris did not allow
it to blind him to his own dire peril. Throwing himself prone on
the ground, he avoided two shots directed his way. By the time
he alighted, he had operated the Winchester's lever action and
was ready to continue fighting. The second bullet he sent met
with a similar response to its predecessor, but the third failed to
produce the same effect. Nor was he granted an opportunity to
try again. Through pure expediency, he was firing at the side
that harbored the most assailants. Although two of them had
suffered as a result of his deadly skill, alerted to the peril he was
posing, the others turned their weapons his way. All four bellowed almost simultaneously and only one missed. Plowing
into his body, the loads from a shotgun and two rifles inflicted
mortal wounds. Desperately trying to respond in kind, he was
unable to do so and, the Winchester sliding from his hands, he
subsided limply with his lifeblood spreading upon the surface of
the trail.

Stimulated by a dose of the cocaine he had received from Dr.
Otto Grantz, Javier Fuentes was wild with elation. Shrieking
what he believed was encouragement to his men, whom he had
reinforced with five of the gunfighters from Flamingo on the
pretense that his older brother had given orders for the ambush, he was firing his elegantly chased and engraved Winchester Model of 1873 carbine with all the speed he could manage.
That his bullets were flying harmlessly over the heads of his
victims and, in fact, posing a greater threat to his assistants,
never occurred to him. Nor did he notice that Asa Coltrane
and the villainous-looking Mexican who had accompanied him

on his most recent visit to the Rancho Mariposa had fallen
victim to the rifle in the hands of Halcón Gris. His only
thought was that, at last, he was being given an opportunity to
avenge what he considered to have been humiliation he had
suffered at the hands of the Cordoba family.

Having their hearing impaired by the detonation of so much
black powder, none of the other attackers were any better able
to hear sounds that should have warned them of the possibility
that danger could be approaching. Not until lead started to fly
and strike some of them did they realize several riders were
dashing along the trail. Those who had already emptied shot-
guns were in the process of loading, or drawing revolvers, to
continue the attack upon their victims. Others still had bullets
in the magazines of rifles. However, all were caught unprepared
by the arrival of this unanticipated menace. Of the three who
were hit, two went down mortally wounded. Being the kind
who preferred murder from concealment to open combat, the
remainder considered discretion the better part of valor and
turned without even waiting to discover who was attacking
them.

Feeling a burning sensation as a bullet grazed his shoulder
and elicited a squeal of pain, Fuentes was brought to an appreciation of the situation. Fortunately for him, it happened in
time for him to become aware the affair was going badly wrong
and to bring about the realization that he was being deserted by
the survivors of the attack. He neither knew, nor cared, who
had intervened to such deadly effect. All he was conscious of at
that moment was that his life was in peril. Throwing aside the
carbine, regardless of it bearing an inscription that could be
considered as offering evidence of his participation in the ambush, he turned and fled to where the party on his side of the
trail had left their horses.

Such was the state of terror that had replaced his earlier
elation, the young Mexican did not attempt to locate his black
Thoroughbred and was oblivious of the fact that it, too, could
serve to establish his presence at the incident. Instead of looking for the animal, catching hold of the nearest reins, he

snatched them free from the branch around which they were looped. Neither knowing nor caring what had happened to the men he had persuaded to help him, but with fear giving speed to his shaking limbs, he hauled himself into a saddle he failed to recognize as being unlike the Mexican-style rig he always used. Moaning in apprehension, he used his spurs with even greater violence than usual and sent the animal forward in a bound that almost dislodged him. However, he retained his seat and turned his attention to making good his escape with all the haste he could produce from his mount.

"Let them go, but a couple of you catch the buggy!" the leading newcomer shouted, after having reined his mount to a halt and listened to the sounds of departure made by the fleeing attackers. Despite an undertone of strain and anguish, his British upper-class accent would have identified him as the owner of the Union Jack ranch to anybody familiar with the population of Bonham County. "We've all we can manage to do here!"

Following a procedure as unvarying as that of the Cordobas, Monocle Johnny Besgrove and the men who had arrived with him had been attending a Protestant church service in Flamingo. Knowing their routine for Sundays, it had been his intention to accompany his friends along the trail to the point where they would be compelled to go their separate ways to their respective homes. Unfortunately, Mrs. Freddie Fog and her party were with him. There were many people who had been unable to make her acquaintance at the dance the previous evening and, being aware of her prominence and social standing in the state, were eager to rectify the situation. Wanting to avoid hurting anybody's feelings, knowing it was advisable to maintain the best possible relationships in the area during the next few weeks, she had allowed Besgrove to make introductions and chatted with those who were presented to her. By doing so, she had inadvertently delayed their departure until some time after the contingent from the Rancho Mariposa had set out.

Because of the threat of inclement weather, the Englishman had decided against sending a rider to ask his friends to wait

until his party caught up. However, on hearing the shooting, he
had not hesitated in the way he responded. Nor had he been
concerned over leaving his cousin behind. He knew she was far
from being defenseless or unprotected. She had what she referred to as an elephant gun loaded and readily available inside
the coach in which she had traveled from Rio Hondo County.
As she was fully competent in the use of both,[3] it would more
than supplement the Colt Storekeeper Model Peacemaker revolver reposing in her reticule. Furthermore, although her two
nephews had accompanied Besgrove, the driver of the vehicle
and another member of the OD Connected ranch's crew who
stayed behind were well armed and equally capable of offering
any added protection she might need.

As was the case with the party from the *Rancho Mariposa,*
Besgrove and his companions had put on slickers. Nor had they
taken the time to remove the restrictive garments. However,
there was one *very* important difference. They, too, were taken
unawares by the shooting, but were not caught in the ambush.
Prior to setting off to investigate, realizing they would be going
into a dangerous situation, they had drawn either rifles from
rifle sheaths or revolvers out of their holsters before sending
their horses forward at a fast run.

Arriving undetected until they opened fire, while inflicting
some casualties upon the men in the bushes, the Englishman's
party had avoided suffering any themselves. The same did not
apply to the group they had come to assist. Not one was standing and their horses were galloping off in every direction. It was
these facts that caused Besgrove to give the order not to pursue
the fleeing men and, having deduced correctly what had happened, for the Cordobas' buggy to be retrieved. Without waiting to make sure he was obeyed, knowing he would be, he

3. *One occasion when Mrs. Freddie Fog displayed her ability with the elephant gun, which was actually a Holland & Holland .465 H & H caliber
double-barreled rifle considered by British sportsmen as being too light to be
used successfully against such massive animals, is recorded in:* BUFFALO
ARE COMING!

swung from the saddle. Leaving his mount standing ground hitched by its dangling split-ended reins, he hurried to the smallest of the shapes lying on the ground. Even before he produced a match from his pants pocket and struck a light, he knew who this was.

"Goddamn it!" the Englishman snarled as he gazed at the lifeless body of the girl, his face savage in the flickering light. *"Somebody* is going to live to regret *this!"*

* * *

Becoming aware of thunder crashing and hearing the drumming of heavy rain somewhere above him, Sergeant Waxahachie Smith found himself struggling desperately against what felt like choking water filling his mouth and nostrils. After a moment, although the sounds of the storm continued, the sensation ebbed away. It was replaced by a similar feeling, except it was even worse, to that he had experienced when regaining consciousness in the bottom of the arroyo where he had been thrown by his horse, and later on his first recovery at the Rancho Mariposa. There was, nevertheless, one major difference. This time he was aware of his identity. The problem facing him was that he knew neither where he was nor what had reduced him to his present condition. While there was no soreness from his ribs, his hands hurt and his head throbbed abominably.

Gritting his teeth, the sergeant tried to raise his head from the pillow upon which it rested. Instantly, he found his already-restricted vision blurring and it seemed the small room, which instincts suggested he had not occupied of his own free will, seemed to start spinning crazily around him. After an indefinite period, which could have been hours or only a few seconds for all he knew, the spasm passed and he opened his eyes without it resuming. For a short while, he felt too weak to do anything more than lie on his back and look at the grimy board ceiling. Then he told himself that he must make an effort to solve the mystery of his presence.

Thinking and doing, Smith warned himself, could prove two vastly different propositions. He had a vague recollection of two earlier resumptions of semi-sentience. On each occasion, presumably having been alerted by the noise he had made in his attempt to rise, a pair of hard-faced men he remembered seeing among the hired guns at Flamingo had entered. One had pinned him down, with an ease that warned just how weakened a condition he was in, while the other had poured some kind of liquid between his lips and, by covering his mouth and nose, compelled him to drink it. They had continued to prevent him from moving, or even shouting for help, until he had lapsed once again into an unconscious state.

Moving very slowly, trying to avoid making the cheap and narrow bed squeak and give notice of his actions, the sergeant eased himself until seated with his back resting against the roughhewn wall. After the wave of dizziness and near nausea subsided sufficiently to make it possible, turning his gaze downward, he found he was wearing the shirt he had had on during the visit he paid to the Cantina del Chili Con Carne, which was his last conscious memory. Although he could feel his boots had been removed, he also knew he had on a pair of trousers.

However, Smith's attempt to recollect what had taken place at the cantina was forgotten as he noticed both hands were wrapped in grubby white bandages. Nor was that all. Something was different about the shape of them. Before he could decide what this might be, another surge of dizziness and nausea flooded through him. Twisting his torso sideways in an instinctive motion, he retched violently albeit without bringing up anything. What was more, when the spasm ended, he was once again prevented from satisfying his curiosity. Hearing the creaking of hinges, he looked around. With a sensation of alarm, he saw the two men entering and guessed what they would do on finding he was sentient.

"He's woke up again, Dip," announced the taller of the pair, taking a bottle from the pocket of his unfastened wolf-skin jacket.

"Looks that way, Skull," the other answered. "I've allus heard's how sleep's good for them's be suffering from his kind of hurt."

"So've I," declared the first speaker, whose completely bald head and cadaverous face suggested how he had acquired his sobriquet. "Which being, let's give him some of this medicine of Doc Grantz's to make him get some."

Realizing the liquid must be some kind of sleeping potion, Smith tried to gather sufficient strength to resist having it forced upon him. Leering in an evil fashion and clearly enjoying what they were going to do, the pair converged upon him. Reaching beneath the blanket, which was his only covering, Dip grabbed him by the ankles and dragged him until he was once again supine. Never had he felt so weak and utterly helpless. The sudden movement to which he was subjected brought a resumption of the dizziness and nausea. He could do nothing more than struggle feebly as his assailant transferred the grip to his shoulders and pressed downward. Preventing Skull from grasping his face and forcibly opening his mouth was beyond his powers. Nor was he any better able to avoid having some of the liquid poured between his opened lips and being compelled by the same means as previously to swallow it.

"Would this here be a private game," asked a voice with a Texas accent just before the sergeant lapsed once more into an unconscious state, "or can anybody sit in?"

13
YOU'VE LOST *BOTH* FOREFINGERS

On hearing the question, Skull and Dip looked at the door through which they had entered the room and started to straighten up from where they were bending over the once-more-limp body of Sergeant Waxahachie Smith. Believing their privacy would be respected, they had not closed the door before crossing to return him to the unconscious condition from which he had just partially recovered; as they were under orders from Teodoro Fuentes to keep doing for the next week. Customers of the small combined hotel and saloon in a dilapidated little village on the northern boundary of Bonham County did not usually show such obvious interest in the affairs of others. The reticence was caused by the owner of the establishment drawing the majority of his trade from the criminal element. His association with outlaws had made him willing to oblige when receiving a request from Don José Lorenzo Rabena, therefore amounting to a demand, to supply them with the necessary accommodation, and they had brought their captive there in the belief that nobody would pay any attention to their activities. However, it seemed the unwritten rule of the place was being broken.

Although it was late on Monday evening, no word had reached the pair of the events that had taken place on Sunday night along the trail between the Rancho Mariposa and the Union Jack, or its aftermath. Being unaware of how drastically the situation had changed, nobody who could have done so having come to warn them, they were continuing to carry out the instructions they had received from Dr. Otto Grantz by ensuring their captive remained in a state of sedation. Their arrival in his room had been by chance, not because they had heard him moving. However, they had no desire for strangers to see him or guess what they had intended to do.

The abductors had seen the speaker and the man by his side in the barroom. They had arrived accompanied by two red-haired young cowhands who were clearly twin brothers and gave the impression of having drunk just a little more than was wise. However, apart from supposing the youngsters were to be relieved of their money and other property by the other two, in keeping with the policy of the place—although one's appearance had been worthy of more than a second glance—Skull and Dip had paid little attention to any of them. What was more, until that moment, they had conveyed an impression of being solely concerned with their own affairs.

Tall, lean, gray haired, in his late forties at least, the one who the hired gunslingers felt sure had addressed them wore the attire of a Texas cowhand and had a deeply tanned face that looked as mean as that of an Indian brave riding a war trail. He stepped forward with a slouching stride, but kept his hands clear of the Remington Model of 1875 Army revolver on the left side and bowie knife at the right side of his gun belt.

While the dark-visaged man might have passed unnoticed, especially in their present surroundings, his companion would have stood out almost anywhere in Texas!

Short in stature, yet sturdily built, the second intruder was considerably younger than his companion. What was more, he

most definitely was *not* a native-born Texan. Good looking by
Occidental standards, his clean-shaven face had Oriental lines,
skin pigmentation, and the so-called slant eyes that had given
the Chinese their derogatory sobriquet. Being bare headed, having removed a black J.B. Stetson hat styled after the fashion of
the Lone Star State and slicker on entering the barroom, established that he kept his black hair closely cropped instead of
having it form the pigtail usually associated with such features.
Furthermore, no member of the Chinese race seen by Skull and
Dip had been clad as he was. Nor, as a general rule when
outside their own communities in large cities such as San Fran-
cisco, did they carry weapons in plain sight. In addition to
wearing a black shirt of Western style, with matching Eastern-
style riding breeches and boots, he had two strange-looking
swords—one considerably longer than the other—in sheaths
thrust through the left side of the red silk sash about his waist.

"What the hell's it got to do with you?" Skull demanded, his
voice becoming charged with menace as he allowed the bottle
from which he had poured the liquid to slip out of his fingers.

"Plenty," the Indian-dark Texan claimed, and gestured
briefly with his left hand toward the little Oriental at his side as
they continued to advance. "When I got word's how you was
holding this gent here 'gainst his will and told Miz Freddie, she
straight off said, 'Well now, Kiowa, that's not rightful' right. So
you and Danny best just go along 'n' fetch him back.' "

Wondering where he had heard the first name mentioned
before and in what context, the bald man made no attempt to
satisfy his curiosity. Instead, silently cursing the impulse that
had led him and Dip to come to see their captive while the
third member of the abduction party was visiting the backhouse, he elected to take action.

"Get 'em!" Dip spat out, dropping his right hand toward his
low-hanging Colt and proving that—while nobody was likely to
consider either of them great—the minds of himself and his
companion were in complete accord over the way to deal with
the intruders.

Already contemplating such a solution to the intervention,

Skull was duplicating the action of his companion. Both were giving their attention to the Texan, feeling sure he posed by far the greater threat. No Chinaman they had ever met had shown any skill in handling weapons, or even displayed the spirit to fight back if abused by them. What was more, even if this one should prove the exception, they did not consider he could provide any danger with his—to their mind primitive—weapons carried in such a fashion.

The pair soon discovered their summations were wrong!

Neither was given an opportunity to think about, much less try to correct, their erroneous conclusions!

While Oriental in racial origins, Danny Okasi was not Chinese.[1] Nor did he possess the meek and mild disposition of the average member of that race to be found in the United States. Born in the Japanese seaport of Kanazawa, he had come to Texas to continue repaying an obligation to the Hardin, Fog, and Blaze clan that a now-dead uncle had incurred.[2] Nevertheless, although he had arrived in Bonham County acting as the driver of Mrs. Freddie Fog's coach, he was far from being a mere servant. From his childhood, despite their special rights having been abolished as a result of edicts issued by the emperor between 1873 and 1876, he had received and become adept at all the training required to qualify him as a samurai warrior. Having acquired proficiency in handling all their traditional weapons and at performing their special bare-handed

1. *As was the case with his uncle, Tommy Okasi, the name of the young samurai was an Americanized corruption of an alias and their true identity cannot be divulged.*

2. *The various members of the Hardin, Fog, and Blaze clan with whom we discussed the subject during visits to Fort Worth, Texas, in 1975 and 1985 stated that, because of the circumstances and high social standing of the people involved—all of whom have descendants holding positions of importance in Japan at the time of writing—it is inadvisable even at this late date to make public the facts concerning the reason for Tommy Okasi's departure from his homeland.*

2a. *Details of some of Tommy Okasi's career and ability as a samurai warrior are given in the* Ole Devil Hardin *series and one occasion when he put to use his skill at karate is recorded in:* SIDEWINDER.

fighting techniques of jujitsu and karate, he was extremely competent in the use of the *daisho* of swords—comprised of a *katana* with a blade thirty inches long and a *wakizashi* approximately half its length—with which he was armed at that moment.[3]

Springing forward, the little samurai sent his right hand flashing across his body. Although he selected the longer sword, despite what appeared to be a cumbersome way of carrying them to Occidental eyes, such was his mastery of the technique known as *laijitsu* that the slightly curved blade slid free of its sheath with a blurring speed. With the possible exception of an ancient Roman legionary's ability to pull out his *gladius,* it was a feat unequaled by the swordsmen of the Western Hemisphere. Yelling a single word in his native tongue, with his left hand joining its mate on the hilt, he struck at the man to his right in a continuation of the motion that set the *katana* free.

Before Skull's revolver cleared leather, with the shining steel glinting in the light of the lantern suspended from the ceiling, the apparently less sophisticated weapon reached its target. Possessing a razor-sharp cutting edge, the power with which it was swung caused it to bite in and pass almost all the way through his right arm above the elbow. As the blade was withdrawn, a screech of pain burst from him. Spinning around with gouts of blood spurting through the terrible gash, he fell against the wall and his Colt still remained in the holster.

Effectively as Danny had dealt with the bald man, it seemed he had made a serious error in judgment. His advance had carried him between Kiowa Cotton and the two gunslingers. By doing so, he was preventing his companion from being able to aim at Dip with the Remington that was brought out of its holster—although not as swiftly as his sword had appeared—with commendable promptitude.

3. *When the* daisho *was carried with the sheaths attached to slings on a leather waist belt, as was preferred by Tommy Okasi, the longer sword was referred to as a* tachi.

However, the samurai proved more than adequate in coping with his apparent mistake. Still continuing to display the remarkable rapidity that had characterized all his movements since commencing the attack, rotating his hands so their knuckles were downward, he twisted his body and reversed the direction of the weapon. Already stained by the blood of his previous victim, the blade blurred around in an upward arc. Passing above Dip's shoulder an instant after his Colt emerged from its holster, the hammer being thumbed back and his forefinger entering the trigger guard, the blow was directed with the intention of preventing him from being able to complete the movement by opening fire.

Nor was the attempt in vain!

Not only did the force with which the gunslinger was struck knock him sideways, it produced an even more devastating effect. The blade pierced the skin of his neck and kept moving like a hot knife sinking into butter. More by luck than deliberate aim, although Danny was aware that such a thing was possible, it made contact with the cervical vertebrae at the point where two of the segments joined. Aided by the extremely sharp cutting edge, the blow was able to part them with greater ease than if striking a solid piece of bone.

Killed almost as instantly as would have been the case had a bullet passed through his brain, the second of Smith's captors was sent reeling involuntarily across the room. Nor had the attack been delivered a moment too soon. In fact, so narrow was the margin, the bullet which left his gun missed the samurai by no more than a couple of inches before flying harmlessly into the wall. Going down, his lifeless body gave a succession of spasmodic jerks much like those made by a chicken after being beheaded. In fact, so effective was a *katana* in competent hands, he had come close to duplicating such a fate.

Running footsteps sounded in the hall and the third of the kidnappers appeared in the doorway. He had come into the building from the backhouse through the side entrance just in time to see the two men with whom he was not acquainted entering the room. Although he was not aware of their purpose, he had been disinclined to take chances. Bringing out and cocking his Colt, he had hurried to investigate.

Despite the man holding his revolver ready for immediate use and the fact that he had heard enough while approaching to indicate it might be required, the sight that met his gaze caused him to pause instead of taking any kind of hostile action. The delay proved fatal for him. Even as his horrified gaze went from Skull to where Dip sprawled, head tilted at a far-from-natural angle, and blood flowing like a fountain from the severed veins and arteries of the neck, he was prevented from doing so. Swiveling around, the Indian-dark Texan brought his Remington into alignment at waist level. Squeezing off a shot, he sent a .44-caliber bullet between the newcomer's eyes. Prevented from using his weapon and rendered a corpse as effectively as Dip had been, the last of the trio pitched backward into the passage from which he had come.

"You all right in there, Kiowa?" yelled a young-sounding Texan voice from the barroom.

"Fit's frog's hair," the Indian-dark man answered, knowing the speaker to be one of the Blaze twins. The appearance they had conveyed on arrival at the hotel of being somewhat drunk had been a pose to avoid arousing suspicion. Once it was established which of the men present were guarding Smith, they had drawn their revolvers and covered the other occupants of the room while he and Danny came to effect the rescue. "How's about you!"

"We've told these gents who we are and what we're doing," reported the twin acting as spokesman. "They all conclude it's between us and those jaspers you followed."

"That's mighty obliging of them," Kiowa declared, having no doubt the passive response was in part due to the potency of the OD Connected ranch's reputation for the toughness of its crew. Holstering the Remington while speaking, he stepped forward and made a quick examination of Smith's motionless body. "One of you go fire off a couple of shots outside, just in case the boys from the Union Jack haven't heard us and'll need to be let know it's time to fetch up the buckboard. We'll need it. He's alive, but he surely isn't going to be able to ride a hoss."

* * *

"Where am I?" Waxahachie Smith asked, thrusting himself into a sitting position and looking at the man and woman who had come into a room that was a vast improvement—like the bed beneath him—upon the one where he remembered having been held a prisoner. Then, attracted by a throbbing ache that each was giving, he stared at his hands. The bandages that covered them were now clean, but once again he realized there was something wrong with their shape. However, he still was not sufficiently over the effects of the drugged liquid that had been inflicted upon him to know what it was. Lifting them so they could be seen by the couple, he went on, "What's happened to me?"

The sergeant had regained consciousness some time ago, at least two days unless he was mistaken, but his assailants had not arrived to sedate him. Despite their absence, when he was not sleeping, he had been in an unresponsive stupor. It had rendered him incapable of knowing more than that, although Juanita had come to feed him with the kind of nourishing stew he had received during his previous period of convalescence, he was not in the bedroom he had occupied at the Rancho Mariposa. Neither the fact that she was clad in somber black nor her massive features being marked by signs of grief had any significance for him. He was even too befuddled to wonder why Ransome Cordoba or her father had not come to visit him.

However, on waking up a few minutes earlier, Smith had felt considerably improved. With his brain starting to function again, he had decided to find the answers to the questions that came flooding into it. His call for the massive woman had been answered by the white couple he recognized as being Mrs. Freddie Fog and Sir John Besgrove. While asking the question, he noticed that they were wearing somber black attire.

"At the Union Jack," the Englishman replied.

"Then *how . . . what . . . ?*" Smith commenced, strug-

gling to decide which piece of information was of the greater
importance.

"Take it easy," Freddie advised gently, still retaining her
British upper class accent despite the number of years she had
spent in the United States. "How much do you remember?"

"Not much, clearly," the sergeant admitted, and his gaze
went to his bandaged hands. "Have I had an accident?"

"No," the Englishwoman replied, after glancing at her
cousin. She realized that she must be experiencing emotions
similar to those of her husband when, shortly after the War
Between the States, he had to tell the then leader of the clan,
General Jackson Baines, "Ole Devil," Hardin that the injury he
had sustained as a result of being thrown from a horse would
leave him a cripple for life.[4] While Smith was not that badly off,
his loss could prove a serious impediment should he wish—
which she suspected would be the case—to remain a peace officer. "It *wasn't* an accident!"

"Then what in God's name . . . ?" the sergeant began, a
realization of why his hands looked so different beginning to
make itself felt.

"Yes," Freddie said as Smith swung his gaze to her with an
expression of seeking confirmation that his eyes were not playing tricks. "You've lost *both* forefingers!"

"Lost?" Smith gasped, raising and staring at the misshapen
bandaged hands. "How . . . *Why* . . . ?"

"They found out who you really are somehow," the Englishwoman explained. Despite Skull having sustained a wound that
would leave him unable to use his right arm, due to having
received prompt attention from Danny Okasi—whose education as a samurai had covered such matters—he had come
through the attack alive. He had told them on being brought to

4. *The incident is described in:* Part Three, "The Paint," THE FASTEST
GUN IN TEXAS.
4b. *In addition to information to be found in his own series, details of Gen-
eral Jackson Baines "Ole Devil" Hardin's later career are given in the* Civil
War *and* Floating Outfit *series. His death is reported in:* DOC LEROY,
M.D.

the Union Jack ranch house by the rescue party the reason for the mutilation of Smith's hands, but he had not known that Talbot Ottoway was responsible for the betrayal. "It seems they didn't want to chance *killing* a Texas Ranger, so Dr. Grantz cut the fingers off to prevent you from carrying out the assignment that brought you to Bonham County."

"He cut them off?" the sergeant croaked, unable to turn his eyes from the white lumps at the ends of his arms.

"Perhaps we'd better get Juanita in to give you one of her sedatives?" Freddie suggested, seeing how distressed the injured man was becoming and having formed a healthy respect for the capability of the massive woman from the Rancho Mariposa where medical matters were concerned.

"No, ma'am!" Smith refused, weakly yet emphatically. "I want to know *all* about it."

"I'm afraid we don't know it *all,*" the Englishwoman replied, sitting on the chair that her cousin had brought for her. "But, as far as we've been able to find out, Teodoro Fuentes is behind the cattle stealing. It's Sheriff Tobin's belief that he had his uncle murdered so he could take over the Rancho Miraflores and to divert suspicion, had Grantz make it appear his story of having been wounded was genuine."

"Has the sheriff got them?"

"No. Javier Fuentes must have arrived and told them what he'd done before John could notify the sheriff and, realizing how everybody else in the county and throughout much of Texas would react when the news got out, they fled across the border to escape arrest."

"What was it he'd done?" Smith demanded, deducing that something very bad had happened.

"Ambushed the Cordobas as they were going home from church last Sunday," Freddie replied, and she was unable to keep a timbre of deep bitterness out of her voice. "Ransome, her father, and five of their hands, including their *segundo,* were killed."

"Killed!" the sergeant repeated, visualizing the girl as he re-

membered her in vibrant life. "Goddamn it to hell, why didn't Tobin go after the stinking son of a bitch?"

"Across the Rio Grande?" the Englishwoman said quietly. "No matter what young Fuentes had done, the Mexican authorities wouldn't have allowed him to be arrested and brought out of the country of his birth."

"Why ask if he could be?" Smith snarled. "Or bother about trying to *arrest* him, comes to that!"

"You *know* the answer without me needing to tell you," Freddie pointed out, but her manner was still gentle. "And don't think what you said wasn't considered. In fact, it was all John and I could do to make ourselves prevent an attempt to do it being made."

"You stopped it?" the sergeant hissed, his face darkening with anger.

"We did," the Englishwoman confirmed, showing neither remorse nor embarrassment over the indignant—close to hostile —response her declaration had elicited. "No matter how justified going after him would be, certain anti-American elements down there would choose to consider it was a lynch mob taking the life of a Mexican citizen; or more than one, if his brother decided to help him resist, as would have been sure to happen. And *that* could have a most detrimental effect upon the relationship between our two countries."

"So he's going to get away with it?" Smith suggested bitterly, despite knowing every word he had heard was true.

"Not necessarily," Freddie answered. "While a person cannot be extradited from the country of his birth, the Mexican authorities might be persuaded to return him when they learn how serious a crime he committed. But such a decision can only be handled at a very high level and any attempt to take revenge outside the law would ruin all chance of it happening."

"Knowing the way things move at a 'very high level,' " the sergeant said, with the cynicism born of past experience, "it's likely to be a fair spell afore any decision's reached."

"That's true," the Englishwoman conceded. "But having things handled in such a fashion is preferable to doing it any other way." Wanting to change the subject, she went on, "Anyway, as there's *nothing* anybody can do about young Fuentes until things are resolved legally, you had better start thinking about your future."

"I've got a real *fine* future ahead of me!" Smith growled, gesturing with his hands.

"What do you mean?"

"What use is a peace officer without a trigger finger on either hand?"

"I don't follow you."

"How can I handle a gun?"

"I don't see why you shouldn't be able to," Freddie claimed. "A friend of my family back in England, old Lord Maidstone, lost an *arm* during the Crimean War;[5] but he had Purdey's fit him out with a gádget and a gun so he could keep on shooting. The last time I saw him, he was bringing down pheasants and partridges as well as he had before it happened. What's more, he was talking about having Hardy's make him a similar kind of aid so that he could start fly-fishing again.[6] Surely you're not going to tell me a *Texan* can't do something that a Limey can."

"That lord gent had him a special gun and rig made so's he could do it," Smith pointed out, but Besgrove could see he was *very* interested in what he had been told.

"He did," the Englishwoman admitted. "And so can you. I don't know what kind of 'gun and rig' would best suit your needs. But, if you'll come and be our guest at the OD Connected, I'm willing to bet we can get together the best men to help you find out."

5. *Lord Maidstone was the son and heir of Admiral of the Fleet Lord Hornblower, the majority of whose distinguished career in the Royal Navy is recorded in a series of biographies written by C. S. Forester. How his injury came about is described in:* Chapter Twelve, "Admiral Of The Fleet," THE LIFE AND TIMES OF HORATIO HORNBLOWER, *By C. Northcote Parkinson.*

6. *The device was produced for Lord Maidstone by Hardy Bros. of Alnwick —now known as The House of Hardy—who were already acknowledged as the manufacturers of top-quality fishing tackle. The company later put a version of it called a Third Arm on the market for the benefit of anglers with similar afflictions.*

14

HE'S A DRIVEN MAN

"Now this is what I call a real fine rig," Sergeant Waxahachie Smith claimed, strapping on the gun belt that he had just received.

"Why, sure," Kiowa Cotton agreed. "While he's not the man his pappy was, young Elvis handles leather 'most as well's old Joe used to."

"Day I hear one of you mossy-horned old-timers allow *anybody* is as good as his pappy," the sergeant asserted, having come to be on excellent terms with the Indian-dark member of the OD Connected ranch's floating outfit,[1] "that's the day I start to vote Republican."

---

1. *Although Kiowa Cotton had ridden under the command of Captain Dustine Edward Marsden "Dusty" Fog in Company C of the Texas Light Cavalry during the War Between the States, it was not until after the events recorded in* TRAIL BOSS *that he became a member of the OD Connecticut ranch's floating outfit.*

A month had gone by since Smith was rescued from his abductors!

Because of the lingering aftereffects of the drug he had had forced upon him, the sergeant had not been able to travel to Rio Hondo County for over a week. However, in one respect, he had not considered the time was wasted. On the third day of his stay at the Union Jack's ranch house, Mrs. Freddie Fog had brought a haggard-looking and clearly distressed Sheriff Daniel Tobin to see him.

It had soon become apparent what was causing the local peace officer to show perturbation!

Furthermore, clearly the beautiful Englishwoman had remained in the room to act as mediator!

Tobin had stated frankly that, in one respect, he had been responsible for the injuries inflicted upon Smith. Despite his having acquired a reputation for being a very competent peace officer, he was also a member of the United States' Secret Service. While he had hoped to remain as sheriff of Bonham County after his mission was concluded, being close to the retirement age for his agency, he was holding the office as an aid to carrying out an investigation. News had reached his superiors that a group of radicals as yet unidentified were plotting to cause strife between the United States and Mexico, with Flamingo as the center for their activities. Unfortunately, the conspirators had been informed of the true reason for his appointment. Hearing that the man responsible was a government clerk foisted upon the Secret Service, Freddie had remarked sardonically that what she termed "civil servants" in the United States appeared to be just as untrustworthy and liable to betray their country as some of those with whom she had had dealings prior to leaving Great Britain.[2]

2. *We asked the present-day members of the Besgrove-Woodstole family whether the dealings Freddie Woods had had with untrustworthy and disloyal civil servants were responsible for her leaving Great—as it was then—Britain. They admitted that she was considered by some people to have gone too far in bringing to an end the activities of three in fairly high positions of trust who were selling military and other information to Russia; then re-*

As a result of having had what a later generation would term "his cover blown," it had been decided by Tobin's superiors that he should remain in Flamingo to hold the attention of the plotters while another agent was sent to continue the work unsuspected. However, they had been given reason to assume that whoever was selected would also be betrayed by other as yet undiscovered traitors amongst the clerks. Therefore, they had arranged—through the office of the state's attorney general —to have the Texas Rangers supply the assistance they required. Regrettably, as it had turned out, they had refrained from explaining the true facts and Tobin was instructed to go along with the pretense that the aid was summoned to help deal with the cow thieves. Therefore, when discussing the situation in the woodlands outside Flamingo, he had not mentioned his suspicions with regards to Teodoro Fuentes. All the available evidence indicated that the rancher was a victim rather than a perpetrator of the thefts, and to have suggested otherwise could have caused Smith to wonder whether there was some other reason for his having been summoned to help with the search for those responsible.

Although Smith had been furious when told of the arrangement, despite knowing at the back of his mind that it was not entirely to blame for the mutilation of his hands, Freddie had succeeded in calming him down by pointing out that Tobin was obeying orders and he would have done the same if it was required by Captain Frank Thornton. Being basically fair-minded and seeing the obvious regret that the sheriff was showing, the sergeant had conceded the validity of the statement. He had been further mollified by learning why Tobin had been absent from Flamingo over the fatal weekend. Having disliked being compelled to keep the sergeant in ignorance of the true state of affairs, he had been determined to rectify the omission.

---

garded as an enemy, particularly where the internal affairs of India were concerned. However, they refuse to supply further details except to say that the affair was not forgotten by the survivor and on at least one occasion he instigated an attempt to take revenge upon her; see DECISION FOR DUSTY FOG.

He had gone to warn his immediate superior that he either was allowed to tell Smith the truth officially, or he would tender his resignation and tell him. Knowing he would carry out the threat, his superior had given him permission to do as he wished.

However, the events that occurred had changed the situation drastically and, in addition to making his apologies for what had happened to Smith, Tobin had described the latest developments!

In addition to the horse and Winchester Model of 1873 carbine Javier Fuentes had left behind serving as evidence of his presence, the men who had been taken prisoner by Sir John Besgrove had established that he was the instigator and a participant in the ambush of the party from the Rancho Mariposa. However, aided by his brother, he had made good his escape. Fearing his own life could be put in jeopardy by his sibling's folly, Teodoro had also returned to Mexico. Dr. Otto Grantz and Don José Lorenzo Rabena—whose implication had been established—had accompanied the brothers and their hired hands, realizing no more pay would be forthcoming from the Rancho Miraflores, had scattered before any action could be taken against them. Sharing the sergeant's supposition that Cousin Cyrus had been an *agent provocateur* for the conspirators and having ascertained he had not returned to collect his belongings from the B Bar D, Tobin had assumed he had taken flight with the others until—having learned of the peace officers' interest in him—the man who had disposed of his body clarified the situation.[3] While the crossing of the Rio Grande had put the main conspirators beyond the jurisdiction of the Texas Rangers, the sheriff had assured Freddie and Smith that the Secret Service would have agents keeping track of them no matter where they went in Mexico, or elsewhere, so they could

3. *As Talbot Ottoway left Flamingo on the afternoon that Sergeant Waxahachie Smith was abducted, wanting to ensure he was not found to be involved should it go wrong, his participation in the conspiracy was not known to Sheriff Daniel Tobin.*

be located should the authorities below the border agree to return them for trial.

In addition to what he had learned from Tobin, Smith had discovered why Freddie had arrived so fortuitously. Seeking to reduce the tension between himself and Bradford Drexell, being aware of her ability as a diplomat—and not unmindful of her influential family connections—Besgrove had written to ask if she and her husband could act as mediators. As was proven by the spirit of cooperation that had arisen and was now even stronger, although Captain Dustine Edward Marsden "Dusty" Fog had not been available, she had justified her cousin's faith in her capability. Satisfied she was no longer needed, she had set out for home as soon as the sergeant was in a condition to travel.

On arriving in Rio Hondo County, Smith had found his hostess had not forgotten his problem. In fact, she had already started to help him solve it. While still at the Union Jack, experimenting with his Colt Civilian Model Peacemaker revolver—which had been retrieved by his rescuers when he was liberated—he had learned he could handle it, albeit awkwardly, in spite of his hands being encumbered by the bandages. Firing, with what had been the second finger operating the trigger and the other two wrapped around the butt, had proved very difficult. In fact, attaining accuracy of any kind was impossible. However, the means to hopefully counteract—or, at worst, reduce—the deficiencies were set into motion shortly after he had been settled in at the OD Connected ranch's house.

Over his first breakfast, the sergeant had been introduced to the local gunsmith, whose name was Abel Smith and who had been collected from Polveroso City by the younger of the Blaze twins. They were not related, but the sergeant had asked whether the other experienced a similar suggestion of dubious acceptance as he did when meeting people or signing a hotel's register. Having admitted this was the case, having been telegraphed from Flamingo by Freddie and told of the problem, Abel had produced what he claimed could help Waxahachie to solve it.

The first item was a pair of specially made black leather gloves, with padded forefingers that could have their curves adjusted. These were to serve the dual purpose of concealing the deformity of the sergeant's hands and, by entering the trigger guard, to lend a modicum of extra support when he was holding his revolver. Next, he was handed a Colt of the same model as his own, but modified in a way he had heard was given the name "slip gun." There was no trigger and, instead of the normal fitment, the hammer had its smoothed and shortened spur set on low. Internally, he discovered, the bolt spring had been removed and the bolt cam on the hammer reduced in length. He did not need to have the advantages offered by the alterations explained. Having no trigger to depress, drawing back and releasing the hammer with his thumb being all that was required to operate the mechanism, he could use the three remaining fingers to hold the butt as previously. However, as an aid to counteracting the way in which it would be held and fired, the rifling of the barrel had been removed and he was advised to load with rounds discharging three balls instead of a single bullet.

On remarking that he had heard multiball cartridges did not offer accuracy at anything other than a short distance, Waxahachie had been offered a solution. Reminding him that he had only relied upon the revolver at close quarters before losing his trigger fingers, Abel had displayed a rifle. At first glance, it could have been mistaken for a Winchester Model of 1873. There was an exposed hammer and the same kind of magazine tube running the full length beneath the octagonal twenty-six-inch barrel. However, it had only a small wooden foregrip and lacked the trigger guard-cum-loading lever that characterized the products of the Winchester Repeating Army Company since the predecessors of the "Gun That Won the West" were being sold as the Volcanic and Henry.[4] A closer examination

4. *Regardless of the popularity achieved by the Winchester Model of 1873, some authorities assert that there are better claimants for the title, "Gun That Won the West." Among those proposed are Colt's revolvers, Sharps's*

informed Waxahachie that it also lacked a trigger and the aperture caused by the removal was covered with a thin steel sheet.

"It's a Colt New Lightning," Abel had explained. "Forty-forty caliber. Takes a load of fifteen and, although I wouldn't advise it with *this* 'n, one in the chamber. Works by what they call a 'trombone slide' slide action. Instead of there being a lever, you pull back on that itty-bitty foregrip, which feeds the bullet into the chamber from the magazine and cocks the hammer. Only there's one *big* difference. Seeing as you're fixed as you are, I've taken out the trigger and rigged it so's shoving the slide forward fires the shot."

Appreciating how the modifications to both weapons could make them more suitable for his purposes, the sergeant had bought them and handed over his own Peacemaker for conversion into a slip gun. He had also purchased an adequate supply of ammunition to allow him to carry out the training that he realized would be necessary to not only accustom him to the vastly different modes of handling required by the new type of weapons, but to return to something like his former expertise. He was helped in covering the cost by a large sum of money that Besgrove, Drexell, and, being equally relieved to know the danger of a range war had departed, the businessmen of Flamingo, had donated to him.

Expending many bullets through the Peacemaker and the Lightning, Waxahachie had found mastery of the new technique called for by the differences between the latter's "trombone slide" and absence of a trigger and the Winchester Model of 1876 was helped by the lighter-caliber cartridges he was using. He had also satisfied himself that he was developing competence in using the former, despite being compelled to operate the mechanism by the thumb and without the assistance of the forefinger. Furthermore, the multiball loads compensated for the slight loss of accuracy caused by having the support of only three digits when shooting at close quarters and, when firing at

rifles and the Winchester Model of 1866, known as the "old yellowboy" because it had a brass frame.

longer range, his double-handed grip still produced an accept-
able number of hits despite their mutilated condition.

In spite of the anxiety which the sergeant had felt, once he
had resumed the exercises with the springs to strengthen them,
he had found his hands caused far less trouble than he had
envisaged. Such was the care with which Grantz had performed the amputations that the pads of skin he used to replace
the digits he removed had healed perfectly. However, the sergeant had discovered that they tended to start throbbing painfully whenever a storm was taking place and they continued to
do so for the rest of his life.

While the means to let Waxahachie fire weapons despite his
disability had presented no difficulty, due to the skill of his
namesake, carrying the Colt so it could be drawn and handled
with the requisite speed had also received attention. Coming in
response to a telegraph message sent by Freddie, Elvis Gaylin
had supplied the answer. Son of a man renowned for making
gun belts of high quality, he had learned much that now proved
of use. The first thing he had announced was that carrying a
slip gun in a conventional rig would not allow its special qualities to be fully utilized. Taking very careful measurements from
his customer, he had returned to El Paso so he could set about
his task. Having completed and delivered the gun belt, he was
called into the house by the Englishwoman before he could see
it strapped on. However, knowing cowhands, he would not
have taken offense if he had overheard the conversation that
took place between the sergeant and Kiowa.

Regardless of the comment he had made on studying the gun
belt, Smith became aware of how greatly it differed from his
previous rig the moment he buckled it into position. The fit was
perfect, being sufficiently snug to avoid it slipping and would
become even more immovable when he followed the advice he
had received from Gaylin when being measured, and slid the
belt through the enlarged loops he had had stitched around the
waistband of his trousers. Nevertheless, it did not feel right. For
one thing, it was higher than the one to which he was accustomed. Furthermore, while the holster was still on the right

side, it was now of the formfitting Missouri Skin-Tite type and rode with an extreme forward tilt just behind his off hip.[5] As if that was not enough, the position and design would mean his Colt was carried with its butt pointing forward instead of to the rear.

"This's going to take some getting used to, *amigo*," the sergeant assessed, accepting his now-modified Colt, which Kiowa had been holding, and slipping it into the holster.

"Young folks these days want everything *easy,*" the cowhand replied, despite agreeing with the summation. "You're not like us mossy-horned old-timers. . . ." The comment ended due to his attention being diverted by seeing one of the Blaze twins approaching at a gallop. "Young Charlie, or is it Henry, looks like he's in one hell of a hurry."

"It's *come,* Wax!" the redhead announced, bringing his lathered mount to a rump-sliding halt and springing from the saddle to wave the bulky letter he was carrying.

"Bueno!" Smith replied, knowing the youngster—even though equally uncertain whether he was Charles or Henry—well enough to have realized only a matter of considerable importance would have made him push his horse so hard and dismount in such a reckless fashion; particularly where he might be seen by his aunt, whose tongue could deliver a lashing to be avoided when necessary. "Let's take it in to Miz Freddie and find out what it tells."

"You're not going to like *this,* Wax," the beautiful English-woman warned, having donned a pair of gold-rimmed spectacles and read both pieces of paper in the envelope that her nephew had brought into her husband's study.

"No, ma'am?" the sergeant queried, and for once he did not so much as glance at the extensive collection of firearms—including the magnificent matched brace of gold-mounted Colt Cavalry Model Peacemakers won by Dusty Fog against *very*

5. *How a Missouri Skin-Tite type of holster was formfitted and made is described in:* Chapter Twelve, "Lieutenant Ballinger Acquires A New Skill," THE LAW OF THE GUN.

stiff competition at the First Cochise County Fair[6]—which were mounted on the walls.

"No!" Freddie confirmed, and waved the sheet of thick paper bearing an impressive-looking official heading in her right hand. "The federal government has decided that no action is to be taken against the Fuentes brothers."

"Goddamn it!" Smith said furiously. "Don't they know what that young son of a bi—"

"They do," the Englishwoman replied, noticing that her guest had not been so filled with rage that he completed a term regarded as an extremely bad obscenity on remembering he was in her presence. She made a gesture with the thinner sheet, which bore no printed heading. "According to my friend, the decision is a matter of political expediency. The Fuentes have powerful friends in Mexico and liber-rad softshells in Washington have helped them by bringing so much pressure to bear on Congress that it's been decided to let the matter drop."

"Now that's what some'd call real *obliging* of Congress," the sergeant said, his voice as quiet and yet latently menacing as the first whisper of a Texas blue norther storm.

"It's called 'political expediency,' as I said," Freddie explained, her face showing none of the annoyance aroused by the news she had received. However, she had had sufficient experience in such matters to be able to see both sides of the issue. Her voice was gentle as she tried to soften what was clearly a great disappointment. "Relations with Mexico are quite good at the moment, Wax. So Congress don't want to do anything which might rock the boat, as we say in Merrie Old."

"Now me," Smith answered, "I'm just a half-smart li'l ole boy from Texas and *somehow* I just can't see things their way."

"My friend warns me that Congress will institute legal proceedings of the most serious nature against anybody who goes after the Fuenteses," Freddie asserted, her manner grave.

"They'd have to catch the feller's did it first," the sergeant countered. Then his right hand dropped to feel at the butt of

6. *Told in:* TRIGGER FAST

the Colt in its unfamiliar position. "If you'll excuse me, Miz Freddie, ma'am, I've got to make a start at learning how to use this fancy new rig. Could be I'll be needing to *know* one of these days."

* * *

The crack of a revolver shot rang out from behind Waxahachie Smith!

Swinging around swiftly, the sergeant started his right hand to move!

In the wrong direction!

As had happened so many times over the past four days whenever he was given some signal to draw his gun, no matter how unexpectedly, Smith had responded with his usual speed. Unfortunately, unless he forced himself to consciously remember the difference in the way he was now carrying the weapon —which he had not on this occasion—his reflexes, honed to a fine edge by many years of habit, instinctively sent his hand down to where the Colt used to be hanging.

"Damn it to hell, Kiowa!" the sergeant said in exasperation as his fingers found only the material of the yellowish brown nankeen trousers he was wearing. "It's *always* the same unless I think what I'm doing, and that slows me down to where I might's well not bother making a draw."

"Uh huh!" the Indian-dark cowhand grunted.

"What I need is something to make me *remember* I've made the change *all* the time," Smith assessed. "But I'll be damned if I can figure out what it's to be."

"I've allus found the quickest way to get a hoss or a hound dawg to change his ways is to use a quirt on him every time he forgot," Kiowa commented. "After he's felt the sting of it a few times, he soon enough comes 'round to doing what's wanted."

"Hell, *yes*!" the sergeant said. "And that's what I want you to do with me."

"What?" the cowhand spat out, coming as close as he ever had to showing surprise.

"Keep close enough behind me on the left side," the sergeant explained, as calmly as if he were doing no more than pass a few seconds in idle chatter. "And every time I start reaching down instead of doing a cavalry-twist draw, lay a quirt across my shoulders so I'll *feel* it."

So began a period that Waxahachie Smith would remember for the rest of his life!

Nor would the means adopted ever be forgotten by anybody else who saw it!

No matter where the sergeant might be, as long as he was wearing his new rig, he never knew when somebody would either shout or give another signal for him to make his draw. Nevertheless, the moment it happened, his right hand was supposed to turn palm out and, coiling the thumb over the low spur of the hammer, cause the single-action mechanism to be cocked of its own volition as the Colt was twisted from level and turned forward. However, should he revert to his old system of reaching downward, Kiowa instantly lashed him across the shoulders with a quirt and, at his insistence, the blows were not delivered lightly.

"Goddamn it, Kiowa!" the younger of the Blaze twins said on the fifth day of the mental conditioning, watching the ranch's cook use powdered witch hazel leaves to staunch the blood flowing out of the welts that resulted from slashes with the quirt. "Why doesn't Wax either quit or leave off until his hurts've healed up?"

"He's a driven man, Charlie boy," the grim-visaged cowhand replied. "And he knows that, happen he's going to be able to do what he's driven to do, he's got to change his ways until he acts right without needing to think what he's doing first."

Drastic though the treatment was, producing scars that Smith would carry to his grave, it eventually proved effective and in less time than the same result could have been achieved by any other means. With each succeeding day, the number of times he needed the painful reminder grew less. Stimulated by suffering, his reflexes gradually and, at last, permanently became attuned to the new responses required from them.

"Well," Kiowa said, after the sixth day of continuous practice without needing the punishment for instinctively making a wrong move, "I'd say you're as ready as you'll ever be."

"I was figuring along those lines myself," Smith admitted.

"You know what you can expect from Congress if you succeed?" Freddie queried, having come to join the men on seeing them approaching the house.

"Yes'm," the sergeant answered, thinking of a letter he had received from Captain Thornton warning him of the possible consequences should he take revenge upon the Fuentes brothers. "But I'm going after them regardless."

"Very well," the beautiful woman accepted. "Dusty will be back by the end of the week and we'll do *everything* we can to help you when you return."

15
LOOK AT HIS *BACK*!

Leaving the stall of the blaze-faced dun gelding, having finished
attending to its needs and those of the roan in the next enclo-
sure, Waxahachie Smith was convinced that nobody he had met
in Flamingo, or most other places for that matter, would recognize him!

Six weeks had elapsed since Smith left the OD Connected
ranch on his mission to avenge the cold-blooded murder of
three people to whom he owed a debt of gratitude!

During that period, the seeker after vengeance had brought
about sufficient changes to his appearance to feel certain his
true identity would not be discovered!

Knowing what he was doing was illegal and that certain
"liberal" factions in the United States would demand that retribution was carried out should he succeed, Smith had had no
intention of allowing his actions to be used by them to besmirch
the Texas Rangers as their kind always tried to do with *every*
law-enforcement agency. Therefore, prior to setting out, he had

sent a letter of resignation, which—knowing the circumstances, deducing what had provoked the decision and approving of the motives—Captain Frank Thornton had accepted. With the aid of Mrs. Freddie Fog and her husband, who had returned before Smith set out and confirmed her promise of support, news of what had been done was circulated to newspapers all through Texas. The reason they had given for the resignation was that injuries he had sustained, in an unspecified accident, prevented him from being able to continue his duties because he was now unable to handle firearms. Although they had realized doing so could serve as a reminder of the nature of his disablement to the men he was seeking, they were hoping it would also induce a sense of false security where the possibility of him seeking revenge was concerned.

Aware of the danger of legal retribution, Smith had refused an offer of assistance from the Blaze twins and Kiowa Cotton even though they had stated willingness to go along regardless of the possible consequences. He had lessened their disappointment by pointing out there was more chance of four men being recognized than one, but refrained from adding that somebody might inadvertently say something that caused the same result. Having engaged in tasks requiring the adoption of a false identity on more than one occasion when younger, Dusty Fog had later stated concurrence with the latter reason.[1]

Needing to discover the whereabouts of his quarry, Smith had gone to Bonham County in the hope that he would find a most useful ally!

The hope had been fulfilled!

Pointing out that there was nothing to prove the Fuentes

1. *Occasions when Captain Dustine Edward Marsden "Dusty" Fog was required to pose as another person are recorded in* KILL DUSTY FOG!; BEGUINAGE; BEGUINAGE IS DEAD!; HELL IN THE PALO DURO; GO BACK TO HELL; THE SOUTH WILL RISE AGAIN; Part One, *"The Schoolteacher,"* THE HARD RIDERS; *its "expansion,"* MASTER OF TRIGGERNOMETRY; Part One, *"The Phantom of Gallup Creek,"* THE FLOATING OUTFIT *and* Part Two, *"A Wife For Dusty Fog,"* THE SMALL TEXAN.

brothers had been compelled to take flight by some other motive than a desire to avoid the consequences of Javier's actions, Daniel Tobin had persuaded his superiors to let him remain at Flamingo in the capacity of county sheriff and continue to look for the men he had been sent to locate. Still believing he was at least partly responsible for the mutilation of Smith's hands and also desirous of seeing justice done—even though it would not be of the strictly legal kind invoked by a judge and jury—he had shown no hesitation before proving he was willing to keep his promise to give every assistance he and his organization could supply.

Going directly to the Union Jack ranch's house, so as to try to keep his return to Bonham County a secret, Smith had word of his arrival sent to Tobin by one of Sir John Besgrove's most trusted men!

According to Tobin, when he had arrived to discuss the situation, he was justified in what he had told his superiors. He had carried out a very thorough examination of the Spanish colonial–style mansion that served as headquarters for the Rancho Miraflores, finding nothing to help him prove the suspicions he harbored about its departed owners. Deputized by him, Bradford Drexell and a force of cowhands from the B Bar D, Union Jack, and Rancho Mariposa had carried out an equally exacting search of the property. All this had established was either the Fuentes brothers were not involved with the cow thieves, or the stolen cattle had already been removed in some mysterious fashion from their range. However, instead of stating his belief that Teodoro was a leader rather than a mere participant in whatever was to have taken place in Bonham County, he had asked for the pair and those associates who fled with them to be located and kept under observation in the hope they would expose whoever they had been working for. As the man to whom the suggestion was made had had a friendship of long standing with the Cordoba family, therefore sharing the wish to see them avenged, it was accepted and acted upon.

One point that was puzzling, yet a source of relief, had been that the men engaged upon the roundup were not finding cattle that had been rebranded on the Rancho Mariposa, Union Jack, and B Bar D. This was considered to be proof of innocence on the part of the respective owners. However, while convinced that the Fuentes brothers were behind the thefts, Smith, Tobin, Besgrove, and Drexell had been unable to decide what had happened to the stolen animals.[2]

Satisfied that the situation was well in hand though he was, Smith nevertheless had found waiting for the information he required to be an irksome process!

Not that the former sergeant had been idle. As the majority of the crew were away helping Drexell on the roundup, which it had been decided to carry out on the day of the murders, he helped with the chores around the property. He also continued his exercises and training to improve the dexterity with which he handled his weapons. Effective though the specially made gloves had proved to be, despite realizing he would always need to wear some form of covering to conceal the condition of his hands, he gave attention to using the Colt Civilian Model Peacemaker revolver without relying upon the additional support offered by the padded and curved leather forefinger.

While Smith had appreciated the futility of attempting any such disguise as dyeing his hair—knowing the roots would require constant attention as time went by and this might not be possible to maintain, he had refrained from shaving and soon had a neatly trimmed beard of sufficient size to make a vast difference to his features. He had, nevertheless, retained the style of clothing he wore—including a jacket with its right side stitched up—but all the garments were different from those he had worn when he was last in the vicinity. Enough gunslingers dressed in the same general fashion for him to believe his attire would not arouse suspicions. On the other hand, appreciating how the big claybank gelding might be remembered by somebody who had been in Flamingo—also that he might have the

2. *Ranchers were continually making changes to their remudas in the Old West and not infrequently failed to alter the brands on the horses that came into their possession.*

need for greater speed over a distance than a single animal could maintain—he had borrowed two of Besgrove's horses that had been trained to work together as a relay, but did not carry the brand of the Union Jack or the other ranches in Bonham County.[3]

At last, the sheriff had received the information that was required from the members of the United States Secret Service assigned to keep the Fuentes brothers under observation. They had not halted their flight until reaching Mexico City, where they had frequently been seen in the company of various middle-class "liberals" known to share the close-to-paranoid hatred their kind throughout the world were already directing toward the United States. However, they had recently traveled to a hacienda near Ascension in the northern part of the state of Chihuahua. They were now engaged in gathering a large herd of cattle and assembling gunslingers of both races.

Smith had considered their activities were simplifying his task to some extent. While he would have gone to Mexico City if necessary, or anywhere else regardless of how far it might be from the Rio Grande, he appreciated how his escape after the successful conclusion of his quest would be made somewhat easier due to the shorter distance he had to travel to reach Texas. What was more, by posing as a hired gun in search of employment, he might be offered an opportunity to reach the brothers, which would have been more difficult to arrange elsewhere.

Finding the whereabouts of his quarry had posed no problem for Smith. The small town was situated where the Rio de Santa Maria flowed into the southern end of Lake Guzmán.

After having seen to the welfare of the two horses at a livery stable, wanting to learn as much as possible about the situation

3. *Waxahachie Smith learned Sir John Besgrove and Bradford Drexell were sincere in the reasons they had given when trying to hire him. In the case of the former, although he did have an arrangement to purchase cattle in Mexico, he had intended to delay sending to complete it until seeing what developed in Bonham County.*

before seeking them out, Smith was meaning to go to the place where the hostler who helped him with the work—proving as talkative as his contemporaries tended to be north of the Rio Grande—had claimed the *pistoleros* from the Fuentes hacienda spent much time.

About to don the jacket he had removed before starting work on the horses, Smith was distracted from doing so by hearing footsteps and a voice raised in protest outside the open main entrance to the stable. Looking around, he felt a surge of grim satisfaction rise mingled with anger.

Javier Fuentes appeared in the doorway!

However, the young Mexican was not entering of his own accord!

Following closely on the young man's heels, in fact propelling him ahead with massive hands grasping his shoulders, was a Mexican so large as to dwarf him!

There was a noticeable change for the worse in Javier's appearance. Twitching in the stress of something greater than fury, not only were his features more haggard and ravaged than Smith remembered, they had a grayish and unhealthy color. Bareheaded, the rest of his dandified attire was grubby and unkempt. His body quivered as if suffering from ague and his hands were shaking as they flailed the air ineffectually in an attempt to halt.

Also without a hat, the other man had a completely bald head and his attire was that of a vaquero, but he was not armed in any way that could be seen. He had a face with brutish lines and from a mouth of snaggled, discolored teeth came only grunting sounds. However, these were not caused by physical exertion as he seemed to be handling his captive without the slightest difficulty. Studying him, although their paths had never crossed, Smith had heard enough when discussing the Fuentes brothers to conclude he must be their mute bodyguard known as the Dumb Ox.

"Goddamn you for the stupid bastard you are!" Javier was screeching as he was pushed into the stable and toward where his black thoroughbred was standing in a stall. "Get your hands off me!"

Although Smith's first inclination was to force a fight and kill the young man there and then, he immediately saw the objections to such a course. These were not restricted to the need he would have to dispose of the massive Mexican first. The noise would bring men to investigate and, regardless of how good an excuse he gave for shooting Javier, it was unlikely to be accepted by them or Teodoro. Nor, with both horses standing unsaddled in their stalls, could he use them to take flight before anybody arrived.

However, hearing the demand, Smith saw what he believed might be a way to achieve his purpose. The hostler had already gone into a room at the rear of the building, leaving the door open, so would serve as a witness to substantiate his story should he succeed in what he decided to do. It was not a scheme that he would have selected if he had had time to concoct several, but was the best he could arrive at on the spur of the moment.

"Don't you try to *rob* that young feller!" the Texas bellowed in English, having discovered the hostler could understand it and knowing the same applied to Javier.

Making the demand, Smith darted forward to catch the Dumb Ox by the right arm. Even as he ascertained the enormous bulk of the bicep he was grasping, the Mexican gave a surging heave that propelled him away in an uncontrollable spin. Brought to halt by the wall, he felt a sharp pain in his back and sensed rather than saw the Colt slide from its Missouri Skin-Tite holster. Rebounding from the planks, the building being constructed of wood instead of the more usual adobe of the district, he heard a tearing sound caused by a partially withdrawn nail against which he had run, ripping open the back of his shirt. However, he gave no thought to the damage sustained by the garment. He realized there were other, vastly more serious, matters demanding his full attention. The most serious, to his way of thinking, was the loss of the revolver and he was not granted an opportunity to try to retrieve it.

Having thrust Javier aside somewhat less violently, the Dumb Ox was rushing toward the Texan. For all his bulk, he was remarkably fast. Too swift, in fact, for Smith to avoid what it was he had in mind. Coming close before his intended victim had recovered from the less-than-gentle collision, he reached out with arms like flexible tree trunks. They encircled Smith's torso, fortunately without also trapping his hands, to tighten remorselessly. It was a hold the Dumb Ox had frequently applied and, unless released before a crucial point, had crushed ribs and, on occasion, broken the recipient's back.

Realizing the deadly peril he was in, Smith reacted with speed. Gratified that his arms were still free, he brought up his hands. Cupping them beneath his captor's jaw, he began to shove with all his might. For a few seconds, benefiting from the regime of exercise that it had long been his habit to carry out, he actually stopped the terrible pressure on his back. Like a steel bar, bending so far and then no further, he quivered motionless in the crushing grip without allowing it to be inflicted more severely. However, he knew the respite could only last for a few seconds at most.

Skilled as Smith otherwise was at defending himself without weapons, at that moment he was grateful for some added knowledge he had acquired while at the OD Connected ranch. Having watched Danny Okasi instructing the Blaze twins in some effective bare-handed fighting techniques he had not previously come across, he had obtained permission to join the lessons. One trick he had acquired was intended to cope with just such a position as he now found himself in.

Removing his hands and feeling the constriction begin to be inflicted without impediment, Smith clenched them into fists and thrust their extended thumbs against the very sensitive area just below the base of the ears and behind the angle of the jawbone. When he had been subjected to such an attack by the little samurai, albeit with far less force than he was now applying, he had found the pain sufficient to make him release the bear-hug hold he had been employing. Feeling as if his ribs were on the point of caving in, he hoped there would be the same response from the Dumb Ox.

For what seemed to Smith to be far longer than was the case, nothing happened!

Then, just as blackness threatened to engulf the Texan and his strength was almost gone, the terrible constriction ended!

Making awesome sounds indicative of rage, the Mexican opened his arms and gave a thrust with his belly. Doing so sent Smith staggering, and he was saved from falling by reaching the open door of an empty stall. Catching hold of it, he hung there gasping breathlessly albeit in relief. Instead of following immediately, the Dumb Ox clasped at his ears. Then, again letting out an inarticulate bellow, he charged forward.

"*Kill* the bastard, gringo!" Javier shrieked.

The young man's never-even temper was already aroused by the condition to which he had been reduced through employing morphine as a substitute for cocaine. Its effect was causing a bitter resentment of the treatment, although this was on the orders of his elder brother, to which he was being subjected at the hands of the enormous Mexican.

Brief though the respite had been, Smith's head had cleared sufficiently for him to be able to assess and take steps to avoid the danger. Although he heard the exhortation and saw how it might be turned to his advantage later, provided he survived the encounter with the Dumb Ox, he had no time to acknowledge it. Instead, shoving himself from the gate, he swerved and snapped a kick with his right foot at the rapidly approaching giant. Reaching its intended target with the skill instilled by the savate fighter who had taught him such tactics, he found the impact from the ball of his foot failed to produce anything like the result he anticipated.

Despite letting out a grunt, the Dumb Ox gave no other sign of having received punishment that would have caused a less muscularly endowed man to be winded and driven into a retreat, if not close to incapacitated. Instead, he made a grab and, catching his assailant's ankle before it could be withdrawn, gave a twisting heave. Feeling himself once more being thrown and unable to retain his equilibrium, the Texan had cause to be grateful for the ability he had acquired as a horseman. Instead of trying to stop his headlong rush, he relaxed and went to the floor in a rolling plunge. Although it carried him almost to the wall, he halted, in control of his movements. Glancing around as he came into a kneeling posture, he saw his assailant lumbering after him. His revolver lay too far away for him to hope to reach it in time, but he noticed something else closer at hand, which he considered might serve his purpose just as well.

Reaching out swiftly with both hands, Smith gathered up the object that had come to his attention. It was the kind of horizontal crossbar from a wagon known as a singletree,[4] to which the ends of the harness's traces were attached. Made from a sturdy piece of wood, with the ends tipped by metal, it proved to be a most efficient extemporized weapon. Thrusting himself upward, with a twisting sidestep that once again carried him clear of the massive fingers reaching to take hold of him, he pivoted and rammed one end of the device with all the strength he could muster into the Mexican's lower body.

Despite the way in which he had withstood the effects of the kick, on this occasion the Dumb Ox was unable to do so. All the air gushed from his body in a strangled roar. Starting to fold at the waist, he stumbled away from his attacker. However, regardless of his obvious distress, Smith did not dare hesitate over what to do next. Nor, having heard of the way in which the huge Mexican had dealt with one man who aroused the wrath of Teodoro Fuentes in Flamingo—only the production of witnesses to imply self-defense was responsible for the fatal injuries inflicted when Tobin had brought him to trial, saving him from dire consequences—did the Texan have any compunctions over the response which was launched. Bringing up and around the singletree, he crashed it against the back of the lowered bare skull with considerable force. Bone splintered and the Dumb Ox collapsed as if he had suddenly been filleted.

4. *The singletree was also occasionally known as a swingletree or a whiffletree.*

Even as he was falling, his assailant heard several sets of running feet approaching the stable.

"What the hell's happened?" Teodoro Fuentes demanded in Spanish, dashing through the front entrance followed by several hard-faced and well-armed Anglos and Mexicans.

Amazed by what he had seen and more than a little worried over how his part in the affair would be received by his sibling, although the question was directed at him, Javier did not reply!

"I thought that jasper was going to rob your brother," Smith claimed, employing his native tongue and, tossing aside the singletree, going to retrieve his Colt. Although the men accompanying Teodoro had formed a rough half circle, they made no attempt to stop him. "So, knowing who he was, I cut in."

"You know my brother?" Teodoro inquired, having glared down at the motionless body without showing concern or any other emotion.

"Not enough to go over and say, 'Howdy you-all, Mr. Fuentes' and have him come back with, 'Howdy you-all, Mr. McCabe,'" the Texan admitted, truthfully as far as it went. "But I saw him when I come into Flamingo to see what was doing thereabouts. Checking the revolver was not affected by its fall and, when satisfied, returning it to its holster, he continued, "Which's why I billed in. I usually tend to my own never-mind, but I'm smart enough to know it's good to stand in well with the *boss* of any outfit and reckoned that's what I'd do happen I saved your brother."

"You *saved* him, that's for sure," an especially villainous-looking Mexican stated in bad English, having crossed to examine the figure on the floor. He was somewhat better dressed than all of his compatriots with the exception of the brothers. Turning his gaze to Teodoro, on whose heels he had followed ahead of the rest, he reverted to Spanish. "The Dumb Ox's dead, *patron!*"

"Do that *'muerto'* mean the jasper's cashed in his chips, Mr. Fuentes?" Smith inquired, wanting to give the impression his knowledge of Spanish was less extensive than was the case.

"It *does!*" Teodoro confirmed.

"That *figures*," the Texan admitted. "Feller with his heft, I didn't aim to take chances with him. He come close to making wolf bait of me afore I got loose and laid into him with that singletree."

"Damn it!" Teodoro snapped. "He was *my* man!"

"I'm right sorry about that," Smith asserted, looking as if he was speaking the truth. "Only, way they come in here and your brother yelled to be turned loose, I reckoned he'd got robbery or *worse* in mind and went to make him stop."

"You thought somebody would dare to *rob* my brother?" Teodoro snorted.

"Most folks'd likely have a heap more sense," Smith replied. "But that big jasper looked a whole lot too mean and stupid to give thought to who-all the feller he was fixing to rob might be kin to. Anyways, your brother didn't do *nothing* to try to make him stop when he jumped me. Fact being, he yelled for me to kill the son of a bitch. So how was I to know how-all things stood?"

"I don't remember seeing you around Flamingo," growled the evil visaged Mexican—who might have had a sign reading Hired *Pistolero* stamped on him, his trade was so obvious— before Teodoro could answer.

"I can't bring to mind seeing *you* there, neither," Smith countered. "Fact being, I rode in on Sunday and, afore I could get to meet Mr. Fuentes, I heard tell he'd lit a shuck over the Rio Grande."

"Well, I'll be damned!" said a white man standing slightly behind the Texan. He had features as close to villainous in cast as those of the Mexican *pistolero,* and they were not improved by a black patch over his right eye. "Will you just take a look at his *back*!"

"How did *this* happen?" Teodoro inquired, as Smith moved until allowing the tear made across his shirt and his exposed back to be brought into view.

"Me and the marshal in Trubshawe couldn't see eye to eye about something," the Texan lied, realizing how he might turn to his advantage the still-visible marks left by the inducement he had had inflicted while accustoming himself to the changed position of his holstered Colt. Aware it was common knowledge that the peace officer in question frequently engaged in such methods,[5] he felt sure his explanation would be considered credible. "The son of a bitch had me whipped while I was in the pokey and I couldn't get at him after I was loose to thank him." Adopting an attitude that implied he regarded the matter closed, he gestured at the body of the Dumb Ox and went on in a tone of annoyance, "After *this,* I reckon I won't be getting hired."

5. *There was no town in Texas called Trubshawe. However, as we have no intention of supplying "liberal" elements with information that—even at this late date—they might be able to use in their campaign to smear the law-enforcement agencies of the free world, we refuse to give the real location.*

16

REMEMBER RANSOME
AND DON JOSE CORDOBA?

"Dan Tobin passed word to me that you'd be coming," explained the man who had brought the condition of Waxahachie Smith's back to the attention of Teodoro Fuentes, as they stood together in the darkness by the corral of the hacienda about five miles from Ascension. "Got the description real good, including the way you tote that Peacemaker. But when I saw those quirt marks, I thought for a moment you wasn't him. Fact being, I still wasn't all the way *sure* until you just now told me that 'eleven, twenty-three, sixty-one' number's Dan allows you keep using."

Despite the comment he had made after explaining how he had supposedly acquired the scars, following some more discussion, the Texan had been hired by the older of the Fuentes brothers!

Called upon for verification, Javier Fuentes had sullenly confirmed that his behavior had been as Smith claimed. On the Texan demanding to know why he had not mentioned Teodoro was in town, the hostler had said he forgot. Then, to lessen the wrath he assumed the omission had aroused, he admitted having heard enough to make him believe Smith considered the Dumb Ox was contemplating a robbery.

Apparently satisfied as to the motives of the Texan, the older brother had asked his name and why he had not come sooner in search of employment. He replied he was Matt McCabe and that, having learned of the flight of everybody from the Rancho Miraflores, he had concluded whatever had been planned was canceled and had gone to look for work elsewhere. Failing to find any, a chance visit to the gathering place for outlaws in the village on the Bonham County line had informed him of the latest need for hired guns and he had decided to come to offer his services. Knowing how quickly news spread, particularly to such places, Teodoro had found nothing unlikely in what he was told. Having admitted that he knew how to handle cattle, although disinclined to do so, Smith had been informed this would be required if he wanted to be employed. Claiming he was too close to the blanket to refuse, but refraining from asking why he would be expected to work as a cowhand—knowing it would be unwise to show too much curiosity—he had been accepted.

Accompanying the Fuentes brothers to the hacienda they were using, the Texan had been accommodated with their men in the bunkhouse. Even though some of them had been in Flamingo, his identity was not challenged. He had concluded this was a tribute to the success of the changes he had made to his appearance. Nor had he discounted the part played by the way in which he was now wearing his Colt Civilian Model Peacemaker revolver. Men experienced in such matters only rarely changed the style of rig in which they carried their weapons.[1] Therefore, it anybody remembered him as he had looked and

1. *An occasion when circumstances required that Captain Dustine Edward Marsden "Dusty" Fog changed the manner in which he carried a revolver is recorded in:* Part One, "Small Man From Polveroso City, Texas," OLE DEVIL'S HANDS AND FEET.

been armed, they would have noticed the gun belt was of a pattern requiring a different kind of draw to that he had used in the town and reach the requisite conclusions.

By careful questioning, Smith had ascertained that the gunslingers were to act as handlers for the vast herd of cattle that was being held near Lake Guzman prior to being split into smaller bunches and delivered to various places in Texas. Too wise to display what might be regarded as excessive curiosity and knowing he would learn more later, he had allowed the matter to drop.

Having emerged from the backhouse after answering the call of nature, Smith had been accosted by the man with the eye patch. After a few seconds of desultory conversation, he had been asked about the newness of his gun belt and replied it was recently purchased to replace its predecessor, which had sustained some unspecified damage. Wanting to change the subject, watching for any suggestion that it might have some meaning to the man, he had told how Sheriff Daniel Tobin tried to order him from Flamingo and was thwarted by him quoting the mythical "Article Eleven, Twenty-three, Sixty-one, legal ruling" used during his first meeting with Sir John Besgrove.

The result was unexpected!

Looking around with great care to ensure they were not being overheard, the man had made a surprising declaration. In spite of his unprepossessing appearance, he was not the vicious hired gunslinger he appeared. Instead, he had introduced himself as Donald Garfew Beech and he was an agent for the United States Secret Service.[2]

"You mean there *isn't* any such legal ruling?" Smith drawled. "Well, I'll be switched if I haven't been leading good folks astray for quite a spell now, thinking there was. Anyways, what's this sending herds to Texas all about, *amigo*?"

2. *Not only did Orville Garfew "Fluency" Beech follow the lead of his grandfather, Donald, by enrolling in the United States Secret Service and wearing an equally unnecessary black eye patch, he rose to be its head during the 1930s. See the* Doc *Savage biography,* RED SNOW, *by Kenneth Robeson.*

"It's something a whole heap worse than what they was trying to do over to Bonham County," Beech replied. "I don't know whether you've figured it out, but it *wasn't* rustlers stealing cattle who were killing off the fellers on the range."

"Back home to Texas we call 'em 'cow thieves,' " Smith remarked, the other having an accent indicative of origins in Illinois. "I knew there was something *mighty* strange had happened, way none of the cattle they wide-looped showed up again and was coming 'round to figuring along those selfsame lines."

"We hadn't got the main idea when we sent word to the boss that something was being planned by the liber-rad softshells down to Mexico City," Beech admitted. "Fuentes's men only went out on rainy nights when their tracks would be washed away, excepting for things like gunning down anybody they came across and enough other signs to make it look like they'd stolen some cattle. Seems like they reckoned doing it would stir up a shooting fuss between the ranchers. Then that'd bring in the other white folks and Chicanos in Bonham County and it'd spread, helped by them, all the way along the border to California."

"Why pick on Bonham County?" the Texan inquired, although he had an idea what the answer would be. "What I was told, more times than not, the white folks and Chicanos thereabouts get along good and friendly."

"That's one reason it was picked. Those sons of bitches in the house are like their scummy breed all over. Stirring up folks of different kinds against one another's a favorite way of theirs to try to overthrow the elected government. A place where white folks and Chicanos get on's not in keeping with what they want. Only this time, that spread the Fuentes's kin had in Bonham County gave them somewhere they could live and work from without over many questions being asked about why they were there."

"I'd say that hophead son of a bitch, Javier, played hell with their notions by what he did."

"You'd say the living *truth*. What I've heard, he's lucky Teodoro didn't kill him. As it was, big brother was so potboiling riled, he personally gave it to one of the yahoos up to the Green River with a knife—which I wouldn't have thought he'd have the guts—and turned loose that overgrown son of a bitch you made wolf bait to break another's back when they showed at the ranch house, 'cause they'd sided the kid in the bushwhacking."

"I'm *pleased* he didn't kill the hopheaded son of a bitch," Smith said quietly, yet there was a chill of deadly menace in his tone. As Sheriff Daniel Tobin had not mentioned finding the bodies of the murdered men, he assumed they were taken away by the fleeing party for some reason and disposed of, possibly by being sunk in the Rio Grande. " 'Cause I've got notions along those lines myself."

"So Dan told me," Beech admitted. "And, even if it wasn't for what they're working on now, I'd be willing to help you."

"I'm obliged, *amigo,*" Smith declared with genuine sincerity. Then, as something in the voice of the secret agent had warned the latest affairs of Teodoro Fuentes went beyond just being of considerable importance, he continued, "Just what is it they're working on now?"

"Have you heard of anthrax?"

"Some. Folks do say it's a mighty fierce kind of illness and real easy to be catching to boot."

"That's putting it *mildly.* Once it takes off, it spreads like a wind-blown prairie fire—And Fuente's crowd aim to see that it gets spread all through Texas."

"How?"

"Seems there was an outbreak down south a ways not too long back, but it was stopped afore it got out of hand. Only these liber-rads got hold some blood from cattle's had it and they're planning to use it on the herds they're sending into Texas."

"I thought you had to be near a critter that had it afore you can catch it," Smith remarked, showing no sign of the grave concern he felt as he visualized what would happen to his home state if the scheme succeeded.

"They reckon not," Beech replied. "They allow it can be given by using a hypodermic syringe to put the blood from one's had it into another that hasn't."[3]

"Is that Doc Grantz's notion?" the Texan inquired, glancing at his gloved hands and realizing he had not seen or even heard any mention of the man responsible for their mutilation since reaching Ascension.

"Not so far's I know," the secret agent answered. "Seems like he lit a shuck when he was told he'd be expected to do some of the injecting, but Teodoro's been letting on's how he ran 'cause he wasn't stopping Javier wanting to sniff down that white stuff copious."

"I'll find him when I'm through here!" Smith asserted, but the words seemed more to himself than his companion.

"And we'll do all we can to help you," Beech promised. "But we've got to stop these bastards *first*. If they get that damned disease going all through Texas, their cruddy liber-rad friends in the U.S. of A. are going to spread word that it was brought in deliberate by cattle from Mexico and figure there'll be such a public outcry that Congress'll have to take what's called 'puni-tive action' to quieten it down. Which'll give us a war, and those bastards hope to be able to get control both here and below the border while it's going on."

"I can't see those hired guns being willing to chance being around anything so dangerous as anthrax," the Texan pointed out.

"None of them know anything about i—" the secret agent commenced.

"Hold the talk down, *amigo*!" Smith hissed urgently, looking over his companion's shoulder. "That greaser who rubs up to Fuentes's coming."

"Mean-looking critter, isn't he?" Beech asked.

"I've seen *pleasanter*."

"Strange thing is, he's got five kids and they're all as cute as

3. *J.F.C. Charriere devised the hypodermic syringe in 1852 and its use was widespread by the period of this narrative.*

a speckled pup. 'Course, his wife's real pretty and I reckon it was a case of the fascination of the horrible that made her take to him."

"I get the feeling you *know* him."

"You *could* say that. His real name's Ruiz Cervantes and he's sure done a good job of apple-polishing to Fuentes. It was him who learned what was doing by listening through the wall with a drinking glass, while it was being talked over with the soft-shells's owns the hacienda and some more of their stinking breed."

"I always heard you spies was real *sneaky* jaspers," Smith claimed, but there was a suggestion of admiration in his voice.

"Aw shucks, we hoped's folks wouldn't *notice* that," Beech answered, then swung his gaze to the Mexican. "How's things, Paco?"

"Bueno, amigo," Cervantes replied, and, gesturing with the bundle he was carrying, he continued in accent-free English, "When I touch some of these off, it'll stir things up more than a little hereabouts, I'd guess."

*   *   *

"I'm responsible for my brother!" Teodoro Fuentes informed the owner of the hacienda in a cold fashion. Never one to take kindly to having his actions questioned, his manner was less polite than might have been expected of a guest and fellow conspirator in a scheme intended to lead to his kind being able to overthrow and replace the present government of Mexico. However, he felt no concern over having left his gun belt in his room. He was armed with a weapon he preferred to use should the need arise. "And I'll make good and sure that he *doesn't* cause any more problems!"

"It's a damned pity that he was allowed to cause the first one in Texas," replied the *haciendero,* a burly "man of the people" who took delight in letting it be obvious his origins were lower on the social scale than those of the brothers and the majority of their compatriots. "I still say you should have left him sniffing that damned white powder in Mexico Ci—"

The rift between the two leaders of the conspirators was not allowed to develop further!

There was the boom of an explosion some distance away, followed by the bellowing of startled cattle and drumming of their hooves as they began to take flight!

"What in God's name . . . ?" Javier Fuentes croaked, having been standing and glowering at their seated host, who had started the dispute by speaking *most* disparagingly about him having caused the death of the Dumb Ox.

"The herd's been stampeded!" the *haciendero* bellowed, bounding to his feet with a violence that sent his chair skidding across the dining room. Without explaining further, he raced into the entrance hall. With the brothers following on his heels, he threw open the front door. Going out, he saw men in various states of dress pouring from the bunkhouse. "Get your horses, *every* one of you. We've got to help the night herders. Move it, damn you. Unless they're stopped, you'll all be riding the hell away from here in the morning without being paid."

Like Smith, all the gunslingers had been hired because they possessed a working knowledge of handling cattle. While they would not have obeyed under normal conditions, having elected for a less arduous means of earning a living, they realized a failure to respond would see the end of their current lucrative employment. With that in mind, they sprinted to where—as they had been instructed by the *haciendero* in anticipation of such a need—each had a saddled horse tethered along the posts of the corral ready for immediate use.

"Are *you* coming?" the owner asked, his manner indicating he did not believe anything of use would result from an answer in the affirmative.

"Of course I am!" Teodoro replied, the question having been directed at him. Although he had no desire to run the risks of helping to try to halt the stampede, he was goaded into agreeing by the attitude of his fellow conspirator. "Tell somebody to have horses saddled for Javier and me."

"Trust *you* not to be *ready*!" the *haciendero* grunted, and set off to where his own mount was waiting.

"Go and fetch our hats!" the older brother commanded his sibling, more after the fashion of addressing a servant, without noticing their host had not given the instructions he requested before swinging into the saddle and setting out for the herd. "I'll make sure there's nothing lying around to show what we're up to."

While Javier was hurrying upstairs, looking annoyed but knowing him too well to argue when such a tone came into his voice, Teodoro went into the owner's office. He knew everything incriminating was locked in the massive safe, but wanted to be able to claim he considered the precaution justifiable when questioned by his host about the delay in his arrival at the stampede. Waiting until hearing the footsteps of his brother descending and the drumming of many hooves fading rapidly away, he strolled into the hall. As he was taking the sombrero he was offered, he saw one of the gunslingers coming through the front door.

"Have you saddled horses for us?" Teodoro demanded, wondering why Matt McCabe was carrying what appeared to be some kind of Winchester repeater by its foregrip in his right hand.

"No," Waxahachie Smith denied, his gaze running from Javier to the older brother. "Do you remember Ransome and Don Jose Cordoba?"

"What if I do?"

Dropping the sombrero while speaking, Teodoro put his hands behind his back in a casual-seeming fashion. Then, deciding that not wearing a gun belt might prove advantageous as it would convey the impression he was unarmed, he started to liberate the knife from its sheath up his left sleeve.

"How about *this*?" the Texan inquired.

Staring at the left hand raised by the bearded man, Teodoro first realized it and its mate were no longer covered by the gloves which had not been removed previously in his sight. Then a chilling appreciation struck home. He realized what it was that looked different.

The forefinger had been removed!

"You!" Teodoro gasped in his native tongue, having believed until the understanding struck home that he was confronted by an ordinary gunslinger whom the friends or relations of the Cordobas had hired to take revenge for their murder as there was no legal way by which this could be brought about.

"Me!" Smith confirmed, also speaking Spanish.

"Get him!" Teodoro close to shrieked and, hoping to divert at least some of the Texan's attention toward his sibling—despite being convinced his secret weapon would prove as unexpected and efficacious as it had in the past—he forced motion into his numb body.

Long addiction to first marijuana, then cocaine and its "harmless" substitute, morphine, had rendered Javier's never-overactive mentality even slower. Having been subjected to adverse criticism over the incident at the livery barn in Ascension, his pleasure at "McCabe's" intervention avenging his humiliation at the hands of the Dumb Ox had changed to hatred. Now, while he was uncertain of exactly what was arousing Teodoro's hostile response—being too dull witted to notice, much less appreciate the significance of the mutilated hand—he was more eager to oblige than was usual when receiving an order. Letting out a hiss of rage, he sent his hands toward the butts of his guns.

As the knife was brought around preparatory to being thrown, its owner discovered its presence was not unexpected and there were indications that it might fail to prove efficacious on this occasion!

On hearing of how Teodoro had killed one of the men who assisted Javier in the ill-advised ambush, Smith had remembered something he had been told in Flamingo. According to Sheriff Tobin, Moses "Cousin Cyrus" Claybone had died as the result of a knife wound in the throat received prior to the mutilations performed on the body. He had realized he could not recollect seeing Fuentes wearing such a weapon. Nevertheless, he had not discounted the possibility of one being carried in concealment and he suspected it was hoped he would be lulled into a sense of false security by the absence of a gun belt so it could be produced with the anticipated surprise effect.

Even as the older brother spoke, the Texan went into action. Tilting the Colt New Lightning rifle forward with his right hand, the left flashed over to meet it. Closing the three fingers and thumb around the small foregrip, grateful for having been granted sufficient time to gain proficiency with the new type of action, he thrust it back and forward to set the firing sequence into action. Aimed at waist level and by instinctive alignment, the weapon crashed in response to his movements.

With a sensation of shock, Teodoro realized his ploy had gone terribly wrong. Not only had his concealed knife failed to achieve the surprise he had envisaged, his attempt to cause Javier to be selected as the greater danger was also coming to nothing. Seeming to be drawn by some magnetic force, the octagonal barrel of the Winchester lifted until it was pointing directly at the center of his chest. Then, before the knife was far enough around to be released in the hope of preventing the shot, it was too late. Flame and white powder smoke erupted from the rifle's muzzle. Something smashed into his torso and he felt himself being pitched backward with his weapon leaving his fingers. He had hardly time to realize it would not go near its intended target before his body struck the floor. However, he remained alive just long enough to have the satisfaction of seeing he would not die alone.

Gobbling similar incoherent sounds to those he had made during the ambush outside Flamingo, except this time they were inspired by terror, Javier tried to bring out his fancy-handled Colts. He had never troubled to take the time required to handle them properly, so fumbled the attempt. Although he managed to get the right-side gun clear of leather while the attention of the Texan was being given to Teodoro, that did not save him. Swinging his way even before his sibling's body arrived on the floor, the rifle spoke again.

And again!

And again!

Operating the trombone slide action of the Lightning with

deft skill, Smith caused it to fire at a speed that even a Winchester in skilled hands could barely equal. Empty cases flew through the ejection slot, to be replaced by loaded cartridges from the tabular magazine. Because of the changes made to accommodate Smith's mutilated hands, there was no slight pause spent depressing the trigger far enough to liberate the sear. Instead, almost as soon as the replacement round arrived in the chamber, it was discharged.

Although the first bullet sent at Javier missed, due to the rifle being turned in a horizontal arc while they were being dispatched, the next two and three of the four following them in *very* rapid succession all found the intended target. Sent reeling against the wall, he was prevented from falling as the flat-nosed .44-caliber bullets—a precaution against an accidental jolt upon the priming cap of the preceding round in the magazine causing a premature explosion—continued to strike his body and tear apart the internal organs.

"There's some might say you've *got* him!"

Hearing the words brought Smith to a realization of what he was doing. Letting out a long sigh and watching the body of his second victim crumpling from the wall now bespattered by blood and shattered fragments of bone, he lowered the rifle with the slide in the forward position. His gaze went to where Donald Garfew Beech was coming into the hall carrying a bundle under his left arm and a can of kerosene in each hand.

"I reckon you might say I have," the Texan agreed. "What's it like out there?"

"The fellers riding to the herd won't have heard you," the agent replied, the removal of the black eye patch proving it was unnecessary as the eye was not in any way affected. "There's only the womenfolk and a couple of old peons left. I told 'em to keep clear of the main house here until I'd found out who was doing the shooting."

"Let's hope they do," Smith declared, then prepared to help with the plan devised by Beech and Ruiz "Paco" Cervantes. The latter had created the diversion he required to achieve his revenge, while also ensuring there would be at least a delay before any herds could be sent to Texas. Now, using more of the dynamite found by his companion, the white agent was going to blow open the safe containing the blood from the infected cattle. However, it was not intended to rely solely upon this to remove the menace. "Leave me spread the kerosene and make ready for the fire. You go fix up the explosion."

17

LOOK AT *THESE* HANDS!

Sitting at a table in the Red Dog Saloon, Dr. Otto Grantz was so engrossed in a game of poker that he was unaware of the baleful gaze to which he was being subjected from beyond the other players!

Almost two months had passed since Grantz had read in a newspaper of the fate that had befallen his former associates!

Following the flight from Bonham County, the doctor had found there was a deterioration in his relationship with the older of the brothers in particular. Despite insisting his medical services were required for the new conspiracy that was planned, Teodoro had clearly been growing increasingly disenchanted by his failure to cure the drug addiction of Javier. To make matters worse, the younger brother had started to blackmail him, demanding a regular free supply of cocaine in return for remaining silent with regards to how the ambush had been carried out at his instigation. Nor were his problems with them his only concern. On learning what would be expected of him in

the latest scheme, he had been all too aware whoever was injecting the blood from the cattle that had died of anthrax into
the animals intended to be sent to Texas would face the possibility of contracting the highly contagious disease.[1] Therefore,
he had decided the time had come for him to part company
with such a potentially dangerous alliance.

On learning how the brothers met their end, although
Grantz had realized he was likely to be another target for revenge by the man whose hands he had mutilated, he felt sure he
had covered his tracks sufficiently well since leaving Mexico to
avoid being located. He had come to the bustling mining town
of Wilson in Colorado by a circuitous route and established a
lucrative medical practice in an assumed name.

What the doctor did not realize was that he had made a
serious mistake!

Serving as medical attendant to Javier Fuentes and a willing
adjunct to schemes upon which Teodoro was engaged had been
lucrative for Grantz. Aware from the beginning that he might
need to escape the consequences of his actions, whether as a
participant in "liberal" political schemes or through selling
Javier cocaine while pretending to be seeking a cure with
"harmless" heroin, he had taken the precaution of ensuring he
would have sufficient money to make this possible. With the
future in mind, taking advantage of being sent to Flamingo—
where one of his earliest tasks had been to pretend Teodoro was
wounded in the first "raid by cow thieves"—he had placed the
considerable sum that had accrued in the bank. Needing the
money to start a new life, also realizing that he dare not return
to Bonham County to collect it, he had telegraphed for his
deposit to be transferred to a bank in Taos, New Mexico. On
receiving it, he had continued his travels.

However, being unaware of the influential support that the

---

1. *How deadly anthrax could be is demonstrated by a man in the United
States of America having died as a result of being infected while working
upon a piece of ivory from the tusk of an elephant that had died of the
disease in Africa.*

man he feared was receiving, the doctor had failed to envisage how serious an error he had committed and believed the possession of the money would ensure his continued safety!

The state of self-deception was about to end!

"Goddamn it!" Grantz growled, watching the winner of yet another pot raking away his money. While speaking, he scowled in a sullen manner at the other five losers—who formed a cross-section of the local population's occupations—in the hope of receiving sympathy, but gave no attention to the rest of the saloon's occupants. "I've *never* had such bad hands!"

"Happen you reckon *yours* are bad, look at *these* hands!"

Although he had established a reputation as being a bad loser, Grantz's position as a medical practitioner offered protection against more than occasional verbal recriminations from those with whom he was playing. However, on this occasion, the comment that was made did not come from any of his six opponents.

Never one to accept criticism or the expression of opinions different from his own, the doctor swung his gaze to the speaker. However, it halted on taking in the sight of the two hands—their skin white as if rarely being exposed to the elements—that were extended by a man who had arrived unnoticed by him to stand between a lean professional gambler and a bulky cavalry soldier at the opposite side of the table. For a moment, he was unable to decide what had caused the comment and the reason for the hands being displayed in such a fashion. Then he stared at the place where the forefingers should have been. It was obvious their removal had been performed with considerable skill.

Then realization struck home!

Grantz recognized the work as being his own!

Filled with a sense of grim foreboding, the doctor raised his eyes. They passed over Levi's pants and a gun belt with a staghorn-handled Colt Civilian Model Peacemaker revolver carried butt forward in a holster set higher than was generally the case, a dark blue shirt, an open brown jacket that had its right side stitched back, and a tightly rolled multicolored bandanna knotted about a throat having darker skin than the displayed hands. Reaching the grim tanned face above them, his gaze confirmed what he feared.

"You!" Grantz gasped.

"Me!" Waxahachie Smith confirmed, remembering the last time an identical exchange—albeit in Spanish—had taken place.

The explosion set off by Donald Garfew Beech had blown open the safe and shattered the bottles containing the tainted blood. To ensure the complete destruction of the potentially dangerous liquid, he and the Texan had started a fire that gutted the hacienda. While this was happening, Ruiz "Paco" Cervantes had removed the other major participant in the scheme by arranging for him to meet his death in what appeared to be an accident while trying to halt the stampeding cattle.

With the mission that had brought him to Mexico ended successfully, Smith had returned to Bonham County and found a letter from Mrs. Freddie Fog waiting for him at the Union Jack ranch. She had warned that, despite exerting all their influence, she and her husband were only able to obtain one concession in his behalf. He had considered it to be a mixed blessing. Although they had been told that criminal proceedings would be instituted against him if demanded by the Mexican government, these would only be enforced if he were found in Texas. She had suggested, to prevent this happening—with the attendant possibility of hostility being aroused by the facts that would emerge during the trial—he leave the state and did not return until he received word from her that the incident was forgotten and it would be safe for him to do so.

Accepting the advice, Smith had set out in search of the man who had removed his forefingers. Nor had this presented too many difficulties, given the assistance he could call upon and his own experience in such matters. After Sheriff Daniel Tobin had learned of the transferred bank account, he went to Taos and picked up the trail. Despite Grantz having adopted an assumed name when the money was in his possession, his appearance and less-than-amiable demeanor had ensured he was remembered everywhere he went.

Already having learned the doctor's nom de plume, Smith had located him within half an hour of reaching Wilson!

However, the Texan had decided to wait until the confrontation could be made in a public place!

Grantz's habit of playing poker regularly at the Red Dog Saloon had offered the opportunity!

"W-What do you want?" the doctor croaked, crouching on his chair with a demeanor very different from his normal bombastic posture.

"You *know* what I want," Smith replied. "Get on your feet and, happen you're not toting a gun, I'll be obliged if one of these gents will take his out, cock it, and put it on the table where you can reach it easily."

Silence, broken only by the scraping of wood against wood as the other players shoved back their chairs and came to their feet, fell over the room. Everybody within hearing distance realized what was implied by the words. Furthermore, although they might have if Grantz had been a more likable person, not even the men around the table offered to point out he was a member of the medical profession or intervene in any other way. In fact, the only response was from the winner of the last pot.

"You can have my gun, Doc!" the big and burly miner offered, dropping a hand to the Colt Artillery Model Peacemaker in his low-hanging holster.

"I . . . I . . . I . . . !" Grantz spluttered, coming to his feet and cringing with both hands rubbing jerkily at his torso.

However, regardless of an attitude of fear that was only partly simulated, the doctor had no intention of trying to avoid the confrontation. He was aware that, as long as Smith lived, he would never be free from the threat of retribution. Nor would pleading his position as a man whose life was devoted to healing gain the sympathy and support he wanted when the crowd heard why the Texan was behaving in such a fashion. Therefore, he knew he must deal with the situation once and for all immediately.

Doing so, the doctor told himself, would be easy!

Like many other medical men in the West, Grantz was always armed. He had realized that his way of life had given him an even more potent reason than many of his contemporaries for doing so. This awareness had encouraged him to practice drawing and using the Remington Double Derringer he carried in a concealed pocket of his vest with reasonable proficiency.

Confident his secret weapon would serve its purpose, the doctor snatched for it under the pretense of acting nervously!

Having heard a story told about Marvin Eldridge "Doc" Leroy following the Western medical habit of carrying a weapon readily available for use,[2] Smith had not overlooked the possibility of Grantz being armed. In fact, he had considered this to be very likely where such a man was concerned. Nor did the suggestion of abject fear lull him into a sense of false security or overconfidence. He knew there were few creatures more dangerous and liable to attack than a cornered rat.

The moment the Texan saw Grantz's right hand change its fumblings into a determined motion, he responded!

Still experiencing a slight twinge of pain in his back, serving as a reminder of his changed circumstances, Smith allowed his trained reflexes to control his movements. Turning his right elbow outward and almost to the level of his shoulder, he twisted his hand toward the staghorn grip of the Colt with the speed of a striking snake. Strengthened by the exercises he had taken, his second and third fingers wrapped firmly about the butt and, as he had discovered doing so offered added support, he hooked the fourth digit under its bottom. While this was taking place, his thumb coiled over the hammer's modified

2. *The incident is recorded in:* Chapter Fifteen, "Kill Me and You've Killed Him Too," DOC LEROY, M.D.
2a. *An occasion when Marvin Eldridge "Doc" Leroy benefited from another doctor following the habit of having a revolver readily available is described in:* Part Five, "A Case Of Infectious *Plumbeus Veneficium,*" THE FLOATING OUTFIT.

spur. By snapping his elbow in, he not only twisted the revolver from its formfitting holster but cocked the hammer without further effort by the thumb.

Even as Grantz's Remington came into view, the four- and three-quarter-inch barrel of Smith's Colt was turned his way!

Aiming by instinctive alignment, the Texan relaxed the grip his thumb was applying. Freed from restraint, the hammer lashed forward to plunge its striker into the priming cap of the waiting cartridge. Leaving the muzzle to the accompaniment of the crash of detonating black powder, the ejected charge was not a single bullet.

Struck in the chest by the lethal triple-ball load, Grantz was thrown backward with the Double Derringer flying unfired from his grasp. Shattering the chair from which he had risen, he crashed to the floor. For a couple of seconds, during which the silence continued around the room, his gross body twitched and writhed. Then it was still.

"I'm not meaning to sound all nosey-like, mister," the burly miner declared, ensuring he kept both hands in plain sight. "But I'd say you must reckon you've a mighty *good* reason for coming after Doc Bother like *this*."[3]

"You *could* say that," Smith confirmed, thumb cocking the slip gun without allowing its muzzle to point at anybody in particular around the table. However, every one of the six recognized the implied threat behind the action and all stood as if turned to stone. Satisfied there would not be any hostile moves against him, once again he displayed the three fingers of his left hand and turned the right to show it was in the same mutilated condition. "He did *this* to me!"

"No matter he was a lousy son of a bitch in *everything* else, he was a damned good doctor," the miner stated. "And it looks to me like he did a real good job of taking 'em off."

3. *In actual fact, the* nom de plume *adopted by Dr. Otto Grantz was the German surname,* Bothe.

"He did *that*!" Smith admitted, satisfied his quest for vengeance was at an end and wondering when he would be able to return to his beloved home state. "Thing being, there wasn't *anything* wrong with them when he cut them off!"

APPENDIX

THROUGHOUT the years we have been writing, we have frequently received letters asking for various terms we employ to be explained in greater detail. While we do not have the slightest objection to such correspondence and always reply, we have found it saves much time-consuming repetition to include those most frequently requested in each new title. We ask our "old hands," who have seen these items many times in the past, to remember there are always "new chums" coming along who have not and to bear with us. J.T.E.

1. We strongly suspect the trend in movies and television series made since the mid-1950s, wherein all cowhands are portrayed as heavily bearded, long haired, and filthy arose less from a desire on the part of the productions companies to create "realism" than because there were so few actors available—particularly to play supporting roles—who were short haired and clean shaven. Another factor was because the "liberal" ele-

ments who were starting to gain control over much of the media seem to obtain some form of "ego trip" from showing dirty conditions, filthy habits, and unkempt appearances. In our extensive reference library, we cannot find even a dozen photographs of actual *cowhands*—as opposed to civilian scouts for the Army, old-time mountain men, or gold prospectors—with long hair and bushy beards. In fact, our reading on the subject and conversations with friends living in the western states of America have led us to the conclusion that the term "long-hair" was one of opprobrium in the Old West and Prohibition eras just as it still tends to be today in cattle-raising country.

2. Clip point: Where the last few inches of the otherwise unsharpened back of the blade—when laid in a horizontal position with the edge down and the handle to the left of the viewer—joins and becomes an extension of the main cutting surface in a concave arc. This is the characteristic which many authorities claim identifies a bowie knife.

2a. What happened to the knife possessed by the alleged designer of such a weapon, James Bowie—many claim this was actually his older brother, Rezin Pleasant—after his death during the final attack upon the besieged Alamo Mission at San Antonio de Bexar, Texas, on March 6, 1836, is told in: GET URREA and THE QUEST FOR BOWIE'S BLADE.

2b. A spear point, which is less utilitarian than a clip, is formed by the two sharpened edges of the blade coming together in symmetrical curves. It was generally used for purely fighting knives such as the Arkansas toothpick or assassin's weapons.

3. Although the military sometimes claimed it was easier to kill a sailor than a soldier, perhaps tongue in cheek, the weight factor of the respective weapons had been responsible for the decision by the United States Navy to adopt a revolver with a caliber of .36 while the Army employed the heavier .44. The weapon would be carried upon the person of a seaman and not —handguns having been originally and primarily developed for single-handed use by cavalry—on the person or saddle of a soldier who would be doing much of his traveling and fighting

from the back of a horse. Therefore, .44 became known as the Army and .36 as the Navy caliber.

4. Introduced in 1873 as the Colt Model P Single Action Army revolver—although with a caliber of .45 instead of the erstwhile traditional .44—was more generally known as the Peacemaker. Production continued until 1941, when it was taken out of the line to make way for the more modern weapons required for use in World War II.

4b. Between 1873 and 1941, over 350,000 were manufactured in practically every handgun caliber from .22 Short Rimfire to .476 Eley; with the exception of the .41 and .44 Magnums, which were not developed commercially during the original production period. However, the majority fired either .45 or .44–40. The latter, given the designation, Frontier Model, handled the same cartridges as the Winchester Model of 1873 rifle and carbine.

4c. The barrel lengths of the Model P could be from three inches in the Storekeeper Model, which did not have an extractor rod for dislodging spent cartridge cases from the cylinder, to the sixteen inches for what became known to the public and firearms collectors as the Buntline Special. The latter was also offered with an attachable metal "skeleton" butt stock so it could be used as an extemporized carbine. The main barrel lengths were: Cavalry, seven and a half inches; Artillery, five and a half inches; Civilian, four and three-quarter inches.

4d. Popular demand, said to have resulted from the upsurge of action-escapism-adventure Western series being shown on television, brought the Peacemaker back into production in 1955 and it is still in the line. During this period, because of interest arising from the use of such a weapon by actor Hugh O'Brian starring in the WYATT EARP series, Colt for the first time produced and gave a model the name, Buntline Special, albeit with a barrel only twelve and a half inches in length.

5. We consider at best specious—at worst, a snobbish attempt to put down the myth and legends of the Old West—the frequently repeated assertion that the gunfighters of that era could not "hit a barn door at twenty yards." While willing to concede

that the average person then, as now, would not have much skill in using a handgun, knowing his life would depend upon it, the professional *pistolero* on either side of the law expended time, money, and effort to acquire proficiency. Furthermore, such a man did not carry a revolver to indulge in shooting at *anything* except at close range. He employed it as a readily accessible *weapon* that would incapacitate an enemy, preferably with the first shot, at close quarters, hence the preference for a cartridge of heavy caliber.

5b. With the exception of .22-caliber handguns intended for casual pleasure shooting, those specially designed for Olympic-style pistol matches, the Remington XP100—one of which makes an appearance in: THE LAWMEN OF ROCKABYE COUNTY—designed for "varmint" hunting at long distances, or medium- to heavy-caliber automatic pistols "accurized" and in the hands of a proficient exponent of modern combat shooting, a handgun is a short-range *defensive* and not an *offensive* weapon. Any Old West gunfighter, or peace officer in the Prohibition era and present times expecting to have to shoot at distances beyond about twenty *feet* would take the precaution of arming himself with a shotgun or a rifle.

6. "Make wolf bait": One term meaning to kill. Derived from the practice in the Old West, when a range was infested by stock-killing predators—not necessarily just wolves, but coyotes, the occasional jaguar in southern regions, black and grizzly bears—of slaughtering an animal and, having poisoned the carcass, leaving it to be devoured by the carnivores.

7. "Up to the Green River": To kill, generally with a knife. First produced on the Green River, at Greenfield, Massachusetts, in 1834, a very popular type of general purpose knife had the inscription, *J. Russell & Co./Green River Works* on the blade just below the hilt. Therefore any edged weapon thrust into an enemy "up to the Green River" would prove fatal whether it bore the inscription or not.

8. "Light a shuck": A cowhand term for leaving hurriedly. Derived from the habit in night camps on open-range roundups and trail drives of supplying shucks—dried corn cobs—to be lit

and used for illumination by anybody who had to leave the campfire and walk about in the darkness. As the shuck burned away very quickly, a person needed to hurry if wanting to benefit from its illumination.

9. The sharp toes and high heels of boots worn by cowhands were functional rather than merely decorative. The former could find and enter, or be slipped free from, a stirrup iron very quickly in an emergency. Not only did the latter offer a firmer brace against the stirrups, they could be spiked into the ground to supply added holding power when roping on foot.

10. Americans in general used the word, *cinch,* derived from the Spanish, *cincha,* to describe the short band made from coarsely woven horsehair, canvas, or cordage and terminated at each end with a metal ring which—together with the *latigo*—is used to fasten the saddle on the back of a horse. However, because of the word's connections with Mexico, Texans tended to employ the term, "girth," usually pronouncing it as "girt." As cowhands from the Lone Star State fastened the end of the lariat to the saddle horn, even when roping half-wild longhorn cattle or free-ranging mustangs, instead of relying upon a dally, which could be slipped free almost instantaneously in an emergency, their rigs had double girths.

11. Chaps: Leather overalls worn by American cowhands as protection for the legs. The word, pronounced, *shaps,* is an abbreviation of the Spanish, *chaperejos* or *chaparreras,* meaning "leather breeches." Contrary to what is frequently shown in Western movies, no cowhand ever kept his chaps on when their protection was not required. Even if he should arrive in a town with them on, he would remove and either hang them over his saddle, or leave them behind the bar in his favorite saloon for safekeeping until his visit was over.

12. Hackamore: An Americanized corruption of the Spanish word, *jaquima,* meaning "headstall." Very popular with Indians in particular, it was an ordinary halter, except for having reins instead of a leading rope. It had a headpiece something like a conventional bridle, a brow band about three inches wide, which could be slid down the cheeks to cover the horse's eyes,

but no throat latch. Instead of a bit, a *bosal*—a leather, rawhide, or metal ring around the head immediately above the mouth—was used as a means of control and guidance.

13. Floating outfit: A group of four to six cowhands employed by a large ranch in the open-range days to work the more-distant sections of the property. Taking food in a chuckwagon, or "greasy sack" on the back of a pack animal, depending upon the expected length of their absence, they would be away from the ranch house for several days at a time. Therefore, as they would not be under supervision by the boss or foreman, they were selected from the most competent and trustworthy members of the crew.

13a. Due to the prominence of General Jackson Baines "Ole Devil" Hardin in the affairs of Texas, members of the OD Connected ranch's floating outfit were frequently sent to assist such of his friends who found themselves in difficulty or endangered.

14. Mason-Dixon line, erroneously called the "Mason-Dixie line." The boundary between Pennsylvania and Maryland, as surveyed from 1763–67 by the Englishmen, Charles Mason and Jeremiah Dixon. It became considered as the dividing line separating the Southern slave and Northern free states.

15. New England: the northeast section of the United States—including Massachusetts, New Hampshire, Connecticut, Maine, Vermont, and Rhode Island—which was first settled by people primarily from the British Isles.

16. "Gone to Texas": on the run from the law. During the white colonization period, which had commenced in the early 1820s, many fugitives from justice in the United States of America had fled to Texas and would continue to do so until annexation by the United States on February 16, 1846. Until the latter became a fact, they had known there was little danger of being arrested and extradited by the local authorities. In fact, like Kenya Colony from the 1920s to the outbreak of World War II—in spite of the number of honest, hardworking and law-abiding settlers genuinely seeking to make a permanent home there—Texas had gained a reputation for being a "place in the sun for shady people."

17. The Texas Rangers were to all practical intents and purposes abolished—their functions being taken over by the more prosaic Department of Public Safety at Austin and the Highway Patrol—on October 17, 1935. This was almost one hundred years to the day after their formation. Although their first purpose was to act as militia, or what in present-day terms would be called a paramilitary organization, to help fend off marauding Indians, they became increasingly responsible for supporting the local authorities in the enforcement of law and order.

17a. Having statewide jurisdiction: As opposed to a sheriff being confined to his county and a town marshal to the community that hired him—the Rangers were supposed to await an invitation from the senior lawman on the spot before instigating or participating in any investigative activities in his bailiwick. However, due to the special conditions that prevailed at the time, during the Prohibition era a special company, Z, was formed and given the right to act without such permission. Information regarding their official "unofficial" operations is given in the *Alvin Dustine "Cap" Fog* series.

17b. During the late 1870s, the governor of Arizona formed a similar force to cope with lawbreaking in his state. A similar decision was taken by a latter governor and the Arizona Rangers were brought back into being. Why it was considered necessary to organize the first force, how it operated, and was finally disbanded is recorded in the *Waco* series.